The Adventures of Atlas Mapp

Michael James

ISBN: 978-1-948582-75-9

Acknowledgments by Michael James

To my father, David, who I knew well, and my mother, Eloise,
who I did not
To my wife, Grace, and my dog, Brooklyn James, for filling
whatever voids were left
Lastly, to Imagination, for always being a constant companion
who saved me from loneliness

ONE
Somewhere in the Western Sahara

Everywhere, there was sand. Dunes and dunes, hills and hills, mountains and mountains of sand, as far as the eye could see.

In the forbidding land of the Sahara Desert, an excavation was under way. Towering cranes pierced the hazy blue sky. Bright yellow tractors and rust-colored trucks surrounded a cavernous hole, hauling great mounds of earth from here to there.

Workers in dirty linen outfits scurried about like fire ants, passing buckets from one to another in a very organized fashion. Atop tall platforms, shouting instructions in Punjabi and Arabic, still others toiled to secure the site's wooden walls. They fought an eternal battle to keep new sand from replacing that which they had already removed.

At the bottom of the hole, Ada was fed up with broiling away in the heat. In a mock fit of rage, he threw his shovel to the ground and declared, "When we are rich, I will move to the North Pole!"

Ada wiped his sweaty face with the back of his bony hand and waited, stealing small glances to see if anyone was actually listening. No one was.

Nearby, Ahib, whose olive skin approached the color of coal, worked on. At the mouth of a tunnel burrowed into the grainy earth, he laboriously scooped the red sand into buckets that were then lifted out of the hole.

Both were children of the desert, but came from vastly different worlds. Ada hailed from the Indian city of Jaisalmer, in the heart of the great Thar Desert. Ahib was from Sunavir, a poor village in the Arabian Desert.

They met as boys in Morocco, when their fathers secured employment with the famous American adventurer and explorer, Compass Mapp.

Now, they worked for Compass Mapp's son, Field, who carried on the family tradition of scouring very inhospitable places for lost relics and treasures. For more than ten years, Ahib had labored alongside Ada, and grown used to such outbursts. He had also grown used to ignoring them.

This, of course, irritated Ada greatly.

"You are an Arab," Ada said, "You were born of the sand and you have developed a great appreciation for it, but I find it utterly useless. Every day here is hotter than the last. When I dream at night, it is always the same. I drown in a sea of sand."

What Ada said *was* true. As he spoke, Ahib toyed with the golden grains of sand lodged between his teeth and flicked them from beneath his fingernails. But, believing that hard work was the honorable way, Ahib chose to suffer in silence. This also annoyed the talkative Ada.

Ada gazed longingly at the rickety wooden ladder leading out of their hole. He could climb it, but to where? There was no escape.

Finding no one willing to share his grand plans for a better future, Ada reluctantly retrieved his shovel, kneeled next to Ahib and resumed digging.

"Trust me," he said quietly, "You will all be envious someday when you receive my postcards from the comfort of the North Pole."

Finally, Ahib, who was in many ways the opposite of the lazy and calculating Ada, spoke.

"I do not think it will be better there, Ada," he said. "Although you are Indian, this sandy earth flows through your veins just as it flows through mine. You dream of the cold of the North Pole only because you imagine it to be the opposite of the desert, therefore better."

Ada considered Ahib's words. Other than the desert, he had never really been anywhere. In fact, the only other place in the world that he had heard about was America, and only then in small bits and pieces. Still, though both were now in their early twenties, Ahib knew more. So, usually, he was right.

"Okay," Ada said, "Maybe I will go to America when Professor Mapp returns home. If the professor finds the treasure we are searching for, we will all be rich. Then, we can go wherever we want to go."

Ahib smiled to himself and checked to make sure the plywood planks around the small tunnel remained sturdy. Sand seeped perilously, as in an hourglass, from the roof of the entrance.

"Since you are so eager to leave this place," he said, "you should have the pleasure of going inside to help the professor. He will need you."

Ada leapt to his feet, looking around as if Ahib could possibly be speaking to someone else.

"But Ahib, you are a single man," he sputtered. "I have a family. That is why *you* should go inside."

Ahib stood to face the tall, lanky Ada. There had been many times like this before. Today, he would not fall prey to Ada's excuses.

"Why not flip a coin between us, Ada? Something democratic?"

Fear arose on Ada's face. He even broke into a cold sweat despite the oppressive heat.

"And you will travel to Delhi to tell Sanji that her husband was smothered to his death in sand?" he pleaded, with eyebrows raised.

Ahib did not budge.

"You used that excuse last time when it was I who went into the lion's den. It is simply your turn."

"Okay, okay… But will you be the one to tell Punji and Puji and Sangri and Ada Junior?"

Ahib was too furious to speak. Ada had him. After all, he *was* a single man and did not have the obligations of family. With a look of contempt, he turned and crawled into the mouth of the tunnel.

Ada was finishing a sigh of relief when Ahib popped back out. "Wait a minute. Who is Ada Junior?" he demanded. "You have no sons."

Ada calmly patted his stomach. "Sanji is, well, any day now…"

Ahib's instincts told him that Ada could be lying, but there was no way to know for sure. During their seemingly endless days in the desert sun, Ada spoke of everything that came to his mind. So why had he held back this very happy news?

"I simply forgot to tell you," Ada offered before Ahib could ask. Defeated, Ahib shook his head and crawled back inside the tunnel. Just then, a man cried out from above.

"Ada! Ahib! Get Professor Mapp. The baby is coming. Come quickly!"

Ada hurried to the tunnel and called inside, "Ahib, tell the professor the baby is coming. Hurry!"

Ahib's faint voice echoed from within, "I'm going as

fast as I can!"

Ahib moved slowly, wincing as sand spilled like water from the ceiling into his eyes. More than once, he thought of death, and how it should be Ada instead of him.

Despite not being one given to anger, Ahib could barely control his emotions as he inched toward Professor Mapp with only a small dim light on his hard hat illuminating the way.

His mind raced. He was sure the tunnel would collapse upon him at any second. He had seen accidents like this happen to others. Maybe now, it would be Ahib's turn to meet his maker. He was petrified by the thought.

But Ahib's blood boiled at feeling that he had once again been tricked by Ada, who would do most anything to escape work.

Suddenly, as if peering into a crystal ball, Ahib saw a vision of the future. There stood Ada, rich and happy with his family – Ada Junior included – lamenting his death with very great sorrow.

"It should have been me," he heard Ada wail, "but Ahib insisted that I stay behind out of love for my family. He *was* a single man, after all."

"If I get out of here alive, I will choke the life from you, Ada," Ahib said aloud, though he really didn't mean it – at least not until he envisioned the headline from the local paper:

AHEEB THE ARAB SMOTHERED
TO HIS DEATH IN SAND

"They have even misspelled my name," Ahib fumed, then, just as quickly, he wiped the mean-spirited thoughts away. "Professor Mapp needs me. That is all that matters."

Deep inside the shaft, Field Mapp dug furiously with a

small shovel.

Wisps of blond hair whipped his sweaty face as he moved the sand with furious determination. Field was twenty-five years old and ruggedly handsome, an adventurer by both heart and blood, as was his father.

He ignored small beads of sweat that dripped from the end of his nose, evaporating before they ever hit the ground. Then he heard the unmistakable sound of metal upon metal.

To be sure, he tapped again with his digging tool. *Ting!*

Field's heartbeat quickened. He positioned a flashlight over the spot and began to dig with his bare hands. As he wiped away the loose earth, a small band of gold reflected in the soft light. He dug even more feverishly, uncovering another gold band wrapped around a wooden mahogany chest.

So intense was his focus that Field didn't notice sand falling from the gaps in the plywood wall before his face.

Something was burrowing through.

Transfixed, Field blew lightly upon the chest and watched the sand skitter away, revealing ancient letters etched into a rectangular nameplate.

Several times, he blinked at the sight. Could this actually be the treasure chest that had eluded his father and numerous others for a lifetime?

He reached into his shirt pocket and took out a rumpled piece of paper torn from a very old book. On it was an illustration of this trunk, and these very same strange letters. With a charcoal pencil, Field quickly performed the translation:

The Diamonds of King Attanan Bushawri.

Field nearly lost his breath. "This is it. I've found it."

Gingerly, he grabbed the sides of the box and pulled it from the sandy grave that had kept it secret and safe for a thousand years. He carefully placed it beside him in the cramped space, unsnapped two gold brackets, and slowly lifted the lid.

Inside were sparkling diamonds, rich green emeralds, blood-red rubies and bright, white pearls. There were gems, big and small, gold pendants and crosses, riches beyond his wildest imagination.

Field grabbed a handful of the jewels and squeezed them tightly, as if to make sure that they were real, then dropped them back into the chest.

Overcome, he leaned against the side of the tunnel and breathed deeply, his eyes glued to the priceless treasure. By now, sand was pouring from the wall before him with urgency, but still, Field took no notice.

Ahib's voice broke the silence.

"Professor Mapp! Professor, the baby comes. Professor?"

Field turned to look as Ahib crawled up on all fours – just in time to see a large brown snake with inch-long fangs burst through the wall.

"Prof-, oh my goodness!" Ahib screamed, recoiling.

Field, however, kept calm, taking note of the bright orange circle in the middle of the snake's head, mere inches from his face. It didn't take long for him to realize that this serpent was one of the most dangerous species of reptile in the entire world.

"Hyperion Sandsnake, Ahib," he whispered. "Don't move."

As much as he tried, Ahib could not help quivering. He had heard many horrible tales of the cunning Hyperion Sandsnake, including one where an army of vipers had devoured an entire caravan. The way Ahib heard it, the snakes first bit the legs of the camels and followed until the camels died. Then, they came and ambushed the stranded merchants.

Field had also heard many of the same desert tales, but considered them greatly exaggerated. His only thoughts now were of survival.

Slowly, Field swayed side to side, keeping clear of the snake's fangs as it mimicked his movements.

Ahib had heard Field's command to stay frozen, but he was so mesmerized by the scene that he also began slowly swaying back and forth. The snake suddenly turned and hissed in his direction.

"Ahib, don't move," Field said evenly, raising his hand to draw the snake's attention back to himself. This time, Ahib became still, as if his life depended upon it. Which it did.

Field stared into the snake's steely eyes while stealthily slipping a hunting knife from a sheath in his boot. Faster than Ahib could blink, Field swiped with the blade, then watched as the snake's disembodied head fell to the floor of the tunnel.

"Professor, are you all right?" Ahib shrieked.

"Better than that," Field said, looking toward the little brown chest that Ahib now saw for the first time.

"The... the Diamonds of Bushawri?" Ahib stammered, his eyes wide. Field nodded. "Now, what were you saying?"

"Oh, Professor," Ahib said, now remembering why he had risked his life to get here, "The baby is coming!"

Field snapped to attention. "The baby? Oh, no... Sarah!"

Ada was startled to see Ahib and Field emerge so quickly from the tunnel and dash toward the ladder. Field's smile was as wide as the ocean.

"Ada, don't let anyone in that hole until I get back," Field said, adding, "I'm going to be a father."

Ahib and Field clambered up the ladder and out of

sight.

Once they were gone, Ada took a few steps toward the tunnel and peered inside, seeing nothing but darkness.

Not far from the excavation site, Ahib and Field came upon a sprawling tan tent city, stopping in front of the biggest tent in the entire makeshift village.

A newborn's cry split the air. Ahib smiled at Field, but said nothing as Field parted the canvas flap and stepped inside.

Colorfully dressed Indian women stood around a large cot covered by a huge mosquito net. They bowed their heads at the sight of Field and moved aside, revealing the beautiful Sarah Mapp lying there. Held closely to her chest was a small bundle that looked more like a bale of cotton than the newest addition to the Mapp family.

Sarah smiled at Field as he ducked under the net and smoothed her long red hair. It was rolled into big, round curls, as it always did in the heat. She was a sight to behold.

From the glow on Field's face, Sarah instantly knew. "You found them, didn't you?" she whispered.

Field nodded.

"But I would have given anything to be here with you," he said, peeling back the layers of soft cloth that hid the newborn from view. "The doctor said the baby would be at least another week!"

"I know," Sarah said, handing the precious infant to Field. "He's a typical Mapp. He came early."

"He?" blurted Ahib, who could not control himself in moments of excitement like this.

"Yes. It's a boy, Ahib," Sarah said, with a soft smile.

"It is a great day!" Ahib proclaimed, with a leap of joy. "Another Mapp joins us, another great explorer. What will you call him?"

"His name is Atlas," Sarah said.

"Atlas Mapp," Field said, stroking the child's pink cheeks and forehead. "I like that. Your grandfather would be proud." From beneath the blanket, a tiny little hand emerged and clutched Field's finger.

"He is not yet an hour old, Professor," said Ahib, "but I am sure that already he understands you. Oh, to find the treasure on the very same day as your first child is born, there could be no greater pleasure."

Field gazed from Sarah to Atlas and said, "If there is, I can't imagine it."

The night air was crisp and cool, filled with music. A wild and festive celebration was in full swing. Drums kept rhythm for sitars, women adorned in marigolds and fabrics all colors of the rainbow danced in the firelight.

Three times a gong sounded majestically. A still quiet fell. From the shadows, Ahib led an ancient man with a long beard and pearl-white hair covered in a purple turban into the center of the gathering.

"The Glorious Neffer wishes to speak," he announced.

Neffer lifted a gnarled hand and beckoned to Field, who sat nearby with Sarah and their newborn child.

"Bring the boy into the light," Neffer said in a strong voice.

Field handed Atlas to Neffer and watched the old man place him upon an altar lined with flowers. Neffer uncorked a small vial and dripped water onto the baby's forehead.

"With this holy water we welcome young Atlas Mapp into the world in the same manner as his father, Field Mapp, and grandfather, the great explorer – and my personal friend, Compass Mapp – before him."

As Field, Sarah, Ahib and hordes of workers watched attentively, Neffer produced a golden round amulet dangling from a strap of brown leather. On the medallion was an image of a proud eagle with its majestic wings spread wide. In the middle of the eagle's face was a single wide eye and across its chest was a pair of crossed swords.

Ahib fingered the amulet around his neck. It was exactly the same as the one in Neffer's hand.

"May the Gods of Mariah bless this child for all his life and keep him safe," Neffer said. "I bestow upon him Agle, the All-Seeing eagle of the Iron Heart and Swift Sword. Agle sees all, knows all, and is fair and just."

Many of those watching the ceremony nodded in agreement. With a most grand gesture, Neffer gently placed the amulet upon Atlas' tiny chest and lifted the baby up to face the twinkling stars.

"May Atlas find peace, love and much adventure, forever more," he said, and then handed the boy back to Field. "Let the celebration continue!"

The sounds of music, cheers and gunfire exploded. People danced joyously, but there was a look of melancholy in Ahib's eyes.

While he was extremely happy for the Mapp family's good fortune, Ahib was troubled as he approached their table. It was dressed for a feast, with all manner of meat, wine, cheese and fruits, as if for a king.

"Professor, if we are to exhume the Diamonds of Bushawri tomorrow morning, I must take my leave," Ahib said.

"It's a day that would not have been possible without you, Ahib," Field said. Ahib managed a little smile, but could not conceal his worry.

"I am sorry to bring up such a personal concern at a time like this, professor, but what will you do now that you are rich? Will you no longer-"

"Don't worry, Ahib. There will be other treasures," Field said.

"That is good to know." Ahib's face lit up as if a great weight had been lifted from his shoulders. "I feared with the new child, you might wish to retire. Then, what would I do?"

"Mapps don't retire, Ahib," said Sarah, rocking Atlas to soothe his cries.

"You are a good man, Professor Mapp," Ahib said gratefully. "I will see you in the morning."

When Ahib was out of sight, Sarah placed a hand on Field's shoulder. She seemed concerned now. "You can take some time off, Field. At least until Atlas is older." Before Field could reply, Neffer approached.

"Might we speak alone, Field?" he asked, smiling at Sarah, as if also asking her permission.

Sarah watched them disappear into the night. Even without the bright light of the large bonfire, Field could see that Neffer was serious.

"Field, I have known your family for a long time," Neffer began, "which is why the news I bring troubles me so. I know you do not believe in such things."

"There's no need to worry, Neffer, we've found them-"

"I am told there is an ancient curse on the Diamonds of Bushawri," Neffer said in an urgent tone. "You must be very careful."

Field's mood changed.

"I'm not my father, Neffer. Nothing's gone wrong so far, and my men are being as cautious as they can be."

Neffer reached into the pocket of his robe and took out

an amulet that was identical to the one he had given to Field's newborn son.

"A curse is a serious thing," he said, holding the medallion out to Field. "If not for me, then take this for your father and his father. I think it will make us all feel better."

Field's face softened. Neffer had been his father's very best friend since well before Field was born and he knew that the old man's intentions were only for the best.

Neffer had been a big part of Field's life forever, and though he believed in things that Field still did not understand, Field took the amulet and closed his fist around it.

"Don't worry, Neffer. I'll be careful," Field said as the two shared a heartfelt embrace.

Neffer nodded and watched Field walk back to his family, feeling only slightly better than before the two had spoken.

The sun broke over the horizon, but already the temperature was well over one hundred degrees when Field was awakened from a satisfying and restful sleep. Outside the tent, he heard anguished cries.

"Professor, you must come now!" the voice said, between gulps of pain and agony.

Field leapt off his cot and reached for his revolver. There had been raiders on expeditions before, but never here in the desert. Still, he had come to the Sahara prepared for anything.

Field glanced over at Sarah and Atlas, who were both still soundly asleep. He dashed out of the tent to find Ahib on his knees in the sand, surrounded by several workers, all with downcast eyes.

"Ahib, what's happened?" Field asked, finally giving

Ahib's shoulders a vigorous shaking to get his attention. Ahib composed himself as best he could, but at first, his words were undecipherable.

"He is... they are ... all gone," Ahib sputtered, with tears streaming down his cheeks.

"Who's gone, Ahib? What are you talking about?"

"The Diamonds of Bushawri," Ahib said. "Ada was seen leaving before the light of day with a small caravan. He is nowhere to be found."

Field's heart sank. He turned and ran toward the excavation site. Ahib trailed, stumbling and falling as he tried to keep up.

When Field reached the spot where the hole had been, he was stunned to see that it was no longer there, now filled in by sand. The only indication that it had ever been there at all were the rusty trucks and yellow tractors.

With Ahib's sobs ringing in his ears, Field gazed helplessly over the barren desert, seeing nothing but sand - dunes and dunes, hills and hills, mountains and mountains of sand - as far as his eyes could see.

TWO
Toxic Soldiers

Atlas Mapp sat in the grass, staring through long wisps of blond hair just like his father's. Around his neck, the amulet of the one-eye eagled dangled from a worn leather strap. All over the spacious backyard, bordered by pine trees and woods, children in birthday hats squealed with delight.

But from his depressed mood, one would never have known that this birthday party was for Atlas himself.

Sarah had watched from the kitchen window and could see that her son wasn't happy. She came outside and knelt beside him, stroking his sullen cheeks.

"Don't worry, Atlas," she said in a soft tone. "Your father wouldn't miss your tenth birthday for the world. He'll call."

"Dad misses everything, Mom," Atlas replied, without looking up. "He promised he would be here this time."

The remark caught Sarah off-guard.

She didn't expect Atlas to understand that his father was forced to continue working to support his family after the Diamonds of Bushawri were stolen, on the very day that he was born. But she did expect him to believe that Field would not break a promise.

"Has he ever forgotten your birthday?" she asked, pulling Atlas' chin up and staring into his eyes.

Atlas shook his head.

"And he won't miss this one, either," she said. "Now,

young man, you go play with your friends and have a good time. Okay?" She gave Atlas a gentle hug and watched him join his friends.

Deep inside, however, Sarah's own worry was growing. It wasn't like Field to have not called home by now. But, like Atlas, she could only wait.

The minutes passed like hours as Sarah sat at her dining room table looking through a box of old family photos. Every now and then she would glance at the telephone, wishing it would ring. But it did not.

One yellowed picture showed Field with Atlas, then maybe five years old, posing with members of a lost tribe in Kunabi. In another, taken several years later, Sarah watched protectively as Atlas fed a banana to a monkey somewhere in the deep recesses of the Amazon Jungle.

Meanwhile, outside the modest Mapp home on 27 Seminole Street, a pickup truck slowed to a stop and parked. A sign on the side of the truck read: *Mapp Excavations, Seattle, Washington.*

Slowly, a man with a streak of grey in his hair stepped out. It was Ahib, exactly ten years older, but wearing the same agonized look as on the day that Ada stole the Diamonds of Bushawri.

For several moments, Ahib leaned against the truck collecting his thoughts and then took small, deliberate steps toward the house.

Sarah was looking at a glass-framed photograph of her family during one of their many happy times, when the doorbell startled her. Through the screen door, she saw that Ahib's face was pale. From his sorrowful expression she immediately knew something was wrong.

"What's happened, Ahib?" Sarah asked in a cautious tone as she opened the door to let him inside. "Ahib?"

After a painful silence, Ahib's tears gushed forth. He grabbed Sarah in an anguished hug and cried, "Professor Mapp is gone, Mrs. Mapp. I am soooo sorry."

Sarah could not speak as she let Ahib's words sink in. Had her worst fears finally come true? Had some horrible, unthinkable accident finally happened to Field? It was not possible, she thought, but then realized that if something bad had befallen her husband, Ahib would know.

"No, Ahib, no!!!" Sarah screamed. Her heart skipped several beats and her knees gave way. Ahib caught her before she could fall, but he could not catch the picture frame. It crashed to the floor, its glass shattering.

"What was that?" Atlas asked, his ears perking up like a cat's.

"What was what?" said Ormon, a rotund, bespectacled boy whose face was buried in a thick book entitled, *Psychology for Smart Kids.*

"I thought I heard somebody scream."

Ormon lowered his book and pointed to a gaggle of young girls. "Women are always screaming," he said, matter-of-factly. "The psychologist Carl Jung says screaming is embedded in their genetic makeup. Why'd you invite them, anyway?"

"I didn't. Mom did," Atlas replied, still puzzled by Ormon, who was only 10 years old, but the smartest friend he had ever known.

Before Atlas could ask Ormon what he meant, Pepper, a thin, rugged boy with thick, mussed hair joined the group at the picnic table. Pepper was only a year older than the two, but he sometimes acted like a teenager, even going on dates with girls.

"You guys wanna play Toxic Soldiers?" Pepper asked.

Both Ormon and Atlas shook their heads.

"We played for four hours yesterday," Atlas said.

"Don't you get tired?" Pepper gave Atlas an incredulous look.

"You're supposed to be the great Adventure Boy and you don't like adventures. What's that about?"

"Get off him, it's his birthday," Ormon said, defending his best pal – and watching Pepper move menacingly close. "You even think about hitting me and you can forget about getting help on your math test."

Pepper smiled slyly. "C'mon, Ormon, would I hit you?"

Ormon and Atlas both shot Pepper a glance.

"Okay, when's the last time I hit you?"

"Pepper, go 'way," Ormon said, "there's lots of girls over there."

Like a robot given a command, Pepper zeroed in on the group of girls gossiping amongst themselves in the corner. "Oh yeah, guuurrrlllzzzz," he said, primping while strutting off.

When Pepper was completely out of hearing range, Ormon sighed in disgust. "He's, like, so Neanderthal."

Atlas was quiet, with his head down on the table.

Feeling his sadness, Ormon asked, "Hey, your dad call yet?"

"Nope."

"He'll call. He always does, right?"

Atlas was too dejected to reply.

In the living room, Sarah sat on the couch facing Ahib, clutching a wad of tissue. Her eyes were puffy and red from crying.

"But they don't know for sure, Ahib," she was saying.

"No, Mrs. Mapp," he said, "but I am told no one could have survived the collapse. They say the entire entrance is impassable and that water may have flooded most of the mine."

"But they don't _know_, do they?" she insisted.

"No, they don't."

"Well, then," Sarah said, composing herself, "you tell them to keep searching until they find him. It's Atlas' birthday, Ahib. I'm not going to tell my son that his father is dead. Not today. Field's alive, Ahib. I can feel it."

Ahib gulped and nodded quietly.

"And don't blame yourself. This isn't your fault."

"Mrs. Mapp, I understand that you might not believe, but I wear the amulet of the one-eyed eagle. Agle protects me and all who wear it."

He pulled out his medallion and showed it to Sarah.

"Professor Mapp chose not to wear the one Neffer gave to him, but I have been with him on every expedition and no harm has ever befallen him."

Ahib choked up.

"If not for the birth of my son," Ahib said, "I would have been with him in Althanar. I did not go, now look what has happened. It is no coincidence, Mrs. Mapp. Believe me."

Once again, Ahib began to sob uncontrollably.

Sarah placed a consoling hand on his back. Suddenly, they heard the sounds of the children at play out in the backyard. Ahib wiped his eyes.

"What will you tell him, young Atlas?"

"The truth, Ahib," Sarah said. "That'll be enough."

Ahib nodded, rose from the couch and walked to the door. They shared a hug.

"I will call if I hear more," Ahib said.

Sarah watched Ahib drive away, and then bent down to pick up the pieces of broken glass from the picture frame, pausing only to take a long look at the snapshot of her once-happy family.

Atlas and Ormon crept like soldiers through a thicket of underbrush, both carrying large yellow and orange Super Soaker water guns.

Toxic Soldiers, a combination of paintball without paint and hide-and-seek (complete with military strategy), was underway. It was Pepper's favorite game – mainly because he'd helped invent it – and, as usual, he was the one being hunted.

"He's got to be around here somewhere," Atlas whispered, as Ormon pointed to Sarah's art studio, a small cottage behind the main house.

"No way," Atlas said, shaking his head. "Pepper knows that's off- limits to Toxic Soldiers. Mom would kill me if we went in there."

"But Pepper doesn't play by the rules." Atlas knew this was true.

"Well, be ready for anything," he said. "I don't want to get hit with the Toxic Rain Spray. If he's in there, he'll be waiting for us."

From a cottage window, Pepper spied Ormon and Atlas closing in. "C'mon, suckers," he said, giggling demonically.

The room was dark as Pepper backed away from the window to find a better spot where he could ambush his prey. Accidentally, he bumped into a table, sending several antique pots flying to the floor with a loud crash.

As Pepper quickly gathered up the little pots, he noticed a large cardboard box beneath the table and crouched to take a look inside.

"AAAAHHHHHHhhhhh!!!!!"

From Pepper's scream of horror, Atlas knew that Pepper had indeed broken the rules and taken refuge in Sarah's cottage.

"He must'a found some of Dad's stuff," Atlas whispered.

"Either that or it's a trap," replied Ormon. "Let's go 'round back."

While Atlas and Ormon maneuvered into position, Pepper's fright quickly wore off. And, since whatever did not kill Pepper made him more curious, he was now investigating the scary contents of the cardboard box.

He flung open a curtain, flooding the room with light, and stood there in awe. On shelves lining the walls were fertility figurines, several ape skulls, primitive weapons and a crossbow – Pepper's kind of stuff.

"Cool!" Pepper exclaimed, as he slid the box out from under the table and fondled a shrunken monkey's head.

"Don't move, Toxic Dude!"

Pepper froze. He was busted and defenseless, with his Super Soaker on the table and the little monkey head in his hands.

"Pepper, we're not supposed to be in here," Atlas said, lowering his weapon. He took the skull from Pepper and put it back in the box.

"But, dude, look at all this stuff," Pepper said, still nosing around.

"C'mon, Pepper," Ormon chimed, "You'll get Atlas in trouble."

But there was no stopping Pepper. While Atlas slid the box back in place, Pepper walked over to an easel by the window. On the easel was a painting bursting with color, depicting an unusual and unfamiliar place. At the top of the canvas were the words, *"The Arch World."*

"What are these?" Pepper asked, fingering a stack of smaller maps on a nearby table. They were all slightly different versions of this same place.

"Wow, there's lots of them," Ormon said, suddenly forgetting that he was supposed to be helping Atlas get Pepper out of the cottage.

"Put them back, guys. That's my mom's stuff," Atlas said.

"What does she do?" Pepper asked.

"She illustrates children's books. She's making a map of our travels."

Pepper studied the large map closely, reading all the labels. "Where's Polema?"

"I dunno," Atlas said, starting to get curious about the maps himself. "It's from her imagination."

Ormon saw a long hand ladder near the canvas' edge. "Wow, that Monkey Bar Bridge over the river is way cool," he said. "Your mom's brilliant."

Pepper focused on another part of the map, and four blips in a boot-shaped place marked, *Haven.* The blips blinked on and off, like lights.

"That's weird," Pepper said, squinting at the little lights. "Does your mom use a special kind of paint or something?"

Ormon noticed the strange blips, too. "Maybe it's an optical illusion. This Haven place kinda looks like Florida."

"Not like any Florida I've ever seen," Pepper said. Suddenly, the boys heard Sarah's voice.

"Atlas? Atlas, where are you?"

Atlas sprang into action, grabbing the others. "C'mon, guys, we've got to get out of here!"

Atlas could barely hide his guilty look when Sarah rounded the corner behind the cottage. He was so nervous that he started explaining what they had been doing without being asked.

"We were just playing Toxic Soldiers, Mom."

But Sarah did not seem to care what the trio had been up to. "Boys, I need to talk to Atlas," she told Pepper and Ormon.

"Okay, Mrs. Mapp," they said, and watched as she took her son's hand and walked toward the house.

"Man, that was close," Pepper said when they were out of sight. "Say, Ormon, can you keep a secret?"

"Sure."

"Swear on the Brotherhood of Toxic Soldiers."

Pepper always wanted to swear on the brotherhood for just about any reason, no matter how big or small.

"I swear," Ormon promised, irritated at having to swear. Pepper wasn't convinced, so he upped the ante.

"And you'll die getting eaten up in a vat of snakes if you say a word."

"I double-swear," Ormon said. "You can't do more than that."

Knowing that Ormon couldn't possibly break the bond of the brotherhood without suffering horribly, Pepper pulled a small map out of his back pocket.

Before Ormon could protest, Pepper reminded him, "Hey Dude, you double-sweared. Let's just check it out and then we can take it back."

"You promise?"

"Would I break a promise?"

Ormon thought for a moment. Of course, Pepper would break a promise, but this time he might actually keep his word. Besides, what harm could it do?

"Okay," he said. "It might lead somewhere."

While Pepper and Ormon were off examining the stolen map, Sarah was wiping tears from Atlas' face. Although it had been hard to break such terrible news to her son, she didn't believe her husband was dead and would not tell Atlas so until she was sure.

"Oh, Honey, Mapps don't die," she said, holding him close.

"But what about Grandpa?"

Sarah had to think fast. Atlas was a smart little boy.

"Well," she began, "I like to think that even though he went away, he's always here. He knows today's your birthday. He can't send you a card, but he knows."

"You think Dad's with him?"

"Not in the same way. Grandpa Mapp went away to a place that's kind of like a safe haven."

Atlas quickly thought of the map, but knew he couldn't ask about it without having to tell the truth about going inside the forbidden cottage.

"Haven? What's it like there?" he asked.

Sarah smiled at the thought of this magical, comforting place.

"In Haven, the sun shines all the time," she said. "People don't feel pain or misery, and they never grow any older. Some people, like Grandpa Mapp, go there to stay. People like your father, well, it's like a place to rest until he can get home."

She hugged Atlas again.

"Don't worry. Your father will make it home."

As Atlas buried his face in his mother's arms, he could see that she didn't look so sure at all.

Later that night, it was dark and quiet in the Mapp house, except for the insistent ticking of the grandfather clock in the living room. From down the hall in Atlas' bedroom came muffled noises. They grew louder.

Atlas tossed and turned, violently thrashing beneath his bedcovers, in the midst of a nightmare.

"Just let me see him!" he cried. "No, ungh, stop! I won't go with you. Noooo!"

In his dreams, Atlas found himself in a dark cave, wildly swinging a torch which cast sinister shadows on the walls. A black, vapory, shapeless figure with pulsing red eyes reached out a dark hand to him. The monster was everywhere, encircling him.

"Get away from me!" Atlas shouted, frantically swinging the torch, its light nearly extinguishing. In a deep, rumbling voice that shook the walls, the shapeless figure called to Atlas, "Come to me, my son. Come."

"I'm not your son. You're not my father.... Where's my dad?"

Atlas' defiance only angered the monster, whose red eyes flickered as he spoke. "You *will* be my son, Atlas."

Atlas tried to run, but could not escape. "I'll never be your son!" he declared. "Daaaaaadddddd!"

Atlas awoke in his mother's arms, breathing heavily and still fighting off the horrible, evil creature.

"It's okay, Atlas. Mom's here," she said.

"A monster was after me!"

"It was just a nightmare, that's all."

"This thing had Dad," Atlas said, clutching Sarah's nightgown.

Sarah tried to reassure him. "I know, Honey. I know."

"But, Mom!"

"Honey, it was a dream," Sarah insisted. "Now, try to go back to sleep."

"Okay, Mom," Atlas said, calming down.

Sarah kissed Atlas' forehead and left a light on in the hall, but Atlas was so troubled by the dream that he did not return to sleep all night.

It was a typical overcast Seattle afternoon as Atlas and Ormon, both deep in thought, rode their bikes to McQuade's Pond, their favorite fishing spot, not far from the Mapp home.

Ormon had listened closely to Atlas' scary nightmare, but, as usual, he did not offer an opinion without seriously contemplating the story.

The boys navigated a thin, worn path and lay their bikes down side-by-side. Atlas sat next to a tree while Ormon skipped pebbles on the lake's smooth surface. Neither said a word for a little while, mostly because they knew each other so well, that was no need for idle chatter.

Finally, Ormon spoke.

"The way I see it, the thing in your dream is a manifestation of your fears that your dad might not come home. It's quite natural, actually."

"But it knew about Haven," Atlas said. "It said Dad won't come home if I don't go. I think it's holding him prisoner."

Ormon shook his head. "Well, that could just be your subconscious mind playing tricks on you," he said, expecting that Atlas would know just what he meant. "I mean, we never even heard of Haven until yesterday, so it might have, like, seeped into your dreams."

Atlas pondered Ormon's words. "Okay, but what if Mom didn't make it up? What if it's really there?"

"I guess it's possible," Ormon said, scratching his chin, "but then you're talking about alternate universes. That stuff's out of my league."

A light flickered on in Atlas' head. It didn't happen often that he had an idea that Ormon hadn't thought of first, but this was one of those times.

"Maybe we can use the map to get there," he said.

Just then, Pepper rode up, excited and breathless. "I think I can help your dad, Dude."

Atlas didn't say a word. Pepper always had crazy ideas.

"Pepper, this is serious," said Ormon.

"Guys, I _am_ serious," he said, "C'mon, you gotta see this!"

Atlas trailed behind the two as they sped toward Pepper's house. It was not as nice as Atlas' or Ormon's and was also not in a particularly good neighborhood, but it was tidy.

Atlas and Ormon had been friends since they were in kindergarten, but Pepper came several years later, moving to Seattle from Oregon with his father. Atlas and Ormon had both of their parents, and Ormon figured that Pepper's quick temper came from not having a mother at home. No one ever asked what happened to her and Pepper never broached the subject.

Atlas slowed as he pulled into the driveway of the drab, gray house that looked much like all the other houses on the street. It was one-story, with an unfinished basement where the boys would sometimes hang out for hours.

Pepper's pride and joy, however, was the rickety garage in back. It was pretty much his because his father rarely used it. With Atlas was out of earshot, Ormon whispered, "You gonna tell him about the map?"

"That's what I'm talking about," Pepper whispered back.

Pepper got off his bike and lifted the garage's creaky, aluminum door.

He then turned to Atlas, his tone serious. "We've got to repeat the Toxic Pledge."

Atlas exhaled loudly. All he wanted to see was Pepper's secret, but Pepper insisted. "Dude, you won't be sorry."

Atlas shrugged and grudgingly placed his hand atop Pepper's and Ormon's. Together, the trio recited their secret pledge.

"If war and death or mishap comes, or enemies bend our fingers, we'll never talk, nor reveal our secrets, 'cause the Toxic Brotherhood lingers."

Then they shook hands and Pepper stepped inside the musty, junk- filled garage. In the corner was a workbench with rusted tools on top. Bicycle parts hung from nails on the walls. This was Pepper's castle.

He closed the curtain over the garage's lone window, explaining, "It's better when it's dark," then walked to an old trunk and pulled out the map, smiling triumphantly.

Atlas' jaw dropped. "That's my Mom's," he stammered. Pepper, entranced by the map, wasn't listening.

"I was gonna take it back last night, but it started glowing like this," he said, unfolding the map, filling the room with a dull light.

Atlas and Ormon were awed by the sight. Two arch-like figures on the right edge of the map glowed brightly. On the other side, in Haven, four red lights flickered rhythmically.

"Ormon, what do you think?" Atlas said, sure that Ormon had a scientific explanation for this.

"Whoa," was all Ormon could say.

"*That* doesn't help," Atlas replied.

Pepper had an idea. "I think these arches are the way in. Now, check this out," he said, walking towards the garage door and watching the lights grow more intense with each step. "See? It gets brighter depending on which way you walk."

"It's a homing beacon!" Ormon exclaimed, "Like GPS."

"Yeah," Pepper said to Atlas, "All you gotta do is wait till it's dark and follow the light. It'll take you right to it."

For the first time, Atlas was afraid. And it showed. "Will you guys come, too?" he asked timidly.

Pepper and Ormon both looked away. Sure, Atlas was their best friend and all, but neither of them had ever really thought about going to another world. Friends or not, this was a very scary thought.

"Uh, I gotta help my dad with some stuff," Pepper said.

Atlas turned to Ormon, who spoke in a near-whisper, "Algebra homework, Atlas. Sorry."

There was an awkward silence. Atlas wasn't sure about Pepper's excuse, but he knew that Ormon was telling the truth. He also knew asking the pair to accompany him on such a journey was a large request.

"Well, what should I do?" Atlas asked.

"Dude, it's your dad. You gotta go," Pepper blurted.

"But my mom'll never let me."

"You gotta be your own man on this."

Atlas looked to Ormon, who shrugged.

"What's the matter?" said Pepper, "I did all the work

for you."

For a moment, Atlas didn't reply. He was thinking about revealing something he had never shared with anyone, not even Ormon. Finally, with a shameful look, Atlas admitted his most-closely guarded secret.

"I, uh... I can't read a map," he said.

Pepper and Ormon look at each other with amazement. "You?" Pepper said. "Dude, you've got to be kidding me."

But Atlas wasn't kidding. Not at all.

THREE
Pepper's Promise

Several nights later, Atlas lay in bed staring into the darkness, listening to the sounds of his mother's soft breathing from the room across the hall. He'd been waiting for what seemed like hours.

Sarah Mapp had been sleeping fitfully ever since Ahib brought the terrible news that Field had been in an accident and gone missing. Days passed, and though workers in Althanar were continuing their rescue efforts, no new information had come.

Once Atlas was sure she was sound asleep, he pulled back the covers, fully dressed, and stepped lightly onto the floor. Just as the numbers on the clock next to his bed flipped over to 11:00 p.m., three short bursts of light came through the window – right on schedule.

Beneath his second story window, Pepper and Ormon were waiting. Atlas grabbed his backpack and tiptoed out of the room. He stopped outside Sarah's room and watched her as she slept.

Sadness overwhelmed him as he thought of having to leave her in order to find his father, but he'd left a note for her to make sure she understood.

Atlas said a silent goodbye and crept outside.

Pepper was dressed in army fatigues with a bandana wrapped around his unruly hair. Ormon wore a dark-colored jacket and black jeans. Both boys had black grease paint smeared under each eye, ready for war.

Their clothes complimented Atlas' dress, although he decided not to wear the war paint, "just in case the people in The Arch World are friendly," he'd said.

"What took you so long?" Pepper asked as Atlas walked up.

"I had to say goodbye to Mom."

"Dude, you weren't supposed to tell her!"

"I didn't," Atlas said.

"Keep your voice down, Pepper," Ormon whispered, digging a piece of paper out of his back pocket. "I've got the checklist right here. We should have everything you need."

Atlas placed the items into his backpack as Ormon rattled them off. "Swiss Army Knife…waterproof matches…compass…four chocolate bars…jerky."

Pepper, with a sly smile, handed Atlas a book. "Map Reading for Dummies," he said. "Thought you could use it."

"Um, thanks," Atlas said, with a sheepish look.

Meanwhile, Ormon continued to check items off the list, "Super Soaker… bottled water…hot dogs," he said, finishing up. "We missing anything?"

Pepper suddenly remembered the map, and pressed it into Atlas' palm. "You can't forget this, Dude."

Atlas looked uneasily at the glowing little map. "Are you sure you guys can't go with me?" he asked.

"We told you, if you're not back in two days, we'll come after you," Pepper said. He looked Atlas in the eyes and added, "That's a promise."

Atlas nodded, hopped onto the handlebars of Pepper's bike, and the trio pedaled off into the night.

Using the map as their own little North Star, the boys rode in silence up and down the dark, empty streets of suburban Seattle. They stopped every once in awhile to take a break and collect their bearings.

When they were several miles from home, the map began to pulsate, as if alerting the boys that they were near to their destination.

"This must be the place," Atlas said, hopping off Pepper's bike even before it came to a stop. "It has to be it."

Ormon and Pepper lay their bikes down and looked around curiously. There were no bright, shiny arches here, only a neat, manicured lawn outside a closed and dark McDonald's restaurant.

"I don't get it, Dude," Pepper said, scratching his head. "The map's glowing like crazy, but there's nothing here."

"Wait a second," Ormon said, walking over to a large, unlit Mickey D's sign. It was almost the same height as the boys, with a red background and two large yellow arches in the center. "This has got to be the way in. Maybe there's a secret password or something."

Atlas took out his flashlight and examined the map, searching for something they might have missed. But there were no other words on the canvas except for *The Arch World*, painted by Sarah's hand.

"It could be like in Harry Potter where he had to run through that wall at the train station to get to the Hogwart's Express," Pepper offered.

"Everybody knows Harry Potter isn't real," Ormon scoffed.

Atlas was frustrated. "What good's the map if I can't get in? Maybe we should forget it."

"Well, it's *your* dad," Pepper said.

"Pepper, that's not fair," Ormon snapped. "You'd be bummed out, too, if your dad was missing and you didn't know how to find him."

"Yeah, but I wouldn't give up so easily," Pepper said. "Toxic Soldiers fight until the end, remember?"

Pepper had Ormon there.

Pepper checked his watch. "It's one o'clock in the morning, Atlas. My dad'll kill me if he finds out I'm not home."

Ormon looked at Atlas. "I'll stay if you want."

"No, you guys go," he said. "If I don't get in, I guess I'll see you tomorrow."

Atlas and Ormon hugged. Pepper offered his hand for a high-five. "Two days, Dude," he said, "or we're coming for you."

Atlas watched Pepper and Ormon mount their bikes and ride away. Once they were gone, he noticed for the first time how cold and gloomy the night was. For the first time, he felt alone.

But Atlas wasn't as alone as he thought. Inside the restaurant, a tall, thin janitor mopped away in the kitchen, dancing to the music piped into his ears from his headphones.

Splashing water onto the floor from a yellow plastic bucket, the janitor swished the water around in circular patterns, sometimes swaying while he worked. He even did a little spin with the mop handle, like he was dancing with a partner.

Now, dancing while mopping isn't the safest or smartest thing to do, and the janitor learned this lesson when he lost his balance and slipped on the slick tiles.

He tried desperately to break his fall, grabbing at a large red lever as he crashed to the floor, but it was no use. The lever flicked to the ON position as he landed on the hard ceramic surface in a heap.

At that moment, Atlas was fast losing hope that he would ever find his way into The Arch World, and, worse, fearing that he would never again see his father. Suddenly, there was an electrical hum – and the McDonald's sign flickered to life, slowly revolving.

Atlas jumped to his feet, staring as the sign rotated with arches illuminated.

"Wow," he said to himself, looking around and noticing that he was still alone. He looked at the map, which glowed brighter than ever.

Pepper's words came back to him: "It could be like in Harry Potter where he had to run through that wall at the train station to get to the Hogwart's Express."

"Well," Atlas said, "There's only one way to find out."

He tightened his backpack, fondled the amulet around his neck and waited for the sign to turn so that the arches faced him head on. Then, he made a mad dash, closed his eyes and leapt into the air with a scream...

"AAAAAAAaaaahhhhhhhhh!!!!!!!!!"

BAM!

Atlas bounced to the ground with a thud, seeing stars. He collected himself and slowly stood up. Light filtered from a large crack in the sign.

"So much for that," he said, rubbing his throbbing head.

There was a slight tremor under his feet that he barely noticed. Growing in intensity, the ground shook and trembled. An earthquake, he wondered?

Atlas whirled in time to see the lush green grass rise as though pushed by a powerful force from beneath. The earth split apart. A large black door materialized in the void.

"Whoa!" he exclaimed, unable to move as the door silently opened outward and fell backwards onto the ground.

Before Atlas could react, he was sucked inside like lint into a vacuum cleaner.

Just as quickly, the door slammed shut and disappeared, as though it had never been there at all.

Inside the restaurant, the dancing janitor arose from the kitchen floor, untangled the headphones from around his neck and rubbed his aching back. He placed the mop into the bucket and turned off the lights. Only then did he notice that the bright red lever marked "Marquee," was in the ON position.

He flipped the lever off and left the room.

Outside, the sign went dark and slowly stopped turning.

Several miles away, ferocious lightning flashed in the sky over Ahib's house. The wind whipped violently, slapping the shutters against the frame of his small simple home with a loud clackety-clack.

Over the din there was a baby's cry. Soft, but a cry, nonetheless.

Ahib was deep in a dream of the past when the storm struck. His beautiful wife, Mahin, was awakened by the commotion, and jostled her husband gently. "Ahib, did you hear something?"

Ahib, talking in his sleep, could not be roused from his slumber. "I will hunt you down and kill you, Ada! You thief!" he mumbled, before he turned on his side and resumed snoring noisily.

Mahin was worried as she quickly put on a robe and tied back her long black hair. She hurried down the hall with flashes of lightning illuminating the way to her newborn baby's room.

What Mahin saw when she walked inside frightened her

to the core. Over her baby's crib, attached to the mobile of cute little orbiting stars and planets, was Ahib's amulet, aglow with the brightest light, jumping and swaying as if being jerked by invisible hands.

Terrified, Mahin snatched her wailing son to safety and rocked him gently, unable to break her gaze from the possessed medallion.

At the same time, a world away near Morocco, a similar storm was brewing. On a hilltop sat Neffer's sandstone house nestled amongst tall palm trees. Above it, lightning fought with thunder. Gusts of wind lifted sand and dust into the air, making it hard to see.

Strangely, however, in the village below, there was no such storm. Candles in the windows there flickered gently. The breeze was light and refreshing in the hours before dawn.

Still, despite the noise outside, on a large bed inside a cramped room, Neffer slept silently, his hands clasped and his long white locks of hair unleashed. On a nightstand nearby lay his turban, several books and a copper oil lamp. Magnificent oil paintings filled the walls and exotic animal skin rugs covered the floor.

He was undisturbed by the howling winds and even the rumbling that shook the foundation of his home. Upon Neffer's chest, his amulet glowed. Suddenly, an eagle's cry awakened him with a start.

AWWWWEEE-AWWWEEEE!

Neffer bolted upright, quickly wide-awake. "Atlas!" he said, breathlessly, clutching his medallion.

Neffer did not know what peril Atlas faced, but he knew there was danger, for Agle's cry had told him so. As he put on his slippers and shuffled out of his bedroom, his thoughts turned to Compass Mapp.

Many years before he had made a vow to his greatest friend that he would do all he could to protect the Mapps, who were as much a family to Neffer as his own. Neffer had kept his promise with Field. Now, he would do the same for Field's only child.

Neffer lit his oil lamp and walked into a room filled with books from floor to ceiling. He put on his rhinoceros-horn spectacles and inspected the dusty shelves. It didn't take long to find the book he was looking for, an old, large tome bound in thick leather: *"A Thousand Years of Curses."*

Neffer lugged the book to a table and opened it, flipping through page after page of demons and majestic figures, tales of dark and unhappy things, ancient evil spells and their remedies.

As he searched, he fingered his amulet, knowing that it would help him discover the answer. Neffer stopped on a page that inspired fear in his heart. He looked up towards the heavens and crossed himself.

"I must get to America!" he said, with urgency, then mouthed a little prayer. "May the Gods protect you, young one."

Outside, the storm raged on.

FOUR
Secrets of Children

The smell of frying bacon, eggs and pancakes filled the Mapp house.

Sarah was up earlier than usual cooking Atlas his favorite breakfast in the whole world before school. Since Field's disappearance, she did all she could to keep up a semblance of normalcy, and making breakfast for Atlas was one way to make sure that things felt, well, normal.

But as Sarah dodged the hot dollops of grease popping from the frying pan, her thoughts were troubled. Things *were* different. Though it was common for Field not to be home for breakfast, because he was often off on long expeditions, Sarah had never before worried that he might not return.

She forced the thoughts from her mind and poured orange juice into cups from a pitcher. "Atlas, breakfast is ready," she called out.

There was no reply.

Maybe he's in the bathroom cleaning up, she thought, as she fixed two plates and neatly set the table. With the sizzle gone from the frying pan, Sarah listened closely, noticing there was no sound of activity; no shower running, none of the usual racket Atlas made as he prepared for school.

She called out again, this time more urgently, "Atlas, your food's going to get cold. Come and eat, Honey."

Still, no answer.

Slightly alarmed, Sarah went to Atlas' room. His bed

was already made. This was not unusual, but what was strange was that the bed didn't appear to have been slept in.

As Sarah turned to leave the room, she noticed the little handwritten note Atlas had left for her on his nightstand, next to a family vacation photograph.

With trembling hands, Sarah picked up the note, which read:

Mom,

Gone to help Dad. Don't worry.

Love, Atlas

Sarah covered her mouth with her hand, a rush of worry already settling in. Her heart quickened. Gone where, she thought? Althanar was on the other side of the world. How could Atlas have gotten the notion that he could somehow help Field?

Sarah ran into the kitchen, nearly wrenching the phone off the wall as she dialed frantically.

When the phone rang, Ahib was in the midst of a spat with Mahin over the frightful actions of his amulet from the night before.

"Agle protects us, Mahin," he was saying, "Surely there must be some explanation for this!" and answered the phone with a high-pitched, "Hello?"

"Ahib, it's Sarah…"

"Oh, hello, Mrs. Ma-"

"Atlas is gone, Ahib," Sarah said, cutting him off. "He left a note saying he went to help Field and I don't know where he is."

Though concerned, Ahib tried to remain calm. "He is but a young boy, Mrs. Mapp. He could not have possibly gone far. I am sure when he tires of his search that he will come home. I would not worry about this."

"How can I not worry, Ahib?" Sarah said. "He's all I've got left."

"I understand," Ahib said calmly. "I assure you, he will come home."

"But Ahib... what if he doesn't?"

For this, Ahib had no answer. He could not fathom that Atlas would not come home. "If he is not back soon, I will go look for him, Mrs. Mapp," Ahib promised.

"Thank you," Sarah said, before hanging up the phone.

Ahib turned to Mahin, who remained upset. She stood there silently, glaring at the amulet in her husband's hand that she was sure had something to do with all of this.

When the bell rang at Peace Elementary School, Pepper and Ormon scrambled out of their seats toward the door, only to be stopped by their teacher, Mrs. Willing.

"Boys, is Atlas sick today?" she asked

Ormon began stammering, before Pepper stepped in.

"I think there's some stuff going on at home with his Dad, Mrs. Willing," Pepper explained. "You know, his dad's a big explorer and he goes all around the world doing this exciting stuff."

"Yes, I know all about the Mapp family, Pepper," Mrs. Willing said. "It's just not like Atlas to miss school without his mother calling in."

"I'm sure everything's all right, Mrs. Willing," Pepper said.

"Yeah," Ormon added weakly, avoiding her gaze.

Mrs. Willing eyed the boys for a moment, and then said, "Okay, you run along. I'm sure everything's fine."

"Bye Mrs. Willing," they replied in unison, and burst out the door.

When they were out on the playground, Pepper scolded Ormon. "It's supposed to be a secret, Ormon. Toxic Soldiers never tell. You know the rules."

"I wasn't going to say anything," Ormon replied. "I was just going to ask her what she knew about wormholes."

Pepper was flabbergasted. "Worm what?"

"Wormholes," Ormon said, matter-of-factly, "are basically openings in the space-time continuum that allow you to travel great distances in the blink of an eye. I figure the way into The Arch World is basically a wormhole. Since teachers know everything, I wanted to ask Mrs. Willing."

Pepper's head was spinning. This talk of space-time travel and wormholes wasn't his thing. All he knew was that they had a responsibility to keep their secret and protect their friend.

"Bookworm, I don't have a clue what you're talking about," he said, "but you can't talk to anybody about this. Not even your dad."

"But, he's a scientist," Ormon protested.

Pepper eyed Ormon seriously. "Are we gonna have to say the Toxic Pledge again?"

Ormon shook his head vigorously. He would do anything not to have to repeat the pledge again for the millionth time.

"Besides," Pepper added, "Atlas probably got tired and cold out there and just walked back home."

Ormon was incredulous. "What are you talking about? You don't believe he got in?"

"C'mon. You don't really believe The Arch World is real, do ya?"

Ormon couldn't believe his ears.

"But you saw the map, Pepper. That was real. Why

wouldn't The Arch World be real?"

"All I'm saying is that Atlas is under a lot of stress with his dad missing and all. I think if we were in his shoes, we'd be willing to believe almost anything, too."

"Well, I believe it's real and I think he got in," Ormon said, defiantly. "Why else would he miss class?"

"I guess we'll find out," Pepper said. "I gotta go. See ya later."

Watching Pepper walk away, Ormon thought of the promise Pepper made that they would rescue Atlas if he didn't come back home in two days. Now Ormon wondered how Pepper could have made Atlas such a promise if he didn't even believe in The Arch World?

Ahib sat alone wearing a terribly worried expression. Mahin had taken the baby to visit her mother and Ahib hadn't been able to convince her that the amulet could not possibly cause harm. He was sure Mahin had believed him, but she was still upset when she left, which, of course, left Ahib upset.

There had been no more news of Atlas since the early-morning call from Sarah. Now, it was late in the afternoon and Atlas' continued absence was beginning to worry him.

Suddenly, there was a knock on the door.

Ahib sprang to his feet wondering who could possibly be knocking – especially with the big brass doorbell that he had so proudly and recently installed himself – right there before any visitor's eyes.

Once Ahib opened the door, however, he understood immediately and fell to his knees. There were no doorbells where *this* visitor came from.

Standing on the front porch before him in purple traveling robes, a white turban and a jeweled walking cane was none other than Neffer. In his hand, he carried an old leather satchel.

"Oh, glorious Neffer, what a surprise to see you. It has been so long," Ahib said, suddenly realizing, "What are you doing here? In America?"

Neffer walked inside. Ahib had forgotten his manners. He leapt up, quite apologetic, but Neffer's tone quieted him.

"The young Mapp is in grave danger. We have much work to do."

"But...but how did you know?"

Neffer pulled his amulet from beneath his robes. "Agle sees all," Neffer said, curtly adding, "How did you *not* know?"

"I hung my amulet over the baby's crib to keep him safe," Ahib said, now understanding that his medallion's strange behavior from the night before *was* connected to Atlas' peril.

Neffer shuffled over and sat at Ahib's dining room table, rummaged through his satchel and pulled out a crusty old book.

"A Thousand Years of Curses?" Ahib said, his face nearly turning white with fright. "Atlas has been cursed?"

"Possibly," Neffer said, calmly. "But we can save him and his father. There is still time."

Ahib was perplexed. "But Professor Mapp was in a mine accident in Althanar, while the boy was here. How coul-"

"There are more worlds than ours, Ahib. Agle's call told me that Atlas is no longer in our world. I believe he journeys to save Field. From what, I fear, even he does not know."

Ahib gasped.

"There have been a million curses over the past thousand years," Neffer said. "We have to find the precise one that has befallen Field and Atlas."

Neffer paused, looking up, "Somewhere close is a Door of Desire."

"I do not understand," Ahib said.

"It is a passageway into and out of our world," Neffer explained. "A door that only opens for those who truly desire to enter."

"So the boy's desire to save his father-"

"Precisely, Ahib. It gave him the power to open one of these doors. Now, you and I must find this place."

"But how?" Ahib asked.

Neffer chuckled. "A child would not go on a journey without telling someone."

"But I have already spoken with Mrs. Mapp, and she has no idea," Ahib said.

"Ah, dear Ahib," Neffer replied, "If one wishes to know the secrets of children, one must ask a child."

Ahib quickly understood the wise Neffer's meaning. And he knew exactly whom to ask.

Not very much later, Pepper and Ormon sat side-by-side on Sarah Mapp's couch, looking quite serious – and quite innocent. Neffer and Sarah occupied chairs in front of the boys while Ahib kneeled close, pleading.

"If you know something, you must tell us. It is of the utmost importance."

Pepper shrugged his shoulders. "We told you everything, Mr. Ahib. Atlas didn't say anything 'cept that he was worried about his dad."

Ormon, not very good at telling a lie, kept quiet and shot Pepper a sideways glance. This, Neffer noticed.

"He's our best friend," Pepper said. "We wouldn't hide anything from you."

Ahib, who believed in the goodness of just about everyone – except Ada, and only after Ada had stolen the Diamonds of Bushawri – was satisfied. "I think they are telling the truth," he said.

Neffer locked eyes with Pepper for a long moment. Pepper betrayed nothing, but Neffer's amulet caught his eye.

"That's the same necklace Atlas has!" he exclaimed.

"I gave it to him on the day he was born," Neffer said, moving closer to allow Pepper to inspect it. "It has protected him ever since."

Pepper didn't bite. "Then, there's nothing to worry about. Atlas never takes it off."

"I hope that is true," Neffer said. "And I hope you have told us all that you know."

Pepper nodded quickly. Ormon, half-heartedly.

"What do you think, Neffer?" asked Sarah.

"I imagine that Atlas believes he can save his Field and will leave no stone unturned until he finds him," Neffer said.

Sarah didn't understand. "I don't know what he could possibly think he can do," she said. "He's only 10 years old, but he knows Althanar's very far away."

Neffer nodded and took Sarah's hand, looking deeply into her eyes. "When a boy goes in search of his father," he said, "distance is of no matter."

Ormon hadn't spoken most of the time during his interrogation, but Neffer's words made him utter the only word he could think of.

"Whoa."

Dusk fell as Ahib and Neffer drove away from the Mapp home – at exactly the same time Ormon and Pepper were riding home on their bikes. They had driven for a while in silence, but Ahib was itching to ask a question. Finally, he did.

"Oh glorious Neffer, why did you not tell Mrs. Mapp the truth?"

At that same time, Ormon also was itching to ask Pepper a similar question. Finally, he also did.

"Pepper, why didn't you tell that Neffer guy the truth?"

Bouncing along in Ahib's truck, Neffer said, "I am not sure she would understand the truth. She has enough worry in her life right now. Do you wish me to alarm her more?"

Ahib nodded, but didn't reply.

About this time, Pepper looked at Ormon and said, "I don't think he could handle the truth. You wanted me to give the old guy a heart attack?"

Ormon nodded, but didn't reply.

"Atlas shares the courageous blood of Compass Mapp and his father. He will fight with all he has," Neffer added. "We simply need him to hold on until we can get there."

"I hope you are right, Neffer," said Ahib.

Pepper seemed to be reading Neffer's mind.

"If Atlas is anything like his dad," he said, "he'll fight like a real Toxic Soldier. He just needs to hold the fort until we can get there."

"I hope you're right, Pepper," Ormon said.

"'Course, I am. We just have to make sure those old guys don't follow us. I know they suspect something."

Pepper was right.

As Ahib pulled into his driveway, Neffer had a thought. "I believe I am right," he said. "We just have to follow Atlas' young friends. I suspect they know something."

FIVE
The Arch World

Atlas opened his eyes and sat up slowly, finding himself on a thin ledge on the side of a mountain. At first, his vision was fuzzy and he shook his head to be sure he was seeing what was actually before him.

The sky was a bright shade of pink and rays of sunlight beamed down from two suns set far apart. *Two suns?* Atlas thought, but his eyes were not deceiving him. There was indeed one large sun sitting on the left side of the horizon and a slightly smaller one on the right that looked like a baby sun.

And that was not all. In the far-off distance to his right, he saw a large golden yellow arch towering up until it was lost in the pink sky and purplish clouds.

To his left, there was an identical arch almost too far away to see, and still another directly before him well past a thicket of trees and strange vegetation that he had never seen before.

Atlas pulled the map from his pocket and tried to get his bearings.

Yes, straight ahead on the map was an image of this exact place - the wondrous and incredible Lazantine Forest.

Atlas glanced at his watch and noticed that it had stopped. It was still ticking, yet the second hand didn't seem to move. He had no idea how long he had been unconscious and no idea what time it was, or even if it was the same day. The only thing he was sure of was that he was no longer in his own world.

It wasn't until Atlas stood up that he realized the ledge was so small that he couldn't take a step forward without falling off. He peered over the edge and realized with terror that the sound of rushing water he heard came from a small river, hundreds of feet directly below at the bottom of a canyon.

Fear overcame Atlas as he felt the little ledge shifting beneath his feet, slowly receding into a groove in the mountainside.

He turned to see the mouth of a cave behind him disappear as if it had never been there. Pebbles spilled over the edge of the shrinking ledge, trickling into the abyss. Atlas screamed and dug in, but the ledge only got smaller and smaller. Soon, it would be gone and he would plummet to a most certain death.

"Somebody help me!" he cried. "Heeeeellllpppppp!!!" He heard his scream echoing, but there was no reply.

Suddenly, he looked up and saw it, the first rungs of an impossibly long ladder leading over the canyon to the other side. He glanced at his map.

"The Monkey Bar Bridge!" he exclaimed, reaching up and grabbing on, just as the ledge disappeared. His sneakers dangled in mid-air. Atlas knew he wasn't strong enough to swing across the Monkey Bar Bridge hand over hand as he did on the playground back home. He had to figure out another way.

Summoning all his strength, he swung his legs forward and latched onto the rungs with both feet, and with great effort, pulled himself atop the bridge, where he could more safely crawl across.

Just as a little internal voice warned, *"Don't look*

down," Atlas instinctively stole a glimpse at the river below.

He was frozen and scared out of his wits as he watched Pepper's gift, "Map Reading for Dummies," slip out of his backpack and flutter out of sight into the canyon.

With a mighty effort, Atlas straddled the Monkey Bar Bridge and took a moment to calm down. He made a silent vow to not again look below into the chasm, secured his backpack and, inch-by-perilous-inch, made his way across toward The Lazantine Forest.

Atlas was exhausted by the time he got to the other side and flopped onto his back upon the pearl-white, sandy ground. It felt just like a beach back home. The biggest difference between this beach and his own world was that there was no ocean or water leading up to it, only a cliff where one could fall over to their doom.

A hundred yards or so from where he was now, The Lazantine Forest cropped up abruptly, just as his mother had painted it on the canvas. The trees were unlike any he had ever seen, some with striped trunks like candy canes, and others with huge leaves and bright flowers. These details weren't evident from his map, but they were here nonetheless.

A butterfly with eight wings flitted by, the first evidence of life in The Arch World. It stopped to study the strange creature from another world, then continued on its zigzag path.

Atlas' hands and knees ached from crawling such a long distance. He had never liked heights much, and when he looked back across, he wondered how he had ever made it.

After resting a short while and pondering the strange color of the sky, Atlas sat up and opened his backpack to take a sip of water. The air was thick and humid, and he was very thirsty.

As he turned the bottle up and greedily gulped away, streams of water spilled down both sides of his mouth to the ground.

Out of the corner of his eye, Atlas thought he saw granules of sand skitter away from the falling water droplets. To be certain, he poured several drops from the bottle onto the ground. Sure enough, the sand was indeed moving away. It was a curious sight, but as he was discovering, this was a curious world.

Atlas scooped up a handful of the sandy substance and sniffed it. Then, he tossed it away and tasted his fingertip.

"It's like salt," he said to himself, spitting on the ground and wiping his hand on his pants. But as his saliva hit the ground, the sand again scattered, as if allergic to moisture. Still, Atlas was not alarmed – until he felt a small rumble, and heard a deep, low growl, growing louder.

Atlas jumped to his feet, eyes searching, but he couldn't tell where the growl was coming from.

"Hello?" he said timidly, not really hoping for an answer. Suddenly, the salt moved, gathering itself, as if alive. Before Atlas' eyes, the salt assembled, molding itself into a shape that at first appeared human, though, much larger. After several more seconds, he saw that the developing form was menacing, like a monster.

Atlas turned to run toward the trees, but hesitated out of fear that even more danger could be lurking there. Unsure what to do, he stood rooted to the spot while a large head and shoulders sprouted from the ground.

The evil figure's coal black eyes focused squarely on Atlas.

"AAAAhhhhhhh!!!" Atlas screamed. "What in the world are you?"

By now, the Salt Monster was almost fully formed, with massive arms and legs and claw-like talons for fingertips. It loomed nearly ten feet tall with a stony body and a voice that made Atlas' blood tremble.

"What are you?" it replied, in a low, rumbling voice. Atlas was petrified as the monster lumbered towards him. "All who trespass here must die!"

Chest heaving, Atlas looked for a place to run, only then noticing that the now-bare ground was littered with skeletons and bones. He tripped and fell, coming eyeball-to-eye socket with a skull.

"AAAAhhhhhhhh!!!!!!"

The Salt Monster mimicked Atlas' cry.

"AAAAhhhhhhhh!!! You must die!"

Atlas desperately scooted away from the advancing monster. "Sir, I don't *have* to die. Really, I'm just here looking for my dad." The monster wasn't listening.

"No one escapes The Arch World."

As frightened as Atlas was, he couldn't help wondering if the monster knew that he was not trying to escape The Arch World at all, and had only just gotten here. But that didn't seem to matter as the monster swiped a mighty claw at Atlas, barely missing and leaving a jagged mark in the ground.

Atlas scrambled to his feet, desperately looking for a way to defend himself against the beast. If he were going to die, it would not be without a fight.

He could see Pepper and Ormon coming after him and finding only a shred of his clothing or a piece of plastic from his Super Soaker. Almost without thinking about it, Atlas grabbed the Super Soaker slung over his shoulder and took aim – just as the Salt Monster prepared to take another swipe with its razor-sharp talons.

"Look Mister," he said in a quivering voice, "I don't want to have to shoot you with the Acid Rain Spray."

But the monster cackled, saying, "Nothing can save you!"

As it reared back, Atlas closed his eyes and squeezed the trigger, sending a torrent of water at the monster. He opened his eyes just in time to see the monster's deadly hand melt like a clump of wax.

"What is this?" the Salt Monster said, befuddled. Atlas stared at his Super Soaker in amazement. "Whoa, this stuff really *does* work!"

The monster waved its stumpy hand in the wind. As it dried, to Atlas' horror, the hand regenerated, returning finger by deadly finger.

"Now, you will die!" the angry monster said.

Atlas furiously fired streams of water at the Salt Monster's legs, sending it crashing to the ground, its wet feet and legs turned temporarily to mush. Even without legs, however, the monster dragged itself towards its prey, digging deep trenches with each powerful swipe of its hands.

Atlas kept shooting while retreating toward the trees, still trying to convince the monster to be reasonable. "C'mon, you don't have to kill me," he said. "I'm just a boy."

"AAAhhh!" the monster replied. "Boy will die!!!"

Atlas was nearly to the trees, and, he hoped, safety. But there was another problem: the monster's legs were growing back and his Super Soaker was running out of water.

Atlas then decided to run for it, dashing as fast as his legs could carry him. He was almost to the forest's edge when he tripped over a skeleton's ribcage and fell to the ground.

The Salt Monster's arms and legs had returned, and it was advancing on him quickly.

His weapon empty, Atlas frantically dug into his backpack and grabbed a bottle of water. He ripped the cap off and stuck the nozzle into the Super Soaker, but when he pulled the trigger - nothing happened.

Not a drop of water came out.

"What?!?" he screamed, snatching the bottle out only to see a protective tin foil safety seal. It was too late. With a roar, the Salt Monster reared back for the death blow.

Atlas' life flashed before his eyes. The images passed quickly and there weren't many things to remember because, well, he was only ten years old and he hadn't lived very long. He shut his eyes and waited for the painful end to come. But there was only darkness. And silence.

Atlas waited before opening his eyes, first one, and then the other. What he saw astonished him. The monster was gone and all that he could see was his own reflection and that of the trees behind him. Bewildered, he stood and looked around.

From nowhere and everywhere, a light voice whispered, "Run into the trees and hide. You'll be safe there."

Atlas whirled, but there was no one there. He still heard the Salt Monster's muffled wails, but he couldn't see it.

"Go, before Waheel realizes you are still here!" the voice said. Atlas didn't have to be told twice. He bolted into The Lazantine Forest and disappeared into the trees.

Later - Atlas wasn't sure how much later because his watch was still not working - he sat alone before a small fire listening to the strange sounds of the Lazantine Forest.

It was dark, but not the kind of darkness he was used to. Instead, the sky pulsed, like the Northern Lights he had once watched with his parents in Alaska. He remembered that as a particularly happy time not only because of the unusual celestial display in the sky, but also because he was allowed to stay up past his bedtime to witness it.

The other thing that told Atlas night had fallen in The Arch World was the emergence of two moons. Like the dual suns he saw earlier, there was a large moon and a smaller one. Still, both reminded him of the big bright moon he saw on clear Seattle nights in the summertime.

As he warmed his hands over the fire, he thought of his mother and hoped that she had found his note and was not worried about him. Then he thought of Ormon and Pepper. Would they really come for him as Pepper had promised?

He could hear Pepper's arrogant laugh when he'd tell him about starting the fire with the waterproof matches he'd stashed in his back pocket, instead of the way the boys were taught by their Boy Scout leader, Mr. Whitaker.

There were more than twenty scouts in his troop, but somehow, Pepper was the only boy who could actually make a fire by rubbing two sticks together. Pepper was very proud of this fact, often taunting the other boys, who tried until their fingers and palms were raw.

Atlas missed his friends, already. When school was in session, Ormon and Pepper were the first faces he saw when he got there in the morning. During the summer, they often began their days together, biking, fishing or playing Toxic Soldiers until nightfall.

Sometimes, they'd even camp outside in the Mapp's backyard and listen to the tales of danger and excitement his dad told when he was home from an expedition. Usually, they'd be too afraid to sleep afterwards.

Sadness gripped Atlas when he thought of his father. He wondered if the selfish thoughts he'd had of his dad not being around for his birthday somehow contributed to the bad luck that had befallen him. Atlas decided then that the first thing he would do when he found his father, after giving him a huge hug, of course, would be to apologize.

Curling up to sleep, he vowed to become the best son in the world.

Atlas hadn't dozed long when a strange sound startled him wide-awake. He bolted up holding the Super Soaker he'd gone to sleep with in his hand. It was already cocked and ready for any danger. He would certainly be ready if he had to do battle with The Salt Monster again.

He remained still and silent, listening intently. For a fleeting moment, he thought of putting out the fire, but quickly abandoned the thought when he considered sitting alone in the dark in this unfamiliar place. He strained his ears and soon heard the sounds again. Were they *voices?*

Against his better judgment, he called out into the darkness. "Is anybody there?"

There was no reply, but the voices seemed to be getting louder.

"If there's somebody out there, you'd better show yourself. I've got a gun and I'll shoot," he said, daring to raise his voice.

Nearby, there was a rustling in the bushes. Atlas leapt to his feet. "I'm serious. I'll shoot."

He backed up against a tree as the rustling grew louder. Then, he heard a voice, very clearly.

"He *is* the one!"

Another voice replied, "I don't think so."

"It _has_ to be him!" a deeper voice said.

The voices came from every direction.

"Who are you?" Atlas screamed, "What do you want?"

A flash of light exploded, nearly blinding him.

Through squinted eyes, Atlas saw a boy standing next to him - aiming an identical Super Soaker. It was *him*. Atlas did a double-take just to be sure. Yes, he was looking at himself.

"Hey, what's going on?" he said, reaching for a rock to hurl at his reflected image. But before he could throw the rock, the image morphed into a monster. Atlas screamed and jumped back.

"AAAAhhhhhhh!!!"

He fell on his rear end. The images before him became even more frightening: Godzilla. A giant, hairy Tarantula spider. Bloody faces.

Suddenly, a voice split the air.

"Reflect, stop! You'll scare the boy to death!"

Atlas was stunned to see a man move into the firelight. Well, it looked like a man at first, except that he was made of reflective material like a mirror. Atlas was speechless as the powerfully built Mirror Man extended a hand to help him off the ground.

"You are the one," he said, effortlessly lifting Atlas up.

"I'm the who?" Atlas asked.

"The one Reflect showed us," the Mirror Man said.

Atlas watched his distorted likeness reflecting off the stranger's body. "There's gotta be some mistake," he said.

"There is no mistake. She has the same power as her father, Vision."

"Who are you?" Atlas asked, as Reflect, a small mirror girl who appeared to be around his age, emerged from the brush with several other reflective beings and stood next to the

Mirror Man.

"I am Image," he said, "And you are the boy from the world above who came through the arches."

"You know about the arches? I thought my mom made them up."

"As I told you," Image said, "Reflect has the power of sight. She foretold us of your visit. That is how we knew to save you from Waheel."

"That big monster?"

Image nodded. "We hid you from him until you could escape."

Atlas was overwhelmed by his new visitors. He was also awed by their shimmering skin. It reflected everything around them. "You're like, like, mirror people," he said.

Image laughed. "I guess you could put it that way. Actually, we are known as The E'lum. Some call us Echoes, because we reflect what we see."

Atlas nodded toward the shiny little girl. "But how did she-"

"That's one of our defense mechanisms," Image explained. "You were about to throw a stone at Reflect and she protected herself by showing you things that you fear. I am sorry she scared you, but she is young and doesn't yet know how to control her abilities."

Other Mirror People emerged and stared at Atlas with wide eyes. "What is your name?" Image asked.

"I'm Atlas. Atlas Mapp... from Seattle," he added, hoping the additional information would help.

Image and the others gave him a blank look.

"I'm looking for a place called Haven," he said, reaching for his map, "Actually, I'm looking for my father. Do you know where Haven is?"

Atlas didn't notice Image and Reflect exchange glances. Suddenly, Image felt uneasy.

Looking around the dark Lazantine Forest, he said, "It's dangerous out here at night and we can't as easily protect you in the darkness. We'd be honored if you'd be our guest."

Atlas nodded. With all the danger he'd faced during his short time in The Arch World, he figured being with the Mirror People would be much better than going it alone.

Image motioned to a pair of large mirror men who gathered up Atlas' belongings. Giggling, Reflect skipped around Atlas while he stamped the fire out.

Image suddenly turned serious. "We must leave now," he said. "It is not safe here."

Image was right. Their every move was being watched under cover of darkness by two evil-looking gargoyles, the massive Boroom and his smaller brother, Sharibu. Spittle dripped off the sharp fangs jutting from the protruding mouths of the ugly creatures, which had small heads and tiny wings on their slimy-skinned, muscular backs.

With a demonic snicker, Boroom whispered to his grotesque sibling, "Master Kibu will be pleased to know that the boy is here. We must inform His Highness that Atlas Mapp is with The E'lum."

But Sharibu was itching for action, ready to attack the E'lum and snatch Atlas right then and there. "Why not just take the boy now, Boroom? Their numbers are small. They cannot possibly stop us."

"No, Sharibu. Master Kibu says that the boy must come willingly, brother. There is no need to fight the E'lum. They cannot protect him, anyway."

"Yes, yes," Sharibu said, slobber dripping off his chin, "Maybe next time. In any event, Master Kibu will be very, very happy."

The goyles laughed ghoulishly and set off, leaping silently from tree to tree in the dual moonlight and disappearing into the night.

SIX
Sarah's Map

It was a cool and clear night in Seattle. Sarah Mapp sat in a chair on her back porch staring up at the moon. Her younger sister, Jenny, who shared the same red hair and fair features, rubbed Sarah's tired shoulders. They looked so much alike that it was easy to see how they were often mistaken for twins.

Jenny lived far away, in Minnesota, but came as soon as she heard that her nephew had disappeared. A family needed each other in times like this. For a long while, neither of the sisters spoke. They just sat together in a way that only sisters can, silently understanding each other.

Evidence of Atlas' party still littered the backyard: birthday hats, toys and confetti were strewn about. Sarah had been too sick with worry to clean up the mess. She stared at the clutter while Jenny poured two cups of tea.

"I don't know what I'd do if you weren't here, Jen," Sarah said.

"C'mon, this is what sisters are for," Jenny said. "You'd be here for me, too. Trust me, Sarah, everything's going to be okay."

Sarah stifled a sob. She had been working hard to keep herself together, knowing she had to be strong for both Atlas and herself. But sometimes, the empty feeling inside was overwhelming.

Jenny moved close and hugged her. "God wouldn't take

them from you now. Not Field. Not Atlas. I know you and you know they're both okay and they'll be home any day now."

As much as Sarah wanted to believe Jenny, it was difficult. "It's just hard. With Field gone all the time, Atlas is all I have. He's never done anything like this before."

"But Atlas never had to worry about his father not coming home before, Sarah. He's a tough little boy and he's resourceful. That came from you."

She tenderly patted Sarah's hand. "He probably just needs time to deal with all of this. It wasn't the best birthday for him, you know?"

The two gazed up at the starry sky.

"Do you remember what Mom used to always tell us when Dad would go away?" Jenny asked.

"Mom told us lots of things," Sarah replied.

"That's true, but I remember how she would take us out in the back yard and point up in the sky. She'd say, 'See those stars? Your father's probably looking at the same stars as we are right now.' Remember that?"

Sarah nodded.

"So, I figure that somewhere, Atlas is looking up at the same stars that we're looking at right now."

It was a comforting thought that actually made Sarah smile. "I hope you're right, Jen," she said, her smile quickly fading. "But where is he? Where could he be?"

Inside Sarah's cottage, a small light emanated from the window. The light came from a painting on the easel; it was brimming with activity. In the place marked Haven, four little red blips beat to their own rhythms.

Far away, in the middle of a place labeled, The Lazantine Forest, a lone red light kept its own time.

Ker-thunk! Ker-thunk! Ker-thunk!

It was early the next afternoon, and Ormon sat quietly while Pepper bounced a small blue rubber ball against the aluminum door of his garage. He was still bothered by Pepper's surprising admission of the previous day.

Ker-thunk! Ker-thunk! Ker-thunk!

Because it was not in his nature to speak about something without deeply considering it, Ormon hadn't said anything. Finally, he spoke up.

"So, you don't believe in the map?" he asked.

Pepper stopped bouncing the ball. He knew this was coming, sooner or later.

"All I was saying is that if something happened to our dads, we'd be just like Atlas, ready to believe in anything, right?"

"Well, I don't think he'd just disappear," Ormon said.

"Atlas isn't really like us, Ormon," Pepper said, as if he and Ormon were the same kind of kids. "He isn't really into big adventures. Heck, half the time I have to drag him out to play Toxic Soldiers."

This was true, but Ormon defended his pal. "Hey, if your dad went on all these great adventures and was never home, I bet you wouldn't like that, either."

Pepper was silent for a moment, then said, "So, we still don't know where he is, do we?"

"Yes we do," Ormon objected. "I think he made it into The Arch World." Ormon looked Pepper square in the eyes and added, "We promised Atlas we'd come looking for him if we didn't hear anything in two days."

Ker-thunk!

Pepper tossed the ball up against the garage door again. "Yeah, so?"

"Well, it's now been two days. Toxic Soldiers don't leave anybody behind. We have an ethical and moral obligation to go find him. And since you don't believe he got in, what's wrong with going to take a look?"

Pepper considered it as Ormon hopped on his bike and pedaled off. He was going with or without Pepper, which was not like Ormon.

Pepper didn't know much about the meaning of words like ethical or moral, but he certainly didn't want to be left behind. He tossed the ball away, jumped on his bike and raced to catch up. "Hey, Bookworm, wait for me!"

Sitting in a car across the street, Ahib and Neffer watched the boys ride away. Neffer smiled softly to himself.

"Do you think they are going to the Door of Desire?" Ahib asked.

Neffer nodded and said, "Of that I am sure. You see, sometimes when a child doesn't reveal their secrets, one must follow them."

Neffer was not only wise, Ahib thought, he was also a genius.

Back at Sarah Mapp's home, the day had not gone well. There was no news of Atlas' whereabouts and she couldn't bring herself to rise from the couch. Thankfully, Jenny was there to provide comfort.

Sarah stared at the phone, looking sleepy and tired, but with both her husband and son missing, sleep was the furthest thing from her mind. She also had work to do, but she simply couldn't concentrate.

In an office downtown at the XL-LENT PUBLISHING COMPANY, Jean Brophy sat in an office whose walls were plastered with covers of the many children's books she had

published over the years. She was in her fifties, with a short
blond bob and a ruddy complexion.

As if suddenly reminded of something she'd forgotten,
Jean Brophy picked up the phone and dialed, waiting
impatiently for an answer.

Jenny picked up the phone to hear Jean Brophy's
gravelly voice. "Sarah? It's Jean Brophy," she said before
Jenny could speak. "We're still waiting for the illustrations to
okay before we go to print."

"I'm sorry, Ms. Brophy," Jenny said, "Sarah's sleeping.
She hasn't been feeling well. It's a family emergency."

"I'm sorry to hear that, but we really need those
illustrations. The project's already six weeks behind," Jean
Brophy said.

"Well, I'll be sure to tell Sarah as soon as she wakes
up," Jenny said, barely finishing the sentence when Sarah
appeared.

"I totally forgot to send those out," Sarah said, taking
the phone. "Jean, it's Sarah. I'm really so sorry about this.
Something came up and I've been very distracted."

She paused, listening, then said, "I know. The book's
really important to Field, too… I'll get them to you right
away."

Jean Brophy hung up the phone and exhaled as though
she was under a lot of pressure. She gazed down at a book
cover design. It was a photo of Atlas' family beneath the title,
"Traveling with the Mapps."

Sarah hung up looking equally stressed. Jenny was
worried.

"Sarah, you really shouldn't be thinking about work at a
time like this," she said. "You've got a lot on your mind."

But Sarah wouldn't hear of it. "I've got to think about

everything," she said, tears forming in her eyes. "If Field doesn't come back, this is exactly the sort of thing that I'll have to worry about. If I don't, who will?"

Jenny embraced Sarah. She had no answer for this.

It was late in the afternoon when the boys finally reached the McDonald's restaurant. They would have gotten there much sooner, but Pepper slowed their progress by ogling pretty girls along the way. Although his dad would not allow him to have a cell phone, Pepper liked to brag about his ability to collect phone numbers. Sometimes, he'd even give out Ormon's number as his own.

"Just tell them I'll be home later, Dude," Pepper was saying, "That's all you gotta do."

But Ormon wasn't listening. Along the way, he had heard just about everything Pepper had to say and didn't find much of it particularly interesting. He perked up, however, at the sight of the McDonald's, hoping to find a clue that Atlas had actually made it through into The Arch World.

In daylight, the area did not look so distant and foreboding. There were neat little homes across the street, families lounging and people walking their dogs. Surely, no one would notice two little boys casually inspecting the sign on the McDonald's lawn.

Several cars waited at the drive-thru and their occupants paid little attention when Ormon and Pepper dropped their bicycles and excitedly scrambled up to the sign.

Across the street, at a safe distance, Ahib's car pulled up. Suddenly, Neffer's amulet began to glow.

"This must be the place," he said.

Pepper kept lookout while Ormon closely inspected the sign. Ormon's eyes lit up when he noticed the large crack where Atlas banged his head.

"See this, Pepper? He made it!" Ormon screamed with joy. "Atlas ran through the sign just like you told him."

Pepper smiled. He had Ormon right where he wanted him. "So, now you're saying Harry Potter's *real*?"

Ormon noticed something lying in the grass, unseen by Pepper. He moved closer and found Atlas' little framed family photo. "There's no way he would have left this," he said, showing the picture to Pepper, who gulped in amazement.

The boys stood there with eyes agog – until a young Indian boy, about 10 years old, broke the silence with a shriek.

"Daddy, come!" he shouted. "These are probably the boys who broke our sign! Daddy!"

Ormon, wrenched from his trance by the commotion, protested. "Hey, we didn't break anything."

But the Indian boy would not listen. "Daddy, I have caught them!" he shrieked, at the top of his lungs.

Pepper didn't need to be told it was time to go. He grabbed his bike and hopped on, yelling, "C'mon, Ormon. Let's get outta here!"

They sped off with the Indian boy's cries still ringing in their ears. Across the street, Ahib and Neffer watched the scene unfold. Ahib looked confused, while Neffer was pensive.

"Maybe this is not the place, Neffer," he said.

In Neffer's fist, the amulet glowed brightly.

"This is most certainly the place, Ahib," he said. "Believe me. Let us go. We must prepare."

Ormon and Pepper were still shaken when they arrived back at Pepper's garage. They had been so anxious to escape the loud little Indian boy that they had not had time to think about what they had seen.

But now, Pepper was a believer, and it was time to make plans. The two sat drinking sodas when Pepper made the decision. "It's the only way, Dude," he said.

"But why don't we just ask, Pepper?" Ormon replied.

Pepper put his hands on his hips and stared at Ormon in dismay. "You know, to be so smart, Ormon, sometimes you're pretty stupid," he said. "What are we s'posed to say? 'S'cuse me, Mrs. Mapp, but we need to borrow one of your maps so we can go look for your kid?' I say we just take one and hit the road. It's not like she's going to miss it."

Ormon always believed it best to be honest, but after thinking over Pepper's plan, he decided there were exceptions. "I guess you're right," he said.

"'Course I am. Now, you in or you gonna be a sissy about it?"

"Why's it always a man thing with you?" Ormon asked.

Pepper stuck out his chest proudly and said, "'Cause I'm a man."

Ormon grabbed his bike and headed off. Pepper smiled and followed.

Ahib trailed Neffer into a great religious temple that was located not far from his home. Neffer had already prepared everything for the ceremony to summon the Gods of Mariah. Ahib was giddy with expectation.

Ahib gazed upon the large burning candle in the center of a circle on the floor next to a large holy book. Neffer removed his turban and placed his amulet in the middle of the circle. Although he had never witnessed such a ceremony, Ahib could not help but feel as though something were missing.

"Excuse me, Neffer," he said, "But should we not have some gift to offer the Gods of Mariah? Will they not seek some compensation for our consultation?"

Neffer was used to questions like this.

"Ahib, the sincerity of our hearts is compensation enough for the gods. They know why we are here… Hand me your amulet."

Ahib hurriedly lifted his prized possession over his head and gave it to Neffer, who placed it inside the circle.

Then, Neffer began a singsong chant.

"Umm Yah, Nay Son, De Oh, Quor Ran."

"This is soooo exciting!" Ahib said, unable to control himself.

"Shhhhh. One must never talk when calling upon the gods," Neffer reminded him.

Ahib dutifully bowed his head. "Oh, I am so sorry."

Neffer continued: "We beg an audience with you, most high of high and omnipotent ones, that we may seek guidance in matters of this world and those beyond."

A swift wind blew through the temple. The candle flared like a torch. "Oh, my goodness!" Ahib said, trembling.

"Quiet, Ahib. The gods come."

Speckles of light formed above the circle, and a filmy apparition appeared, floating, like a ghost. It was a woman, The Goddess Mariah, regal in a white gown, her long hair flowing as if in a perpetual breeze.

Neffer and Ahib both were surprised at seeing, well–

"What did you expect – a man?" Mariah said, her voice echoing. This time it was Neffer who sputtered.

"Oh, Holy Mariah, I have never called upon you before, so I ex-"

"Yes, Neffer," she said, "It's a man's world, even amongst the gods."

Ahib marveled, having never seen such a wondrous

sight.

"You are so beautiful, Goddess Mariah."

"Thank you, Ahib."

"But, but… how did you know my name?"

"She knows all," replied Neffer.

"Not all," said Mariah. "What I know is that the boy who seeks his father has traveled to The Arch World."

"The Arch World?" said Ahib.

"Yes. It is the one upon which your world rests, the only place where there is a portal to The World Below."

Although Ahib was not supposed to be the one talking, he did so, anyway. "But why has he gone there?"

"The boy is being lured by an evil spirit who wishes to exchange his soul for the life of his father," she said.

"Professor Mapp is still alive?" Ahib asked.

"For now. Whether he lives or dies depends upon the choice of his son."

Finally, Neffer spoke. "Can you tell us more of this spirit?"

At that moment, it became cold in the room. Even the Goddess Mariah seemed to feel the chill.

"They call him Kibu," she said. "In The World Below, he is king. My powers are not limitless, but the amulet will protect the boy until his choice is made. You have the wisdom to know what to do, Neffer. Good luck."

In a flash, Mariah was gone. Ahib was not pleased.

"Is this all?" he asked Neffer. "These riddles? Surely, there is more?"

But Neffer did not need the goddess to speak any more than she had. "It is enough, Ahib," he said. "Mariah's words only appear as riddles because the gods are complex, while we are simple. It is up to us to figure them out."

It was dark when Ahib and Neffer drove away from their meeting with the Goddess Mariah.

As usual, Ahib was at the wheel because Neffer, having been raised to ride camels, had never learned to drive a car. Besides, all of his life there had been someone just like Ahib to drive a vehicle whenever Neffer needed one.

While Ahib drove looking irritated, Neffer studied his big book.

"I do not see the purpose of consulting with the gods if they do not give you a straight answer," Ahib said.

Neffer, engrossed in his readings, did not hear Ahib, but he had found what he was searching for. "Aha," he said. "It is right here."

"What is right where?" Ahib asked, barely able to keep his eyes on the road.

"A curse that involves an exchange is one where a spirit comes to claim payment for what is owed," Neffer said.

"And what does this mean?"

"It means that one has taken something belonging to the spirit, which sets the curse in motion."

"So, Professor Mapp excavated something that unleashed a curse?"

"Evidently," Neffer replied. "And the price of whatever he recovered must be the cost of his child."

Reading on, Neffer saw it, "Yes, a first-born son."

"But this cannot be," Ahib protested.

"It is," Neffer said. "Sons pay for the sins of their fathers."

"But how?"

Neffer closed the book of curses and turned to Ahib, whose face was as pale as the ghostly Goddess Mariah.

"While spirits cannot usually harm us, they can affect *things* in the material world," Neffer explained. "The wind that brings chills to a windowless room, an object inexplicably knocked over. In this case, I fear the spirit was powerful enough to cause the mine collapse that imprisons Field."

"And the spirit lures the son," said Ahib, "who is faced with the terrible decision to trade his life for that of his father's?"

"Not his life, Ahib – his soul," Neffer replied. "A life is nothing to a spirit. Field unknowingly set the curse in motion of his free will, thus Atlas' choice is to accept the exchange of *his* free will."

"Or else the father … dies?"

Neffer didn't reply. He was already thinking of a plan.

"But on which excavation did this occur?" Ahib asked. "And how would a boy know how to get to this Arch World?"

"*That*," Neffer said, "is what we must find out."

Understandably, Sarah Mapp didn't understand the tale Neffer related (with Ahib's constant intervening), of ancient curses, spirits, gods and goddesses. But she did trust Neffer, whom she had considered part of her family since the day they met.

Neffer had been there for nearly every important occasion for as long as Sarah had known Field. And, of course, he was there on the day Atlas was born and she approved of his blessing her first-born child.

But Jenny was not so understanding. She felt that Neffer and Ahib's story was causing even more stress for Sarah, and did not want to hear more.

"I'm sorry, Neffer, but all this talk of curses is upsetting Sarah," Jenny said. "I don't believe it and I don't think that she does, either."

Sarah tried to wave Jenny off, but knew how headstrong she could be. Neffer, however, was used to skepticism in matters of the supernatural, so Jenny's words did not bother him one bit.

"I understand that this is a little much for you," he said to Jenny, "but it is my duty to tell Sarah. She may hold the key to helping them both."

Jenny said nothing as Neffer slowly crossed the room and knelt before Sarah.

"Tell me, Sarah," he said in a calm voice, "was there anything unusual in Atlas' behavior once he heard of his father's mishap?"

Sarah strained to recall. "Well, he cried a little bit, but he seemed to feel better when I told him that I thought Field would come home."

"Was there anything else? It does not matter how small."

So much had happened since the day Ahib relayed his terrible news that the days had run together for Sarah. Now, they were mostly a blur.

"Well, there was one thing," she remembered, "The first night, he had a nightmare, and that hasn't happened since he was very, very young."

Ahib's eyebrows arched inquisitively at this news.

"Did he tell you of this dream?" Neffer asked.

"He started to, but I stopped him. I didn't want him to have to relive it. He was talking about this thing... a monster, coming after him saying, 'You will be my son.' Something like that. He was convinced it was real."

Neffer and Ahib exchanged looks.

Neffer lowered his voice as if revealing a secret, which,

in fact, he was.

"Sarah, although I have told you of the curse, I have not told you all. I must ask one question: Did Atlas mention a place called The Arch World?"

Sarah's jaw went slack and the color drained from her face. "Neffer, how did you know-" she said, unable to finish the sentence.

"You are familiar with this place, Mrs. Mapp?" Ahib asked.

"I've been drawing fictional maps of it for a book that Field's been working on," she said, still incredulous. "I was going to send them out to the publisher today."

Now, even Jenny was confused. Sarah couldn't possibly believe any of this, she thought. But from the look on her sister's face, Jenny could tell that something strange was going on.

"Do you still have these maps?" Neffer asked. Sarah slowly nodded.

Neffer jumped to his feet with a start. "I must see them at once!"

Unaware of the happenings in the main house, Pepper and Ormon slinked around with flashlights inside Sarah's cottage out back. Ormon was anxious, but he couldn't pull Pepper away from the large map on the easel.

"C'mon, Pepper, let's just take one and go!" he whispered urgently.

But Pepper was too busy comparing one of the smaller maps to the big one. "Just wait a second!" he snapped, shushing Ormon.

Pepper's eyes scrunched up as he compared the two, moving slowly from one to the other and back again.

"We got a problem, Bookworm," he said.

"What's that?" Ormon asked with trepidation.

"These maps aren't the same."

"You have GOT to be kidding me!" Ormon replied in disbelief.

Pepper held out his miniature map. "Nope. Look at the big one," he said, allowing Ormon a couple of moments to scrutinize it. "Now, look at this one."

Ormon saw it instantly. "Oh, man. The little one's got no Monkey Bar Bridge!"

"That's right," Pepper said, but his sense of triumph at being right was tempered by the fact that he didn't know how to solve the problem. After all, solving problems was Ormon's thing.

"There's a couple of other differences, too," Pepper added. "So, how are we gonna find Atlas if we don't have the right map?"

Before Ormon could answer, the boys were startled by Sarah's voice. "Pepper! Ormon! What are you boys doing here?" she said.

Without waiting for an answer, Neffer eyed Pepper and said, "I suppose they are here for the exact same reason that we are."

Ormon and Pepper hung their heads. They had lied to Sarah and the others, and even though they had done so for a good reason, it would take a lot of explaining to get out of this one.

As Pepper stealthily slid the little map into his back pocket, Ormon uttered a shameful, "We're sorry, Mrs. Mapp, but we had to!"

But Sarah walked past the apologetic Ormon, her eye caught by something unusual. Confused, she stared at the large map.

"What is this?" she said, to no one in particular.

"What's wrong, Sarah?" Neffer asked.

"These blinking dots… and this dark foliage at the bottom…"

"I don't understand," Neffer said, "Is this not the map you created?"

Sarah was stunned. "This is the map I started," she said, turning to the others, "but I didn't paint all of this."

Jenny's cry made everyone in the room jump.

"Oh, my gosh, Sarah!" she said, pointing at the easel, "Look at that!" Sarah turned slowly back to the canvas.

Before everyone's eyes, the image began to grow as if painted by an unseen hand. At the bottom, beneath The Arch World, darkness began to spread. Gnarly, diseased tree roots took form, intertwined with vines that looked like poison ivy.

It was so surreal that nobody said a word. Neffer's amulet glowed as if sounding a warning.

Jenny, a non-believer only moments earlier, was being converted.

Ahib was ready to flee from the room. Pepper's unruly hair stood on end and Ormon wiped his spectacles.

The canvas stretched, squeaked and strained to accommodate the developing new horrific picture. Staples popped out of its sides, allowing it to expand.

"What's happening, Neffer?" Jenny screamed.

"I believe that the evil spirit Kibu is showing Atlas how to get to The World Below," Neffer replied.

"We've got to do something!" Sarah shrieked.

But Neffer had seen so many strange things in his time that he was not afraid. While everyone else scurried away from the animated painting, he moved closer. After several long moments, he turned to Ahib and asked, "How many men were with Field in the collapsed mine?"

Ahib, cowering behind the boys, said, "I am told there are three."

They all watched as Neffer pointed out four blinking dots in Haven, then slowly traced a path to a lone blinking blip in The Lazantine Forest.

"So, *this*," he said, "must be Atlas."

SEVEN
The Black Pyramid

By the time Atlas and the Mirror People reached E'lum Village, he was sure that time worked a little differently in The Arch World.

On one hand, he felt as though their journey through the dark and spooky Lazantine Forest had taken half a day's hike. But on the other, the trek seemed much shorter than he imagined.

He was tired, but felt a sense of exhilaration upon first laying eyes on E'lum Village, set in a clearing somewhere in the middle of the forest.

Grouped together as far as he could see were clear, pyramid-shaped structures of varying sizes. Inside the crystal structures, hundreds of E'lum worked, talked and relaxed.

Atlas was astonished. "You can look right into everybody's house here," he said.

"We are all one, Atlas Mapp. We have nothing to hide," Image said.

Atlas' eyes were bursting out of his head at all of these unimaginable sights. But then he saw something that left him truly speechless.

In the center of the village, towering high above all of the see-through dwellings was a humongous black pyramid – the only one he couldn't see inside. Atlas hadn't noticed it at first because it blended in so neatly with the darkness, but as his eyes adjusted, there it was, taller than any man-made building he'd ever seen.

In front of the entrance, a large glowing orb was suspended in mid-air, surrounded by four free-standing columns. At the base of the structure, Mirror People kneeled in prayer. Atlas felt drawn to the ball of light, though he didn't know why.

Image noticed his curiosity and answered the question before Atlas could ask. "That is the Sphere of Norova," Image said, walking towards it so that Atlas could get a closer look.

"It's like a little sun," Atlas said.

Reflect skipped ahead to the sphere and stuck her hand inside. She giggled as small beams of light flared up with each movement of her hand. She waved Atlas over.

"Come on, it won't hurt you."

At Image's urging, Atlas edged forward. He felt intense heat the closer he got to the sphere, but, unlike the sun, there was a point where the temperature grew no hotter. The light dimmed as he approached, almost welcoming him.

Reflect guided Atlas' shaking hand into the center of the large sphere. He was filled with a soothing warmth that he couldn't describe. He watched as his hand, then his arm, took on the golden color of the orb. Suddenly, he didn't feel tired anymore, or afraid. Outside of a hug from his mom, Atlas had never felt so safe.

He shared a laugh with Reflect, remarking, "This feels weird."

"We-eerrrd," she said, repeating the strange word.

"It is our life source," said Image. "That is why we honor it."

Atlas' hand and arm took on the same shiny sheen as that of the E'lum. He put his hand to his face and was stunned to see his own reflection. "Cool," was the best word he could think of.

He looked toward the kneeling Mirror People who approached and appeared to bow to Reflect, who was standing close to him. "Are they doing that for you?"

"No," she said. "It is for *you*, the one sent here to help rescue my father."

"Me?"

"Yes," Reflect replied. "Image says you are The One."

Atlas was bewildered. "But I came here to find *my* dad."

Reflect's expression changed. Suddenly, she seemed hurt. She turned to Image, "But you said he was the-"

She never finished the sentence. From a distance, Image shot her a stern gaze, then raised a brow. She appeared to listen – though Image didn't say a word.

"I know it's not polite, Image, but the Novi will converge soon and we have–"

She stopped again, silently admonished.

Finally, Reflect said, "Okay. I'm sorry," bowed her head and sadly walked away. Atlas had watched the exchange with eyes ping-ponging back and forth between the two.

"It's *telepathy*," he thought. "They can read each other's minds."

"Language is not the only way to communicate, Atlas Mapp," Image said, reading *his* mind. "We have many ways of speaking."

"What was she talking about, Image? Who are the Novi?"

Image tried to calm Atlas' fears. He did not want his young guest to feel uncomfortable. "I know that you have many questions. Let us go to a place where we can talk."

As Image led Atlas into the huge, dark pyramid, the

others watched as if their lives depended on him.

A short time later, Atlas found himself sitting at a great, long table that looked like marble, but was made of a material he'd never seen. Before him was a bowl made of gold and a platter covered by a cooked bird the size of a hog. None of the E'lum were eating. The feast was just for him. Atlas was very hungry, but he didn't know where to start.

"The Ah-wal is a great bird that does not fly," Image said, motioning for Atlas to eat. "You will need energy for your journey."

Atlas stared at the curious bird for a moment, then reached over and grabbed a piece. He took a small, tentative bite, then looked relieved.

"It tastes just like chicken," he said, with a smile.

Image made a confused face. He had never heard the word before. But Atlas didn't notice. He was munching greedily away, even forgetting his table manners.

Image sat beside him. "I am sorry for Reflect's directness," he said, "but she speaks the truth. We need your help, Atlas Mapp."

Atlas abruptly stopped chewing and wiped small pieces of Ah-wal from his soiled lips. "I don't know how I can help you, Image, but if I can get to Haven and find my dad, maybe he can help."

Atlas wiped his hands, pulled out his map and unfolded it for Image. "I've got this if you can show me the way. I don't really know how to read it. See… I think we're right here-"

Atlas stopped and stared at the map in disbelief. It had transformed. "Whoa. This wasn't here before," he said, pointing to the decayed, bark-less trees and dark, deathly images at the bottom of his map.

But Image recognized it quickly.

"It is just as Reflect showed," he said. "Your map includes The World Below."

"You know this place?" Atlas asked.

"It is where our leader, Vision, is being held by Kibu," Image explained. "Vision is Reflect's father."

"Who's Kibu?"

"Kibu is the dark lord of The World Below, a place where the evil ones reside. He has sent you this map for a reason."

"But, I don't know any Kibu," Atlas stammered. "Why would he want me?"

Image slowly shook his head. "I do not know the answer to that, Atlas Mapp. But he wanted you badly enough to kidnap Vision so that he could use Vision's power to reveal our world to you."

Reflect entered the room with several curious E'lum who wanted a closer look at the boy who they felt had come to save them.

Atlas, however, didn't feel like a savior. In fact, he was so confused now that he wasn't even hungry anymore.

"But, I told you my mom painted this map," he said, adding, "well, at least the part with The Arch World on it."

"Yes, but she did so from a picture Vision sent to her in her dreams." Image nodded to Reflect. "Can you show him?"

Reflect nodded and turned to Atlas. She closed her eyes and contorted her torso into the shape of a large flat screen television. Atlas' mouth hung open at the sight, until he saw an image on the screen slowly developing, like a Polaroid snapshot.

"Hey, that's my Dad!" he shouted.

There, on Reflect's screen, Atlas could clearly make out the face and form of his father, as well as those of three other men. They appeared to be in a dimly-lit cavern. The image was so grainy that Atlas couldn't be sure. But as he stared at the familiar broad shoulders filling out the khaki shirt, and despite the stubble on a usually clean-shaven face, Atlas had no doubt that the man on the screen was his father, Field Mapp.

"Is this happening now?" he said, unable to avert his eyes. "Yes," said Image, as Atlas approached the screen to touch his father's face.

"He's alive," Atlas said in a low voice. "I knew it."

Reflect began to tremble and shake. She tried mightily to keep her focus, but the strain was too great. The picture flickered out. "I am sorry," Reflect said. "I could not hold it any longer."

Atlas turned to Image. "Was that from Haven? Is that where my father is?"

"I do not know," Image said. "But wherever your father is, we believe the fate that has befallen he and Vision is connected to Kibu. You, Atlas Mapp, are the one who can save them both."

"But how?" Atlas cried. "If this Kibu has all these evil powers, how can I stop him? I don't have any powers."

Image stepped forward and placed a shiny hand upon Atlas' shoulder. "You are wrong, Atlas Mapp. You are much more powerful than you realize."

Atlas did not understand. "Why do you say that?"

Image spoke slowly to make sure that Atlas understood every word. "In darkness, Kibu can take whatever he wants," Image said. "Light is our only protection. You were alone in The Lazantine Forest, yet he did not take you then. I can think of only one reason for this."

Image paused and looked into Atlas' eyes, waiting for the child to figure out the answer on his own.

Atlas was thinking, too. Soon, the answer came. "Because he couldn't?" Atlas said.

Image nodded and smiled. It was as if Atlas had read *his* mind.

A world away in Althanar, a large hairy hand slapped the side of a dimming lantern, briefly causing it to flicker brightly.

Boulders and splintered wood littered the small space; it was filled with sharp, jagged black rock, making it hard to tell how anyone could have survived the collapse.

Field, in a soiled khaki outfit, tended to Denai, an injured young Indian man whose legs were pinned beneath a large piece of wood.

Watching closely was a large, hairy Arab man, Habbibi, muscular and sweaty with scary eyes peering out from below his head wrap. On the other side of the mine, Mahmoud, older with thinning hair and spectacles, watched Habbibi closely, expecting danger.

The air was musty, thick, and filled with the specter of death. "Save your light," Field said to Habbibi, who continued banging on the lantern. "They know we're here. They'll break through soon."

Habbibi scowled. "We must be able to see in this prison of darkness that you have brought us to, Professor Mapp," he said in a deep, gruff voice.

Mahmoud was antsy. For hours now, he had worried that there might be a confrontation between Field and Habbibi, for Habbibi made no secret that he blamed Field alone for their predicament. They had been trapped here for days. Food, time and patience were all running out.

Mahmoud tried to be the voice of reason.

"Habbibi, this is no more the fault of the professor than are sandstorms in the desert," he said. "He is right. We will be found."

Habbibi and Field shared a tense glare. "Yes, but dead or alive, Mahmoud? What do you prefer?"

Mahmoud didn't reply. He watched quietly as Field pointed to several unlit torches. "Use those," he said. "There's still air coming in. We've got enough oxygen."

How much longer they could survive in this hellish place, Field did not know. Field thought only of his family and his vow to Denai that they would indeed survive this ordeal.

Denai was just twenty-four, not much older than Field had been when he led his first expedition. He was much too young to die, and Field promised to do all in his power to make sure that Denai got out alive.

But, with each passing hour, Field was finding it difficult to keep his own worry at bay.

He heard the slosh of water beneath Habbibi's feet when the large, angry man rose to light a torch. Mahmoud noticed it, too, and placed a small stick into the water to gauge its level.

Field read the bad news on Mahmoud's face. "The water has risen more than an inch over the last hour, Professor," he said. "May the Gods have mercy on us."

Denai awoke and screamed in agony.

"I cannot feel my legs!" he howled. "Are my legs still there, Professor?"

Field dipped a handkerchief into the shallow water, wrung it out and applied the cool compress to Denai's forehead.

"Easy, Denai," he whispered. "The beam has cut off

your circulation, that's all. Just try to relax and stay calm."

Field lightly tapped each of Denai's legs near his knees. Denai smiled. "Yes, I feel them now, Professor," he said. "Have we had word from the outside?"

"Not yet, but they're coming," Field said. "They know what to do."

"Which is more than we can say for the famous Professor Mapp," Habbibi barked.

Mahmoud once again tried to provide calm, moving close and patting Habbibi's massive shoulder. "I know the origin of your feelings, Habbibi," he said softly, adjusting his wire-framed glasses, "but we are now all in this together. Fighting will not help."

Habbibi was not encouraged by Mahmoud's words, but he did respect them. After all, Mahmoud was a university professor and Habbibi did not want to bring him into his dispute with Field.

"We will die here," Habbibi said. "I will not join my merciful God with unsaid words upon my tongue. What do you expect me to do?"

Mahmoud gently grasped Habbibi's hand and bowed his head. "Pray, Habbibi. We can pray."

The two kneeled together. For the moment, the storm had passed.

Field knew it would flare up again, but for now, he was just grateful to have such a man as Mahmoud with him.

For days, the pattern had been the same; they would sleep as best they could; eat minimally from their meager rations; take turns watching the injured Denai – and wait for Habbibi to vent his frustrations upon Field.

Sooner or later, something bad would happen. Field hoped that help would come before he had to deal with

Habbibi's rage.

"Do you think that we will die here, Professor?" Denai asked. "This would be a terrible way to die, to not see our families again, alone in this terrible, cold and forsaken place."

Denai weakly reached for Field. He was afraid, and although he had already cried several times, this time he held back his tears. Field gripped Denai's hand tightly.

"We'll die, Denai, but not today," he whispered. "We'll make it out of here.... I promise."

Even in the midst of prayer, Habbibi listened to every word Field said. He stopped to scowl at Field once again.

"One should not make promises that he cannot keep, Professor." Field glanced from Denai to Habbibi and back, but did not reply.

In E'lum Village, Atlas lay on a bed of feathers Image had brought. He was not comfortable, not because of his makeshift bed, but because the weight of not one, but two worlds, weighed heavily upon him.

He wondered how his journey to save his father had turned into something else so quickly. Sure, he *was* fascinated by the Mirror People, their wondrous power, and The Arch World, but all that really concerned him was getting to Haven and finding the one man who mattered more to him than any other in both worlds.

Atlas sat up and put the map on his lap, gently tracing the outline of Haven with his fingertips. He didn't know how to help the E'lum save their leader, Vision, but he was sure his father would know what to do. After all, there was no problem his dad could not handle.

When Reflect walked in, Atlas was trying to remember the last time his father had been home.

"Hi," he said, struggling to get used to the sight of a girl who looked as though she were made of metal and mirrored glass.

"Hi," Reflect said, sitting down.

For several moments, neither said a word. Finally, Atlas thought of something.

"Reflect, have you ever been to Haven?"

"No," she replied, "But I have heard of it."

"Well, do you know anyone who has been there?"

Reflect shook her head. "You are anxious to find your father, Atlas Mapp. Are you sure he is there?"

"He *has* to be," Atlas said, showing Reflect his map and pointing out the little red blips. "See these lights?"

Reflect leaned close, her head nearly touching Atlas'.

"Well, I figure they're heartbeats," he continued. "One of them *has* to be my dad."

Reflect sat back and looked at Atlas curiously. "Heartbeats? What does this mean?"

Atlas had to think about her question. He had never been asked to explain something so simple as this. Back home, everyone had a heart and everyone had a heartbeat. It was generally understood. But he realized that for Reflect, some of his words were as foreign as he was.

"Give me your hand," he said.

Reflect did as she was told and watched intently as Atlas guided her hand to the middle of his chest and placed her palm flat against it. Her bright, shiny eyes lit up as she felt the gentle thump of his heart.

"Do you feel that?" he asked.

"Yes," Reflect said, "It is unusual."

"Well, that's my heartbeat. It's the source of our lives, I mean, human beings. It pumps blood that we need to live throughout our bodies."

Reflect considered this while feeling the *thumm-thump, thumm-thump* of Atlas' heart.

"Does it do anything more?" she asked.

Now, Atlas really had to think. Reflect's questions were tougher than his science exams at Peace Elementary School. Where was Ormon when he needed him, he thought? Ormon could clearly explain just about anything.

"Who is Ormon?" Reflect suddenly asked.

Atlas had forgotten that the E'lum could read minds.

"Ormon is one of my best friends back home," he said, wistfully. "I've known him ever since I can remember."

"And he knows things of heartbeats that you do not know, Atlas Mapp?"

"Ormon knows lots of things," Atlas said, "I just think he might be able to explain it to you the right way."

Reflect giggled. "I think your way is just fine. Tell me more."

Atlas realized that Reflect's hand remained on his chest. He almost thought of how awkward this would have felt had it been Penelope Brockington from school or one of the girls who came to his birthday party – but quickly stopped himself from thinking about them for fear that Reflect would know more of his innermost thoughts.

"Well," he began, "when we lose things, it kinda hurts in there. I don't really know why. I'm only in the fourth grade and you don't learn about that stuff 'til high school."

"So, this is what you feel when you think of your father?" she said. "This hurt?"

Atlas stifled a sniffle and muttered a quiet, "Yeah."

Reflect smiled, seeming to understand.

"Well, even though we are different, I feel we are also the same," she said. "This is what I feel when I think of my father."

The two shared an understanding glance.

"Before I got here," Atlas said, "I was kinda mad at my dad. I mean, he's never home because he's always somewhere working. I thought that when I grew up, I wouldn't want to be anything like him. But, the more I think about it... he's the only dad I've got, you know?"

Reflect nodded. "Image says it is important to be a good father, and just as important to be a good child. My father is responsible for everyone here. It is a heavy weight to bear. Is your father this way, too?"

Atlas nodded.

"So, maybe it is *we* who have to be more understanding," Reflect said, as she stood to leave. "I cannot think of anyone that I would wish to be more like than my father."

Reflect's words were comforting. As she spoke, Atlas felt the same soft, warm glow as when she had placed his hand inside the Sphere of Norova. For the first time, really, he thought of how he had not considered all the people that his father was responsible for; the many people who worked for Mapp Excavations, his mother, Ahib, Neffer, and many others that Atlas had never met.

Atlas suddenly felt selfish for not seeing all of this before.

"We will find our fathers," she said. "I must go. Image calls. You should get some rest, Atlas Mapp. You have a long journey ahead."

Atlas nodded, although he was no longer thinking of just his own troubles. Reflect had given him a new and different way of thinking. Maybe there was a way that he could help the E'lum and his father at the same time. After all, the

Mirror People had saved him from the Salt Monster, and they had also rescued him from danger in The Lazantine Forest.

He thought of how they had asked for nothing in return.

Reflect smiled as that thought crossed Atlas' mind, then she walked to the door, turned and giggled.

"Heartbeats," she said. "I like that."

And she was gone. Atlas smiled and lay down with his head on his backpack, soon falling into a deep, deep sleep.

EIGHT
Kibu's Minions

It was dank, dark and dirty in The World Below, but the slimy flesh-eating gargoyles, Boroom and Sharibu, were right at home trudging through the swampy muck on their way to Kibu's Castle.

Fearlessly, they made their way through the poisonous foliage and twisted trees that somehow flourished without the nourishment of light. In this evil place, a thick fog hung in the air and a permanent dampness made it hard to breathe. Worse was the smell; it reeked like a landfill in the heart of the summer.

From the shadows emanated sounds of suffering, the silence broken by a sloppy slurping noise of some unthinkably hideous creature feasting upon a weaker, equally hideous creature.

All manner of things that crawled, crept and bit were here, even though you couldn't always see them – until it was too late.

But none of this caused fright or concern for Boroom and Sharibu, minions of Kibu, the powerful and evil lord of The World Below.

They made their way down the crooked path by torchlight, ignoring the trees that swayed as they passed, spying an opportunity for a late dinner.

Vines snaked underfoot, trying to wrap around their ankles and pull them towards a suffocating death in the overgrown brush.

"Nasty vines!" Boroom shouted, when one encircled his waist, nearly causing him to lose his balance. Boroom swiped through the vine with a sharp, pointed finger. It recoiled and oozed a foul, malodorous goo.

"They must be hungry," Sharibu said.

"No, brother, they've eaten well," said Boroom, lifting his torch high to illuminate a wall of spindly vines above them clutching bloody carcasses.

"*Mmmmm*," said Sharibu, with a lick of his lips. "Tasty."

Ahead in the distance was an enormous castle, a place that reeked of wickedness and which never saw the sun.

At the shadowy entrance, other gargoyles lurked, sentries on guard against any and all foolish enough to attempt an attack.

The Goyles growled un-pleasantries to Boroom and Sharibu as the pair made their way up steep stone steps to the castle's massive entrance.

Misshapen dog-like figures tethered to heavy chains lunged with razor-sharp teeth, hungry for a morsel of flesh. They cowered and slunk back into the darkness when Boroom hissed and bared his fangs.

Boroom was afraid of nothing, which is why Kibu had made him king of the Goyles and his most trusted slave. Sharibu was simply the bumbling sibling who often found trouble in vile places, knowing he could always run to his big brother for protection.

Sharibu was merely tolerated by Kibu, nothing more.

The ghoulish pair navigated an endless maze of narrow halls, descending more steps to a cavernous room decorated with intricate artwork of famous demons, fallen gods and spirits. There were furnishings of solid gold and blood-red tapestries hanging from a high ceiling covering windows that were never opened.

At the far end of the room was the entrance to a cave. This was Kibu's favorite place in the entire castle. With each step Boroom and Sharibu took towards the cave, torches flickered to life, signaling their approach to the evil one inside.

But he already knew they were coming.

"Do you bring news of the boy?" came a voice so deep that the torches on the walls flared with every word.

Sharibu slowed a step so that he could cower behind his brother. "Yes, Master Kibu," Boroom said, his eyes searching the inky blackness inside, but unable to catch a glimpse of anything. "He is in The Arch World, in The Lazantine Forest."

For a moment, there was a tense silence. "Why did you not bring him?"

"He is with the E'lum, Sire," said Boroom. "They reached him before we found him."

Suddenly, familiar sinister red eyes glowered from the cave mouth. "The E'lum!" Kibu thundered.

Sharibu trembled at the sound of Kibu's fury. "Y-y-you told us that he must come of his own accord, Master," he stuttered. "That is why you sent him the map."

"Fool!" Kibu shouted, his evil, gaseous breath nearly blowing the torches out. "How dare you question me!"

Boroom tried to quiet his little brother, but it was no use. Whenever Sharibu began talking, he simply could not stop.

"W-w-well, it wasn't really a question, Sire. We did as we were-"

A great flash of fire erupted from the cave, catapulting the goyle into a wall with a most frightening sound. Sharibu slumped to the floor in a heap, while Boroom lowered his head.

The torchlight dimmed as a shapeless creature filled the room, its rancid presence everywhere. The red eyes focused on Boroom, who did not dare move an inch.

"I have waited a thousand years for this, Boroom," Kibu whispered with malice. "You and your idiot brother will make sure that the boy comes to me."

Boroom did not look into Kibu's eyes, not out of fear, but out of respect for his immense power. "We will not fail you, our King," he said.

"That," Kibu threatened, "had better be true."

In an instant, the air was sucked away as Kibu vanished to the recesses of his favorite cave. The room brightened, but only slightly.

Boroom helped Sharibu to his feet.

He hissed at his brother and whispered to him a word of warning, saying, "Next time, let *me* do the talking."

NINE
Heartbeats

The large map from the cottage now sat on its easel in the Mapp family's living room with Sarah's eyes firmly glued to the horrible new addition of The World Below.

On a table nearby, Ahib and Neffer pored over old, weathered stacks of books and papers from Field's past expeditions. Jenny, Pepper and Ormon watched, waiting and hoping that a clue would materialize.

Ahib brought over another pile of books and plopped them down upon the table, sending scraps of paper flying to the floor.

"Oh, I am so sorry, Neffer," he said, quickly picking up the documents and pointing to the old record books he had just delivered. "This is all, a complete accounting of every excavation the professor has ever done over the course of his long and illustrious career."

Neffer was studying a list they had already compiled.

"Many here include tales of legendary curses. But which one?"

Ormon peered over his shoulder hoping to help.

"The Chalice of Corinthia?" he said.

Ahib shook his head. "No, my cousin unearthed that one. His teeth and hair fell out, but that was all."

Another interesting find caught Pepper's eye. "How about the Scroll of Sayeer?"

Again, Ahib shook his head.

"That one made the dogs go blind."

Jenny was now as interested as anyone in all things mystical and supernatural. She chose the title of a romantic-sounding expedition.

"What about the Diamonds of Dubai?" she said. "That sounds nice."

"Diarrhea," Ahib said, matter-of-factly.

"*EEEeeeeewwwwww*," said the boys, cringing.

But their distaste did not stop Ahib, who remembered that particular expedition as if it had happened yesterday.

"Oh, that one got me," he said, absentmindedly rubbing his bum. "It was absolutely horrible. For days and days, the Professor and I did nothing but-"

Thankfully, Neffer's stern words halted Ahib's musings. "Ahib, please! They are children."

Chastised, Ahib told no more. "So sorry, Neffer. You are right. But, it *was* mightily unpleasant."

Neffer regarded Ahib with exasperation.

Suddenly, Sarah shouted, "So, *that's* what they are!"

Everyone crowded around the map to see what she was talking about. "What is it, Mrs. Mapp?" Ahib asked.

She pointed to the blinking red dots. "They're heartbeats. Can't you tell?"

Neffer, Ahib, Jenny, Ormon and Pepper watched for a moment, each slowly coming to the realization that Sarah was right. They *were* heartbeats.

"It appears that anyone who is not of The Arch World can be seen on this map by the beating of their hearts," Neffer concluded.

Sarah pointed to a dim little blip in Haven. "This light isn't bright like the others. What do you think it means, Neffer?"

Neffer studied the other blips. They were all beating strongly. "Someone may be weak or injured," he said, then off Sarah's worried look, added, "but we have no way of knowing for sure… or whom."

Sarah sat down and clasped her hands tightly beneath her chin. "So," she asked slowly, "what happens if the light goes out?" Jenny shared a concerned look with Sarah.

Pepper and Ormon exchanged glances. Ahib looked at Neffer, who looked away. But no one said a word.

In the rubble of the collapsed mine in Althanar, it was Denai's heart that was fading. He drifted in and out of consciousness and dreamed of terrible things like death and the misery that would fall upon his family with the news of it. Denai replayed memories of his short life and thought of things that he might never do if eternal darkness chose to take him.

Several torches flickered weakly, casting eerie shadows. Field lay drowsy against a boulder next to Denai and Mahmoud slept as comfortably as he could despite their predicament, but Habbibi sat stoically, wide awake, glaring daggers at Field.

Denai stirred and slowly opened his eyes. His slight movement awakened Field, who was relieved to see that Denai was still alive. Denai looked weakly into his eyes.

"Do you believe in God, Professor?" he asked, softly.

Field could barely hear him.

"What, Denai?"

"I asked if you believed in God?"

"Why, yes," Field said. "Yes, I do."

"So, you believe in Heaven, also?"

Field nodded. Habbibi, now awake, frowned.

Denai struggled to lift his head. Field fluffed the jacket beneath Denai's neck to make him more comfortable.

"I was thinking of what I would say to God if we don't get out of here," Denai said. "I wonder would I be okay with the life I've lived."

"And?" Field replied.

"I don't know. I feel that I have been a good and honest person, and that I have worked hard, but that is all." He paused. "I might ask Him for a little more time. Do you know what I mean?"

"You are a young man, Denai. You have a lot of time ahead of you."

Denai coughed, then said, "You are very optimistic, Professor Mapp, but I think we both know that is not true."

Field looked at Habbibi, who was still glowering.

Denai continued, "If you had more time, what would you do differently?"

"I'd spend it with my family," Field said, without hesitation.

"Is that all?"

"That would be enough," Field said.

For a while there was silence. Over the long days and nights they had been here, Field's thoughts constantly drifted to Sarah and Atlas.

Until he found himself trapped in this mine, he hadn't truly realized how important they were to him. Of course, like most fathers, he loved his family, but it wasn't until now, at this moment, when he feared he might never see them again, that he really understood just how much they meant.

Field recalled the first time he met Sarah, at a high school dance. She was not even the girl he had gone with, but from the moment he saw her smile, and the way her beautiful red hair curled in the humid courtyard air, he could see no other.

Their love affair began that day and had never ended.

He thought of all the times thereafter, momentous events in their lives leading up to and after the birth of Atlas. Now, in this time of crisis, those cherished memories kept him going, but he also felt the pain that came with knowing he might not create more memories to share with them.

Field was startled from his daydream by Denai's question.

"Your family, will you tell me about them? I have not seen them since shortly after Atlas was born, and, well, that was a long time ago."

Field knew exactly how long it had been.

"Ten years," he said, wistfully. "You know, Atlas just had his tenth birthday. I was on my way to call him when the mine collapsed. He's probably disappointed."

Field choked up a bit. "He probably thinks I've forgotten him. And I know Sarah's worried sick."

Denai saw the anguish in Field's face.

Field continued, "I've worked so much since he was born, it's a wonder that he remembers me. But I've never missed calling Atlas on his birthday. When we get out of here, I'll be there for everyone."

"I am sure he will understand," Denai said. "Life is difficult sometimes!"

Denai coughed violently, waking Mahmoud.

"Is the boy okay?" he asked, wiping sleep from his eyes.

Field grabbed a canteen and gave Denai some water. Suddenly, Habbibi leapt to his feet and ripped the bottle from Field's hands.

Field recoiled from the large hairy man in shock.
"Habbibi, what are you-"

"You waste our precious water on a dying man,"
Habbibi snarled, as he replaced the cap on the bottle.

Mahmoud was incredulous. "Habbibi, have you gone
mad?"

"If I am mad, Mahmoud, it is for placing my life in the
hands of a Mapp, as my uncle did so many years ago," he
thundered. "We all know what happened then. Isn't that right,
professor?"

Field didn't reply.

"You cannot blame him for that," Mahmoud pleaded.

"I can and *do* blame him. He shares the same arrogant
American blood as his father."

Habbibi locked eyes with Field, who still said nothing,
but was obviously upset.

"You tell young Denai stories of your God and your
beautiful family that you so desire to see again," Habbibi said,
adding, "but as he lies there dying, why not tell him the rest of
the Mapp story – the one that no one hears of how history
repeats?"

"Habbibi, please," Mahmoud desperately urged.

Field got to his feet. He and Habbibi shared a tense
stare.

It's okay, Mahmoud," Field said. "I understand
Habbibi's anger. This isn't the first time I've-"

Denai cut him off. "It is not necessary to tell me of
these stories, Professor."

But Field had grown weary of Habbibi's rants.

"No, Denai," he said, his jaw set firmly. "If Habbibi
wants you to hear it, I'll tell you."

Habbibi sat back with a satisfied look, waiting for Field

to begin.

As Field prepared to revisit an unpleasant tale of the
past, at his home, a world away in Seattle, Neffer, Ahib and
even Ormon were hard at work trying to discover a way to save
him and Atlas.

It was getting late, and Sarah stared groggily at the
large map. Jenny was already in a deep sleep with her head in
Sarah's lap. Ormon sat at a table reading a book entitled,
"Mythological Curses from A-Z," while Neffer and Ahib
studied an assortment of books and papers.

Pepper, bored with sitting around, busied himself by
sifting through Neffer's open leather satchel. He knew that the
old man was too preoccupied to complain. Despite his
advanced age, however, Neffer showed no signs of tiring, and
even if he did, he was so old that it would be hard to notice.

Having spent several hours with Neffer since their first
encounter, Pepper found himself drawn to the ancient and
mysterious stranger. Even more, he was fascinated by all the
curious artifacts that Neffer owned.

Pepper stuck his hand into Neffer's bag and pulled out a
vial marked "Holy Water," and held it up to the light.

"Does this stuff work?" he asked, shaking the vial as
though expecting something magical to happen.

Neffer shot Pepper a glance and muttered, "I should
hope so."

"What's it used for?"

Though annoyed, Neffer patiently explained, "There are
many uses. Holy Water repels evil spirits and some use it for
cleansing or blessings."

"Whoa," Pepper said, using his favorite word for just

about everything that was new or unusual. "That's really cool."

"Yes. I should hope so," Neffer sighed.

From the couch, Sarah saw that the boys' presence, Pepper's in particular, was hindering Neffer and Ahib's progress.

"It's late, kids. Your parents will be worried," she said.

"My dad knows where I am and Ormon told his parents that we're here, Mrs. Mapp," Pepper offered.

"That may be true, but I'm going to take you home. You can come back tomorrow. If anything happens before then, I'll let you know."

Ormon closed his book and sat back deep in thought.

"I can take them if you like, Mrs. Mapp," Ahib said.

"No, Ahib. You stay here and help Neffer. I need to get out, anyway." She placed a pillow under the still-sleeping Jenny's head, put on a sweater and grabbed her car keys.

Ormon stood and walked over to the large map, giving it a long look before leaving. Pepper, once he was sure that no one was looking, stashed Neffer's bottle of Holy Water in his jacket pocket.

"What are you looking at?" he asked Ormon, whose face was scrunched into a thoughtful expression, something he often did when his brain was hard at work.

"I'm just thinking how strange it is that all this stuff happened on Atlas' birthday, you know?" he said, "Professor Mapp in that mine collapse, us finding the map and all. It just seems like it's more than a coincidence. It's almost like it was *planned* to happen this way."

Neffer and Ahib stopped working and looked quizzically at Ormon.

"You just need some sleep, Bookworm," Pepper said, dismissing Ormon's hypothesis. "That big brain of yours is overloading."

"There's got to be something to it," Ormon insisted.

"Let's go, boys," Sarah called, heading for the door.

Ormon followed Pepper out, both boys turning in unison to chime, "G'night Mr. Neffer. G'night Ahib."

"Good night," Neffer and Ahib replied.

As the door closed, Neffer stared off, lost in thought. Ahib noticed. "Is something wrong, Neffer?"

After a long pause, Neffer said, "What's wrong is that I think the child is right. The curse we are looking for must have happened ten years ago – exactly to the very day."

"On the anniversary of Atlas' birthday?" Ahib said.

Neffer snapped his fingers. "How could we have missed it?" The revelation hit them both at the same instant.

"The Diamonds of Bushawri," they said together. Quite quickly, Neffer was energized.

"Ahib, we must find all we can of these diamonds," he said. "Time is of the essence!"

Not long after, Ormon and Pepper stood in front of Pepper's house watching Sarah Mapp drive off. The ride home had been silent because the boys really didn't know what to say to Sarah, who told them she wasn't angry with them for stealing one of the maps from her cottage. In fact, she even said she understood and was glad that Atlas had such good, caring friends.

She had hugged the boys - a little too tightly for Pepper's taste - and assured them that she would call should there be any news of Atlas' whereabouts. Then she hugged them once more and said goodbye.

In the darkness, the pair stood on the street as a light rain fell. Just several hours from now, two full days would have passed since Atlas had left for The Arch World. Already, it felt like an eternity.

Ormon, who was still thinking about the weird coincidences of the past several days, turned to Pepper with a serious expression.

"It's almost been two days," he said, pausing to see Pepper's reaction.

"I know, Bookworm," Pepper said. "I was just thinking about that."

Ormon waited for Pepper to say more. Pepper acted annoyed.

"What???" Pepper asked, although he already knew what Ormon was thinking.

"We promised Atlas we'd come looking if he wasn't back in two days," Ormon said, wiping his rain-streaked glass with his shirttail.

"I know," said Pepper, digging into his pocket and pulling out the vial of Holy Water. "I just wanted to make sure we were prepared."

Ormon eyed the little vial and rolled his eyes.

"Hey, I'll only use it if it's absolutely necessary," Pepper said, with his usual sly smile. Then he produced a bandana and wrapped it tightly around his shock of unruly hair.

Ormon knew what this meant, as Pepper wore his bandana for one thing and one thing only – Toxic Soldiers.

"So, what do you wanna do?" Pepper asked.

Ormon was already a step ahead of him, running to the porch to retrieve his bike.

"I've gotta go home and get my stuff," he said. "I'll meet you back here in an hour. I already told my dad I'm staying at Atlas' house tonight."

"So did I," Pepper said before Ormon rode off.

Pepper watched until Ormon turned the corner, raised his face to the dark sky and yelled, "Look out, Arch World, the Toxic Soldiers are coming!

TEN
The Convergence of the Novi

The sound of shuffling footsteps on the dusty rock floor of Kibu's castle echoed off the walls as three large gargoyles ambled down a dark corridor. At the end of the hallway was a thick, heavy door with an enormous steel bar barring the entrance, as if to keep in something very dangerous.

There were no windows here, because, for the prisoner inside the dungeon cell, light was an ally that Kibu and his minions had to keep away. Held captive behind the door was Vision, the powerful leader of the E'lum.

The largest of the gargoyles placed his torch in a holder a short distance away. The two others lifted the bar out of its cradle and pulled on the large door. It opened with a noisy creak.

Despite the darkness of the windowless room, a faint glimmer of light shone from one corner. The goyles peered inside, and then took up guard positions on either side of the door as the sound of a terrible *whhhoooossshhhh* filled the hallway and a gloomy shadow took residence there among them.

"Prisoner, stand before the honorable Kibu!" said the large goyle.

A slight stirring was heard inside as the emaciated Vision struggled to his feet. Unlike the other bright and shiny Mirror People, Vision's skin was sallow and dull. He had a long beard and his cheekbones and eye sockets were hollow.

He appeared to have been denied nourishment.

But, somehow, even in his poor state of health, Vision was a regal presence, a king despite his captivity.

With quickness, the dark shadow flew into the cell, its sinister red eyes focused menacingly on Vision, who showed no fear.

"Your imprisonment is near an end, Vision," Kibu said in a deep, airy voice. "My prize is within sight."

"You must allow me to leave now, Kibu," Vision demanded. "I have done your bidding."

"I will make that decision," Kibu cackled. "When the boy is here, then you may go."

Although Vision knew it was useless to try to reason with evil, he protested, anyway.

"The convergence of the Novi is near," he said, as strongly as his frail body would allow. "I must return to E'lum Village to seal the Black Pyramid or many will die. Does your word mean nothing?"

Kibu's eyes glowered, and then stole a glance at the torch on the wall. He sensed that Vision was gaining strength from it. "What should I care of the lives of those in the Arch World?"

"Living in darkness is your choice, Kibu," Vision replied. "Those above do not deserve to die for the desires of an embittered spirit."

There was no mistaking the power in Vision's voice.

"Even from the flicker of a torch you grow strong, Vision. I believe we have talked enough."

Vision stared deeply into Kibu's eyes. "I must be freed now!" he demanded, spawning concerned looks from the goyles standing guard.

Summoning all his might, Vision extended his hand in

Kibu's direction and strained mightily as a spark harmlessly fluttered from his palm. He stumbled, exhausted from the effort.

But Kibu had seen enough.

"Without light, you cannot hope to fight me, Vision. I will keep to my word. When the boy from the World Above is here, you will be set free."

With a whoosh, Kibu was gone. Vision weakly tried to pursue, only to be pushed to the floor by a burly gargoyle.

"Your kind is no match for the Dark Lord," he whispered to Vision, saliva dripping from his fangs. "Be happy that he spares your life."

Vision stared up at the big, ugly creature, but was too weak for words. He watched helplessly as the goyles slammed the door and slid the steel bar back across the entrance of his prison cell.

Later, the creepy, giddy laughter of Boroom and Sharibu filled the castle as they entered the room outside of Kibu's private cave. From within, they could see their master's evil eyes fixed upon them.

"Why do you disturb me?" he thundered.

"We have great news, Glorious One," Boroom said in an excited tone, "a foolproof plan to get the boy from the World Above here with haste."

"Fools making foolproof plans?" Kibu asked. The skittish Sharibu could not help himself.

"Oh, this is the work of sheer genius, Sire-"

Boroom shushed his brother with an elbow to the ribs. "It is not exactly genius, Master Kibu, but it will bring the boy here," he said. Kibu's silence told the goyles that he wanted to hear more.

"We have sent one who has sought refuge in the Black Pyramid in the past to tell the E'lum that he has knowledge of the whereabouts of Vision," Boroom continued. "He will meet with the E'lum in the morning and tell them a rescue can be planned in time to save The Arch World races."

"Interesting," Kibu said slowly.

Equally pleased, Sharibu rubbed his scaly hands together.

Encouraged, Boroom added, "He is one the E'lum trust. The boy can be here by tomorrow night."

Kibu's eyes flared brightly.

"Tomorrow? I shall have to prepare. A celebration is in order."

Sharibu cackled under his breath as Boroom retrieved their torch and the self-satisfied goyles trudged out of the room.

Dawn broke in E'lum Village. A light breeze that smelled of cherry blossoms filled the air; large bird-like creatures took flight; E'lum villagers stirred in their crystal-clear pyramid homes. On one side of the horizon, the sun rose. On the opposite horizon, a smaller sun did the same in tandem.

It was a quiet and peaceful morning, but gloom hung over the village. Small gatherings of E'lum gazed fearfully from one sun to the other.

Image stood in the middle of a gathering of elder E'lum, studying the rapidly rising suns, his face filled with concern. "The convergence is imminent," he said. "Soon, the races will come seeking shelter."

Shine, a short and stout E'lum, was extremely worried.

"What good will it be if they arrive and Vision is not here to seal The Black Pyramid?" Shine asked. "They cannot withstand the cleansing light of the Novi. If the pyramid is not sealed, they will die. We all will die!"

Shine paused and allowed the others to consider his words. "Without our protection, there is only one place for them to go."

"I know, Shine," Image said, "The World Below."

The other E'lum traded terrified glances. "What shall we do?" asked Shine.

"We have no choice," Image said, his voice calm and clear. "We must journey to The World Below and rescue Vision."

"But what of the boy from above?"

At that moment, a voice from behind startled the group. It was Atlas.

"I'll go with you," he declared, as the others turned to him. "If you think I can help you fight this Kibu guy, I want to help."

Image smiled and nodded.

"Shine, assemble the most fierce E'lum warriors. We meet at the Sphere of Norova." Image then placed his hand on Atlas' shoulder and said, "We thank you, Atlas Mapp. You are very brave."

Although his face looked determined, it concealed a tinge of fear Atlas felt as the E'lum lined up to shake his hand.

"I believe in you," one whispered.

"You are most certainly The One," said another.

"I am honored to be in your presence," said still another.

"Um, thanks," Atlas mumbled, at the outpouring of gratitude.

Still, he was very afraid. He was just a kid. What could he possibly do against an evil spirit that imprisoned the

E'lum's powerful leader? And how could he prevent whatever horror might befall The Arch World?

Many thoughts tumbled in his mind. He thought of Reflect, and how even though she was a girl – and from another world – she understood things that he didn't. She knew the importance of being a good child and thinking of others. She even wanted to be like her father, who held the lives of everyone in The Arch World in his hands. Reflect was right, such responsibility was a heavy weight to bear indeed.

This weight now sat squarely upon Atlas' narrow shoulders.

But looking into the faces of the grateful E'lum before him, Atlas resolved then and there to carry that weight, no matter the cost. After all, he thought, this is what his father would do.

For a long while, Atlas walked around E'lum Village pondering the task before him. As he did, he realized that other than their shiny exteriors, the gentle people here weren't much different from those back home or on expeditions he had taken with his family to strange and exotic places around the world. His world.

A Mirror Mother cradled a crying child; a Mirror man tossed a ball of light back and forth with his son. Other E'lum sat and pondered the future.

For the first time, Atlas wondered about the universe and the possibilities of still more worlds beyond Earth. Like most kids, he and Ormon had contemplated life on other planets, but Atlas always imagined their inhabitants to be hostile little gray men with ray guns.

He never dreamed there were other races and civilizations that, well, mirrored his own. But that is exactly what the E'lum did.

They were extraordinary beings who led fairly ordinary lives. They had simple desires and did simple things, and, like Atlas, when they lost something that was important to them, they would risk their lives to find it. The thought brought a smile to his face.

As he walked back inside the towering Black Pyramid, Atlas saw Reflect walking into a large room that he hadn't noticed before. He followed. Inside, at the end of a long aisle, Image knelt before a pyramid-shaped altar with a miniature glowing sphere inside.

He watched as Image pulled a thin, golden crown down around his forehead. In the crown's center was a sun symbol.

Atlas was riveted to Image's ritual when Reflect approached. "What is this place?" he asked.

"It is called The Hall of Relics. It is where we come to pray before we go to battle. Image is preparing."

"Do you think he can beat-"

Reflect shushed him. "Evil's name is never spoken here."

"Oh, sorry," Atlas replied sheepishly, his curiosity still piqued by all the huge glass cases throughout the cavernous hall.

Suddenly, he spied something familiar. Before he could ask, Reflect explained, "These are relics that have made their way through The World Above into The Arch World. My father says that your ground is our sky."

Atlas couldn't take his eyes off the object. It was a very large shoe with a familiar Nike swoosh on the side.

"It's a sneaker," he said, pointing to his own.

A gathering of E'lum who had entered the room repeated the word in hushed tones.

"It is a very big sneaker, then," said Reflect.

Atlas walked from case to case. They were filled with items of everyday use back home. He saw TV dinner trays, a broken radio, a ruined compact disc, a lamp, and other objects that were normal sights for him. But here, for the Mirror People, they were all something special, something out of the ordinary; things worthy of being encased in glass and called relics.

"Why do you keep all this stuff?" he asked.

Reflect smiled. She had been reading his thoughts all along. "What is familiar to you is foreign to us, Atlas Mapp."

A crowd gathered around the pair, entranced as Atlas explained what their treasured relics were and how they were used in The World Above.

Deep inside, however, he felt ashamed that trash from his world was being spewed into this beautiful and pristine place, even if it did have value to the E'lum.

Image walked over carrying a golden box. "Our most prized relic," he said.

"That one nearly started a war," an elder E'lum added with a frown.

"I will show it to you," Image said, handing the box to Atlas and gently removing the cover. As he did, a ray of yellow light shone from within. Many of the E'lum watched Atlas closely, wondering if he would know much of this particular relic.

Shocked, Atlas pulled the object out to reveal – a Coca-Cola bottle. "It... it's a soda bottle," he said.

"It is made of a material similar to our pyramids, which were created by the Gods," said Image.

"It's called glass," Atlas explained, hoping not to offend his hosts, and trying to conceal his true thoughts of this relic, lest the E'lum read his mind.

"Glass," they repeated among themselves, whispering the word as if the Coke bottle were a precious diamond.

Before Atlas could utter another word, there was a loud commotion outside. Shouts of excitement echoed throughout the chamber as the E'lum hurried from the Hall of Relics.

Without the power of telepathy, Atlas had no idea what was going on. Did someone say, *Teddy Bear*, he thought?

Atlas followed the throng outside where many Mirror People were gathered around something, or *someone*. To his surprise, the newcomer who caused the hubbub was a man. A *human* man.

Atlas couldn't believe his eyes when Reflect ran to the tall stranger and wrapped her hands around his waist, crying, "Freddy Bear!"

The thin fellow wore tattered overalls, had a scraggly beard and bright, friendly eyes. To Atlas, he looked like a mountain man.

"How ya doing, Reflect?" Freddy said, lifting her up in a mighty hug.

Once again, before Atlas could ask, Reflect answered his question. "He came from The World Above long before you, Atlas Mapp," she said.

Freddy marveled at the sight of Atlas. "Well, I'll be!" he said with a loud, Southern drawl. "Where did *you* come from?"

Atlas was speechless as Image and Freddy shared a hug.

"It has been a long time, Freddy," Image said.

Freddy looked up at the two suns growing ever closer in the sky. "With the convergence comin', I didn't want to take no chances, Image," Freddy said, turning to Atlas. "Who's this young feller?"

Freddy thrust his hand in Atlas' direction and issued a hearty greeting, "Freddy Bearer from Tennessee!"

"Uh, Atlas Mapp... from Seattle," Atlas replied, shaking his hand and wondering how Freddy came to be in The Arch World.

"Seattle?" Freddy said, raising his eyebrows. "That's where I was when I fell into this place. Boy, I haven't heard that name in a while."

"Atlas Mapp will help us rescue Vision from The World Below," Image told Freddy. "Have you not heard?"

Freddy lowered his eyes and shook his head slowly.

"Yeah, evil old' Kibu. I wouldda come sooner, but I was way over in the Valley of Fear. 'Sides, I didn't know what I could do, anyway."

Image looked off into the distance. As far as an eye could see, beings off all shapes and sizes made their way toward the safety of The Black Pyramid. They were the strangest creatures Atlas had ever seen.

Some had fur from head to toe. Others had skin covered with scales. And some of these beings had three legs or more. Some walked upright, like human beings; some crawled, and others slid along the ground like snakes.

Atlas knew that it wasn't polite to stare, but could not avert his eyes. "They come not knowing that Vision himself must seal the pyramid," Image said.

"So, you're going to fight Kibu?" Freddy asked.

"There is no choice," Image said without emotion.

Freddy scratched his chin through his wiry, speckled beard. "Well, I can't let you go alone," he said, finally. "'Sides, I'm probably the only one here who knows the way to The World Below."

"You've been there?" Atlas asked.

"Once," Freddy said, his face looking as though he had a bad memory of the happening. "A long time ago."

"It will be dangerous, Freddy," Image said, drawing a concerned look from Atlas.

"Image, ain't a wild boar could stop me from going with you. If you're gonna fight Kibu, I'm with you."

Image nodded. The Mirror People crowded around Freddy, jumping up and down with joy, hugging and dancing.

As the jubilant scene unfolded, Atlas saw a bald baby wearing a loincloth, no more than three years old, waddling towards the group.

Trailing the child was a tall, hairy man of immense proportions. They looked like human beings, but Atlas sensed something different about them. He simply couldn't figure out what it was.

"Is that a... baby?" he asked, to no one in particular. Freddy looked at the visitors and laughed loudly.

"No, no, no, Mr. Mapp. That ain't no baby, 'least not any baby you ever seen before," he said. "That little guy's very old. Now, that big feller? *He's* a baby."

Atlas' eyes nearly popped out of his head.

Only when the unusual pair came closer did he see that the large fellow was actually twice the size of a normal human. In fact, he was even bigger than Habbibi, the Arab who sometimes worked with his father.

Habbibi was the largest man Atlas had ever met.

Atlas had also seen old bald men before, and it was easy to see how they could resemble a baby, but this? He simply couldn't believe it.

"They're from a tribe called the Byab," Freddy said.

"But they almost look just like regular people," Atlas said. Freddie shook his head.

"They're not like us. They age backwards."

"You mean, they start off big like that guy and turn out like the little one?"

"You got it, young feller."

"Wow. People who age in reverse? Ormon would love this," Atlas said, more to himself than anything. Atlas then noticed even more Byab headed towards the Black Pyramid.

"Why are they coming here, Freddy?"

Freddy pointed up at the dual suns. High in the sky, they were much closer together than Atlas first noticed.

"The Byab's life cycle is tied to the convergence," he said. "See, when those suns come together, that's it for the little guy."

"He's going to… die?" Atlas said with a gulp. Freddy nodded.

"Yep. That's why he's bringing the big ones here, so his people can survive."

The little Byab, who had thin wisps of hair protruding from his shiny head, and wide round eyes, approached and shook hands with Image.

"It is good to see you, Ekim," Image said. "It has been many mirons. I regret that I cannot be a proper host, but there is an important task that I must undertake."

"I heard, Image," Ekim said, in a gravelly voice that sounded very much like an old man's. "I don't have a lot of time left here, so I would be honored if you would allow me to accompany you on your quest. I may be small in stature, but my heart is large. I believe that I can help you rescue Vision. In fact, I feel that it is my duty."

Image was troubled by Ekim's request. "Your time is so short!"

"Exactly," Ekim interrupted. "I have nothing to lose."

Image introduced Ekim to Freddy and Atlas, who politely shook Ekim's hand, but couldn't get over the fact that he was no more than two feet tall.

"Pleased to meet you, Atlas Mapp," Ekim said. "Word of your arrival has spread all over The Arch World."

"Guess that means you're famous, Mr. Mapp," Freddy said, slapping Atlas on the back.

Atlas' face flushed a bright red hue. "I didn't come here to be famous, Freddy. I came to find my dad."

Before Freddy could reply, Image appeared with a small golden crown, just like the one he wore. He gently placed the crown on Atlas' head.

"Now, you are ready, Atlas Mapp," Image said.

"Ready for what?" Atlas asked.

"For war."

As an endless line of beings from The Arch World made their way to the safety of the Black Pyramid, Atlas watched the E'lum get ready to go into battle.

Atlas didn't fully understand the whole convergence of the Novi thing, but what he gathered from Freddy Bearer and Image was that every so many years the big sun and the little sun – called Novi – would converge, or come together.

According to Freddy, the light would be so bright and intense that no being could survive it without the protection of The Black Pyramid, which no light could penetrate once sealed.

Freddy said most of The Arch World races were decent and peaceful, and the E'lum had built The Black Pyramid to protect them.

The war-like evil ones escaped to The World Below,

where they fell under the spell of Kibu, its evil ruler. Freddy knew a lot about The Arch World and its people, which brought comfort to Atlas.

Despite his stringy hair and unkempt appearance, Atlas quickly felt a kinship with Freddy, probably because they were from the same place. Not only had Freddy figured out a way to survive here, with its monsters and evil spirits, he had also made friends. From what Atlas could see, the Mirror People adored Freddy and he, in turn, adored them.

More importantly, Atlas thought, if Freddy knew so much about this world, there was a chance that he could help Atlas get to Haven to rescue his father. After all, that was the reason Atlas was here.

With Freddy Bearer as his new ally, Atlas was sure that helping the Mirror People was the right thing to do.

Image moved atop a podium and called for silence. Many of the E'lum fighters who would accompany him on the journey gathered around, their grim faces gleaming in the bright sunlight.

"E'lum warriors, citizens," Image began, "We come to a critical time in the history of The Arch World. Though we are a peaceful people, there is a time when peace must be put aside. That time is now!"

Everyone was riveted as Image spoke.

"As keepers of the light, it is our obligation and honor to ensure the safety of those who would perish in the face of the cleansing effects of the convergence of the Novi.

"This is a dangerous mission," Image said, looking into the eyes of the E'lum warriors before him. "Some of us may not return. We must rescue Vision from The World Below or all is lost. We cannot fail."

Atlas felt power and determination in Image's words.

And though he had never met Vision, he knew that Vision must be wise indeed to have appointed Image as his second-in-command.

Atlas was energized even more when Image raised his fist to the sky and declared, "We... will... not... fail!"

The E'lum and peoples of the Arch World races cheered wildly. Not until Reflect touched his shoulder and smiled did Atlas realize that he was deliriously cheering, too.

Image then walked over to the Sphere of Norova; it glowed almost as bright as the suns in the sky. He stepped inside, and brilliant golden light enveloped his body. Image drew energy from the light, and his shiny muscles swelled before Atlas' eyes.

"Wow," Atlas remarked, when Image stepped out of the sphere looking much more like a warrior than before.

One by one, other E'lum warriors repeated the process. When the last warrior walked out of the glowing orb, Image waved his hand and a large surfboard of light appeared, hovering less than a foot above the ground.

Image stepped on and turned to Freddy and Atlas. "You will ride with me," he said.

Freddy and Atlas gingerly climbed onto the craft. It lifted higher into the air under their weight. Atlas, who was afraid of heights, quickly sat down beside Freddy. He had so many questions about this strange vehicle, but was too frightened for words.

Image quickly calmed his fears.

"The Skyrider is controlled by thought," he explained, demonstrating with a small circling maneuver. And just when Atlas was thinking about plunging to his doom in flight, Image added, "Do not worry about falling off, Atlas Mapp. When we are in motion, a field of energy invisible to you surrounds us.

There is no danger."

Atlas could only nod, while Freddy crowed, "Sounds fine to me." All around, E'lum warriors and their lightboards lifted into the sky. "The best way to Polema is to take the shortcut through the mountains," Freddy said. "That way we can sneak up on 'em."

"Yes," Image said. "Kibu has sentries everywhere."

As Image prepared to fly off, Reflect ran over to his sky craft.

"No, Reflect," Image said. "You must stay here."

"But, Image-"

"There is no debate," Image sternly replied. "You are Vision's heir. I cannot risk your life."

Shine came over and gently pulled Reflect away. Her face was a pool of sorrow. She buried her face in Shine's chest to hide her mirror tears.

"I can't blame her," Freddy said. "I'd want to go help my father, too."

Atlas knew just how Reflect felt – and he sent her a little message with his mind. "Don't worry, we'll find our fathers, both of them."

Reflect gazed into Atlas' eyes and managed the slightest of smiles.

Then, Image raised his hand and fifty lightboards sped off. Atlas watched Ekim waving his arms in the air on a Skyrider behind him. He was awed by the sight of the majestic E'lum warriors so bravely heading out to battle and felt proud to be among them.

"This is really something, huh, Mr. Mapp?" Freddy said, his long hair whipping wildly in the wind. "There ain't nothing like this back home."

"I wish my friends could see this," Atlas shouted back.

"It's fun!"

But as Image guided the board over the lush greenery of The Lazantine Forest toward the dark thunderclouds and ominous mountains well off in the distance, Atlas had a disturbing thought.

He might not live to see E'lum village - or home - ever again.

ELEVEN
When Worlds Collide

Sarah Mapp opened her eyes and looked around the room. On a recliner in the corner, Ahib snored softly. At the dining room table, Neffer was still awake, reading from one of the large, old books he had collected to try to find the source of the curse afflicting Field and Atlas. He hadn't slept a wink all night.

At the other end of the couch, Jenny looked like a sleeping angel, her red hair perfectly framing her face, just like it did when she was a little girl. Sarah was happy to have her here. When she called to tell Jenny of Field's accident and that Atlas was missing, Jenny was on the first plane to Seattle and would not take no for an answer.

Jenny was right. Times like these were what sisters were for.

As Sarah sat up and rubbed her eyes, her attention was drawn to the large map on the easel. She noticed quickly that the red blip in The Lazantine Forest had moved from where she last remembered seeing it.

But the red blip that she believed was the heartbeat of her only child wasn't what captured her attention. What made Sarah's heart race was seeing something that was not there before.

Next to the red blip was a new gray one that seemed to be moving slowly across the canvas with Atlas, not far away from a place that was now marked on the map, *E'lum Village.*

Sarah mouthed the strange new words that had appeared on the canvas overnight along with the new gray blip. What was an E'lum Village, she wondered?

"Neffer, Ahib, something's happening!" she shouted.

Neffer quickly walked over from his perch at the dining room table. Ahib awoke with a start, flailing his arms briefly as though emerging from a fight with a dream enemy. "What is it, Mrs. Mapp?" he asked, gathering his bearings and stumbling over on uneasy legs.

"There's a new blip on the painting, Neffer," Sarah said, pointing it out with alarm in her voice. "It's like a heartbeat... but it's... gray."

Neffer closely examined the blip, but did not immediately offer an opinion as to its origin. Ahib stared with his mouth agape. Jenny, who had also awakened, wore an expression that mirrored Ahib's.

"A heart that does not beat red?" Neffer mused.

He and Sarah exchanged glances, and then looked back to the map. Whatever this new gray blip was, they only hoped that it was not a threat to Atlas.

It was Ahib who brought that point home.

"Mrs. Mapp, although I have no idea of this strange heartbeat, I would think that you should not worry as long as Atlas' heartbeat remains strong. Quite possibly, this new heartbeat belongs to someone of this Arch World who he has befriended to help in his search for Professor Mapp."

"I hope you're right," Sarah said in a whisper.

Then, Neffer, Ahib, Jenny and Sarah watched helplessly as the red and gray blips moved together across the map.

Neffer traced a path with his finger from the pair of blips to a place ahead full of dark, angry clouds and jagged mountain peaks. It was only then that the foursome noticed that this place also had a name: *Polema.*

"I wonder where he's going," Jenny mused.

"I suppose," said Neffer, "Atlas goes into the arms of destiny."

Ormon was angry and red-cheeked as he struggled to pedal up a hilly street in the pale light of dawn. Pepper, looking sheepish, lagged a short distance behind. It wasn't often that Ormon got mad, but when he did, it usually meant that Pepper had done something wrong.

Out of breath, Pepper stopped at the top of the hill. "C'mon, Bookworm," he shouted, "It was an honest mistake. Everybody makes mistakes."

Ormon turned his bike around and rode back to face Pepper. "You can't make a mistake at a time like this, Pepper! Anything could have happened to Atlas by now," he said. "You told him two days. Toxic Soldiers always keep their promises."

Pepper hung his head. He knew Ormon was right.

"Well, I said I was sorry, Bookworm," he said in a soft voice. "I even double-checked to make sure the alarm would go off at eleven."

"Yeah," Ormon scoffed, "Eleven A.M. instead of P.M."

"That's never happened to you?" Pepper retorted.

"It was your idea to get some sleep," Ormon said. "If you remember, I wanted to camp out in The Arch World and start tracking Atlas after we got some rest. If I hadn't woken up, we'd still be asleep."

"There's nothing we can do about it now," Pepper said. "We'll just be a little late, that's all. 'Sides, I checked the map and Atlas is fine. See for yourself."

Pepper pulled the map from his pocket and handed it over. He watched as Ormon unfolded it and took a long look.

"Whoa!" Ormon said, raising his eyebrows. "This is crazy!"

"What?" Pepper asked, scrambling over for a look.

Pepper saw the gray blip right away.

"Whoa!" he said, mimicking Ormon. "What is that?"

"I dunno," Ormon said, his anger washed away. "It's beating just like a heartbeat, but it's not red. And whatever it is, it's with Atlas."

"They're moving, too - and fast," Pepper added, pointing to where their little map now read, *E'lum Village.* "Atlas was over here last night."

Ormon read the words aloud and turned to Pepper.

"This E'lum Village place is where we have to go," he said, handing the map back. "Maybe somebody there can tell us something."

Ormon pedaled off, but Pepper was so mesmerized by the gray blip that Ormon was nearly out of sight by the time he tore his eyes away from the map. He shoved the map back into his pocket and hurried to catch up.

"Hey, wait for me!"

It was still early when Ormon and Pepper reached the McDonald's restaurant Atlas' map had led them to. The streets were fairly deserted and only a smattering of cars waited in line at the drive-thru.

That they weren't alone made Ormon nervous.

"That's why we should have come when it was closed, people are here already," Ormon said. "And that little Indian kid might be around, too."

Pepper spied a bike rack in front of the restaurant.

"It's too late to worry about that, Bookworm," he said,

anxious to put his mistake behind them. "If we lock our bikes up over there, maybe nobody will notice us. Then, we'll just wait until they're not looking and run through the sign just like Atlas did."

"That's the problem, Pepper. We don't know for sure if that's the way he got in. We need to investigate."

"Well, you got a better idea?"

Ormon didn't reply. Their plan was off to a bad start; they were late, the new gray blip could mean that Atlas was in more trouble than they realized, and now, they had to figure out how to get into The Arch World.

Ormon knew there was little time to waste.

He nodded to Pepper and the duo headed over and chained their bikes to the rack. Several early-morning customers sat at a picnic table nearby drinking coffee and eating breakfast.

"Maybe we should go in and buy something so we don't look suspicious," Ormon said.

Pepper rolled his eyes. "Don't be a wuss, Ormon. Nobody's paying attention to us. And, if they do notice anything strange, by then, we'll be gone."

Reassured, Ormon followed Pepper to the grassy lawn near the slowly revolving McDonalds sign. It had been repaired. For a while, they simply stared at it, neither sure what to do.

Pepper was surprised that Ormon was as confused about their next move as he was. Ormon could figure out just about anything, but watching Ormon study the sign, Pepper saw that his brainy friend was at a loss.

"Maybe we should say the Toxic Pledge," Ormon said, finally.

Now, Pepper was positive that Ormon had no answers.

In the past, he always had to twist Ormon's arm to get him to recite the pledge of the Brotherhood of Toxic Soldiers. However, with Atlas' life at stake, Ormon was actually hoping the pledge would help.

Ormon was equally surprised that Pepper didn't jump at his offer, for Pepper used any excuse he could find to state the pledge. When Pepper asked timidly, "You think it'll help?" Ormon knew Pepper was scared, too.

"It can't hurt," Ormon replied, and placed his hand atop Pepper's, both realizing that it wasn't the same without their missing comrade.

Together, they repeated the pledge:

"If war and death or mishap comes, or enemies bend our fingers, we'll never talk, nor reveal our secrets, 'cause the Toxic Brotherhood lingers."

They shook hands and turned back to the slowly revolving sign. "You ready?" Ormon asked.

Pepper was silent. He seemed distracted.

"Hey, Pepper!"

"I heard you, Bookworm," Pepper said, averting his eyes. "I'm just thinking… well, what if something bad happens to us in there? I mean, we don't really know anything about The Arch World. We could get killed. We might never see our families again."

There was real fear in Pepper's eyes, a look that Ormon had never seen from him before. Pepper prided himself on never being afraid of anything. He could always be counted on to pick up a creepy bug with his bare hands, or be the first one to go into a dark room. But this, taking a leap into the unknown, had shaken him.

Ormon had to think fast. His word was everything, and they had made a promise to Atlas. Nothing could stop their mission. If Pepper chickened out, he decided, he would go alone.

"Pepper, this isn't about us," he said. "Going to The Arch World is about something bigger than us. It's about what friends will do for friends."

Pepper swallowed hard, but didn't say anything.

"My father says that a person is lucky to have a handful of friends in a lifetime," Ormon continued. "The way I see it, we've got a head start. We've already got two best friends and a lifetime ahead of us to get the rest.

"Now, I won't blame you if you don't want to go, but I won't feel good about the rest of my life if I don't ever see Atlas again when I know there was something I could have done about it."

Ormon stared into Pepper's eyes. "I'm going with or without you."

For a long while, Pepper was quiet. He turned away so that Ormon couldn't see his watery eyes, then nodded to himself several times, as if deciding what to do. When he turned back, he'd made up his mind.

"Your dad's a smart guy, Bookworm," he said. "I'm glad you're my friend. Let's go."

As they faced the McDonald's sign, neither of the boys noticed the ground tremble, slightly at first, then more violently. Just behind them, the earth split apart, revealing The Door of Desire.

Ormon turned slowly just as the door swung open, a black and purple vortex of swirling matter appearing in the abyss. Before he could warn Pepper, they were sucked off their feet into the dark hole – and the door slammed shut.

Nearby, at a picnic table, a bald, middle-aged man sat holding his cup of coffee frozen in mid-air, his mouth agape.

Next to him, a blonde woman wore the same incredulous expression.

Both looked like they'd just seen a ghost.

On the other side of The Door of Desire, invisible to those in The World Above, something magical was happening.

Ormon and Pepper tumbled lightly, head over heels, down, down, down, into a seemingly bottomless pit. They had no idea how long they'd been falling, only that it was useless to continue screaming. They weren't falling so fast that they would be turned into piles of goo when they hit bottom; it was more like the weightlessness of Outer Space. Or a gravity-defying ride at Disney World.

As they fell, Ormon and Pepper saw a strange, pink luminescent light far below. It looked like clouds, but they couldn't be certain.

The sights became very interesting. It was like being inside the Earth's stomach – and they could tell what it had eaten for dinner. There was a thick and scaly crust which seemed to stretch for miles, and colorful, crystal formations called geodes that Ormon recognized from his Introduction to Geology class. They sparkled like diamonds all hues of the rainbow.

Intact fossils of dinosaurs and other prehistoric creatures lay frozen in time within the rock walls that they passed by. Further down, they felt heat rising from magma, angry red and yellow molten rock that sizzled deep inside the planet.

"This is incredible," Ormon said. "We must be close to Earth's core."

"Yeah... or China," Pepper replied, with a laugh, surprised that they could actually hear each other talking. "All this stuff is amazing," he continued, "but how come we're not dead? I thought we were goners when that big door opened up like that."

"Me, too," Ormon said. "I was screaming like a little baby."

"I won't tell anybody," Pepper said, "'Sides, I was squealing like those girls at Atlas' birthday party for a minute there, myself."

Ormon smiled, happy Pepper didn't force him to point out that fact.

"You think this is how Atlas got to The Arch World?" Pepper asked.

"It's got to be," said Ormon. "It makes more sense now. The Arch World must be beneath our world and just above The World Below on Mrs. Mapp's map. I don't know how long we've been in here, but we should be able to see it pretty soon."

"That's if we don't end up like road kill when we land."

"I don't think that's going to happen," Ormon said. "It's not like we're plummeting through space. It's almost like there's some kind of gravity here that's controlling our fall, like a vacuum. Plus, Atlas made it there in one piece, so I think we'll be fine."

"I hope you're right, Bookworm."

"I'm pretty sure I am," Ormon said. "Who would have thought of this? A world within our world? You know, my dad always said the universe was too big for just us. He's always thought that other life forms existed somewhere in space. He's gonna freak when I tell him that he's been looking in the wrong direction."

"I don't think you're going to have to worry about that," Pepper said. "There's no way he's going to believe you. Nobody's going to believe this. It's not like anybody knows we're here."

Pepper's words made Ormon think. He'd never really done anything or gone anywhere without at least telling his parents.

He wondered if they'd be worried when they found out he wasn't at the Mapp's house as he had told them. He'd also lied to them, something he had never done before, but he figured they wouldn't have understood.

As he plummeted slowly ever further into the recesses of the earth, he wished he'd told someone where he was going. Surely, Neffer and Ahib would have believed him, even though there was no way they would have let two little boys go to The Arch World alone. And Mrs. Mapp would certainly have believed them, especially after seeing her painting magically transform right before her eyes.

Ormon forced himself to stop thinking about what he could have done differently. Now, all he could do was take in the mystical and magical insides of the Earth as he and Pepper continued to fall, each secretly praying that a sudden death did not await them at the bottom.

Back inside the collapsed mine in Althanar, beads of sweat pooled on Habbibi's forehead, but his gaze remained riveted to Field's sleepy face. As though locked in a trance, this had been Habbibi's posture for the past several hours since demanding that Field tell Denai of an unpleasant chapter in the Mapp family's history.

Field agreed to do so, but the injured Denai had been much too weak to stay awake to hear it. He would awaken in fits and starts, sometimes hallucinating, other times screaming in pain, and still other times lying calmly with his eyes wide open staring up into nothingness.

Mahmoud had once again drifted off to sleep, and Field was fighting to stay awake. Every few minutes, his head would lower to his chest, and then snap up quickly, only to see the restless Habbibi staring back.

Field worried that their oxygen supply might soon run out, but so far it had not. Hunger was the enemy now; the weary men had lost track of time and had no idea how long they'd been trapped. Now, Field was sure that if they were not rescued soon, Habbibi would be proven right.

They would die.

In his most lucid moments, Field passed the time daydreaming of Sarah and Atlas. Just the thought of his family gave him strength, but in between - especially when he considered how powerless he was to alleviate Denai's pain – his thoughts turned to accepting the real possibility that he and the others would perish in this place.

Field was about to give in to his desire for sleep once again when Denai stirred from his slumber.

"Professor?"

"I'm here, Denai. Right here."

"Are the rescuers coming? I don't know how much longer I will last."

Habbibi sighed loudly, drawing Field's attention. Even through the dim light, Field could see Habbibi sitting atop a boulder, staring with hateful, evil eyes.

"They're coming," Field said, edging closer to Denai. "It will take a lot of work for them to reach us, but they won't give up. We can't, either."

Denai craned his neck to look upon Habbibi and Mahmoud. He could hear the gentle rhythm of Mahmoud's breathing. Satisfied that both men were still alive, he smiled to himself.

"How did we come to be in such a predicament, Professor?" he asked. "To have delved into the Earth to mine her riches, only to have her turn on us so horribly?"

Field had no answer and hoped that Denai would not ask again, but Habbibi did not let that silence linger.

"He is awake now, Professor," Habbibi prodded, "Tell him the story."

Denai looked into Field's eyes expectantly, as though he didn't remember telling him that he did not need to hear the tale.

Field sat for a moment, exhaled, and then began to speak. "I was seventeen when my father died," he said. "For as long as I can remember, all he ever talked about was finding the Diamonds of Bushawri. He talked about them so much that I think they might have been my first memory."

Denai smiled at Field's feeble attempt at humor.

"Anyway, his search for those diamonds made my mother a widow and became my obsession!"

"Tell Denai the *real* story!" Habbibi interrupted.

"It's all part of the story," Field said sharply, his growing impatience with Habbibi showing through. "You demanded that I tell him, so let me tell him my way."

Habbibi cracked his huge knobby knuckles, but said nothing.

Field continued, "My father didn't want the diamonds for himself. He wanted to prove that a time in history existed and he knew that those diamonds would be evidence of that. He was never in it for the money."

Habbibi coughed rudely to signal his disagreement.

"Anyway, my father got a tip that the diamonds might be found on a treacherous mountaintop in the Virunga Chain off Uganda."

"In The Impenetrable Forest?" Mahmoud asked excitedly, even though he had just awoken.

Field nodded.

"He assembled a group of men," Field said, looking straight into Habbibi's eyes, *"warned them of the ri*sks, and they set off. It was the last time I saw him. He was killed in an avalanche. Everyone was killed. Some," he paused, "obviously, blamed my father."

"Tell him how many died," Habbibi demanded.

"Thirty," Field said, slowly.

"Including my beloved uncle," Habbibi interjected.

"Excavations are dangerous work, Habbibi. Accidents happen."

Habbibi's voice rose. His tone was angry and terse. "But who will explain this to my cousins, who struggle still for my uncle's following a man without regard for the lives of others?"

Habbibi stood up, his head nearly hitting the rocky ceiling.

"Habbibi, he has told the story," Denai said, sensing the growing tension in the air. "Where is your forgiveness? You are a religious man."

Mahmoud was also wary. He had worked with the gargantuan Habbibi on several occasions before and had seen first-hand the devastation he could wreak when his passion boiled over. Usually, Mahmoud could talk to Habbibi and soothe the savage beast in him before things got out of control.

But Mahmoud knew things would be different this time once Habbibi pulled his prized dagger from its sheath.

"What are you doing, Habbibi!?!" Mahmoud shouted, recoiling.

Habbibi saw and heard no one else as he approached

Field with the dagger poised to strike, its shiny, sharp tip gleaming in the torchlight.

Field scrambled to his feet and watched as Habbibi carefully and deliberately stepped over boulders and splintered wood, his eyes firmly fixed on his prey.

"We will not get out of here alive, Mahmoud," Habbibi said. "The Professor will not breathe one more breath than I. This I promised to my uncle's family."

Mahmoud pleaded with Habbibi, who had lapsed into madness. "Habbibi! You came on this expedition with the intention of killing Professor Mapp?"

"It is my duty," Habbibi replied, inching closer to Field, who picked up a large rock to defend himself.

"Habbibi, no!" cried Denai, who was helpless to do anything more.

"Be reasonable, Habbibi," Field reasoned, raising the rock. "We can talk about this when we get out of here."

"Habbibi, come to your senses!" Mahmoud screamed.

"There will be no more talk!" Habbibi declared, his booming voice echoing off the walls of the unstable mine surrounding them.

Mahmoud screamed once more just as Habbibi raised the knife.

Then came a low rumble, almost like the tide rushing in from the ocean. Habbibi stopped in his tracks. Suddenly, heavy rocks rained down. It was another collapse.

Field dove on top of Denai, covering the young man's body as best he could, while shielding his own head with a free hand.

Outside of the collapsed mine, workers scattered, shouting, "Get out! Everybody out! Run!" as a huge black cloud plumed from the entrance.

In seconds, it was over. Inside, there was nothing but dust, and then silence.

Back at the Mapp house, Sarah, Neffer, Ahib and Jenny followed the progress of Atlas and the gray blip that accompanied him.

Suddenly, there was a happening in the boot-shaped place called Haven. The four heartbeats pounded quickly, faster and faster still.

And then, just as swiftly, there were just three heartbeats, two beating hard and fast, and one very weakly.

"Neffer, something's going on," Ahib said.

"I see, Ahib, I see," Neffer replied.

Jenny and Sarah looked on, helpless and too horrified to speak. Ahib turned to Neffer, who turned away.

"Do you think-"

Neffer held up a hand to quiet him.

"If you please, Ahib," he said, "right now, I would prefer not to think at all."

Outside the McDonald's restaurant, several police cars sat with lights flashing. The middle-aged couple talked with an officer, while the little Indian boy stared at the lush parcel of neatly manicured green grass. It bore no evidence of the Door of Desire beneath.

The police officer frowned as the couple told their story yet again.

"I'm telling you, sir, there were two boys right here!" the man insisted. "My wife and I both saw them, and several other folks did, too. They were just standing there, and then the ground opened up and swallowed them. I've never seen anything like it."

The policeman took notes, his face stoic and skeptical.

"I know it's hard to believe, officer," the woman said, "but we have children and somebody's going to miss those boys."

"Well, ma'am," the officer said, closing his book, "nobody's reported any boys missing so far. There's nothing more we can do here."

"So, you're just going to... to leave?" she said in disbelief.

"Like I said, there's nothing more we can do."

The officer walked toward his car, then turned back to the couple. "Please don't take this wrong folks," he said, "but do either of you drink... I mean, alcohol or anything like that?"

The woman shook her head. Her husband flushed a deep red. "No officer," he said, "but I think I'm going to start up again."

Whizzing over The Lazantine Forest, Atlas was drinking in the unusual sights and sounds of The Arch World. Every now and then, Freddy pointed out a flying creature or a strange-looking tree and explained to Atlas what it was. Atlas was glad to have Freddy with him, but he couldn't digest all that he was seeing. There was simply too much to take in.

"It's beautiful," he repeated over and over, wishing to have Ormon and Pepper there beside him on Image's Skyrider. Ormon always knew the right words to describe things and Atlas knew he'd have a hard time explaining it later.

"It is beautiful, Mr. Mapp," Freddy said. "That's why I gave up trying to get back home."

"How long have you been here?" Atlas asked. Freddy shrugged his shoulders.

"I don't really know. Time works a little differently here."

"But didn't you ever want to go back home?"

"In the beginning I did, but when I thought about it some more, wasn't nothing to go back to," Freddy said. "When I was up there, I wanted out so bad that when I got swallowed up, I just felt like God answered my prayers. Then, when I met the E'lum and got to know the place, well, I guess I kinda forgot about home."

Atlas stared hard at Freddy Bearer's face and wondered if he might someday feel the same way. He couldn't imagine not wanting to return home. He didn't quite grasp what Freddy meant about time working differently in The Arch World, either, but when he glanced at his watch, the second hand hadn't moved far from where he'd last seen it.

Atlas thought of his mother and could see in his mind's eye an image of her sleeping on the night he left. He hoped it would not be the last time he would see her. He tried to picture himself as a man of Freddy's age and wondered what Pepper and Ormon would look like, or if he would remember them if they ever saw each other again.

He closed his eyes and tried to burn their images into his mind. As beautiful and interesting as The Arch World was, Atlas never wanted to forget home – or his desire to get back there.

Suddenly, Image pointed to something in the distance. "There," he said, "Fossil Mountain."

Atlas tore himself away from his thoughts and saw the largest mountain he had ever seen. It reached majestically into the pink-purple sky, its peaks barely poking into the ominous black clouds overhead.

"Better tighten up your britches, Mr. Mapp," Freddy

said in a serious tone, "This is one scary place."

As much as Atlas needed Freddy to explain so many other things on their flight over The Lazantine Forest, he didn't need Freddy to tell him that they were approaching danger. He could see that much with his own eyes.

Sarah stared at the large map on the easel, watching her son making his way toward the mountain with the dark clouds hovering above.

The telephone rang, shattering the quiet. Sarah answered and turned slowly to Ahib. "It's for you," she said, looking perplexed.

Ahib took the phone and said hello, then quickly changed to his native Arabic tongue. Although Sarah and Jenny couldn't understand Ahib's words, they could easily translate the look on his face.

He hung up slowly, then said, "There has been a secondary collapse at the mine in Althanar. The men refuse to search more. They say it is simply too dangerous."

"No!" Sarah insisted, "They have to keep searching."

"I will go to Althanar," he said, "but I fear they will not listen to me."

"No, Ahib. I will go. If not to you, they *will* listen to me," Neffer said, in a voice that left no room for debate. "I will leave at once."

"Thank you, Neffer," Sarah said, giving Neffer a hug.

While this was happening, Jenny cried out, "Look at this!"

Everyone joined her before the large animated map. To the far north, just before The Lazantine Forest, there were two *new* bright red heartbeats.

Instantly, Ahib knew. He could feel it in the pit of his

stomach. "That can only be-" Ahib began.

"Ormon and Pepper," Sarah said, burying her face in her hands, and crying, "No, boys! No, no, no!"

TWELVE
The Five Kings

Ormon was lying on the salty ground when he opened his eyes to gaze upon a pink sky with two suns. He thought he had died and gone to heaven – until he heard Pepper's voice behind him.

"Bookworm, do you see what I'm seeing?"

Ormon turned to find Pepper sitting on the ground not far away. But what caught Pepper's eye wasn't the pair of suns in the sky. Instead, Pepper was looking at a long hand ladder behind them spanning a chasm to a mountain on the other side.

"It's the Monkey Bar Bridge!" Pepper exclaimed, scrambling to his feet. "We're here! We're really in The Arch World."

Thanks to Pepper's keen observation, Ormon knew this definitely wasn't heaven. He quickly figured out that they must have been unconscious when they landed because though he remembered falling through the milky pink sky, he certainly didn't remember - or feel - hitting the ground.

He didn't feel any pain, and he and Pepper weren't piles of goo as he'd feared. Somehow, they were here in one piece, in a spectacular new world that they didn't know existed until just days before.

Ormon searched for signs of life, and saw several creatures that looked like birds slicing through the unusual sky, but little else.

Stretched out a hundred yards or so before them, he

recognized the dense greenery of The Lazantine Forest, and, in the distance, saw mountains and large arches towering into the sky.

There were no buildings or houses or anything man-made that resembled the world he was familiar with. Aside from the water rushing at the bottom of the canyon below, it was eerily quiet. So quiet, in fact, that Ormon could almost hear himself thinking.

Pepper walked to the edge of the cliff and peered over.

"A couple more feet and we'd have been fish food," he said.

Looking up at the strange-colored sky with a big sun and a smaller one, Ormon said, "Dorothy, we're definitely not in Kansas anymore."

"Who you calling Dorothy?" Pepper asked.

"It's just a figure of speech, Pepper."

"Where do you s'pose we are?" Pepper asked.

"I think that's The Lazantine Forest," Ormon said, pointing ahead. "Check the map to be sure."

Pepper pulled out the map and the boys took a long look. Then another. Pepper pointed to the long hand ladder.

"Whoa, the Monkey Bar Bridge isn't on this map."

"Remember how all those little maps were different?" Ormon asked. "Maybe that's why we landed here instead over way over there. Atlas probably had to climb across."

"You think *Atlas* was able to climb across that thing?" Pepper said, with a look of disbelief.

"He's looking for his dad, Pepper. You can't underestimate anybody when they're on a mission like that. There's all kinds of stories about people doing incredible things and displaying superhuman feats of strength in stressful situations," Ormon said. "So, yeah, I think Atlas did whatever he had to do to. You should have a little more faith in him."

Pepper nodded, reached inside his backpack and took out a bottle of water.

"I wasn't saying I didn't think he could do it. It's just that Atlas, well-"

"I know, I know. He doesn't like big adventures."

"Well, you said it, not me," Pepper replied, turning the bottle up and taking a big gulp. "Ahhhh, I needed that. It's hot out here."

Water dripped off Pepper's chin onto the sandy earth. Ormon watched the salt curiously scatter. And he heard a low growl.

"Did you see that?" he asked.

"See what?"

"When you spilled water on the ground," Ormon said, "the sand just kind of moved away."

Pepper smirked.

"Bookworm, you need a drink," he said, handing the bottle over. "I think those two suns are getting to your head."

"No, *I'm serious*," Ormon said, tilting the bottle so that several drops fell to the ground. The boys watched the salt disperse, and heard the growl grow louder. They scanned the area with their hearts in their throats.

"Tell me you didn't hear *that*," he said.

"I... I heard it, Bookworm," Pepper said, as the hairs on the back of his neck stood up. "We're not alone."

But the boys saw no one on the pristine white beach, nor lurking in the trees of The Lazantine Forest. That's when the sand began to gather itself into the shape of the Salt Monster. Ormon, watched, too terrified to move, but Pepper sprang into action, cocking his Super Soaker and pulling out the vial of holy water.

"I still can't believe you stole that from Neffer," Ormon said through chattering teeth.

"It was for a good cause," Pepper retorted, pouring a few drops of the liquid into his Soaker. "You better take some, too!"

Ormon hurriedly poured some holy water into his weapon while Pepper watched Waheel the Salt Monster emerge, snarling and growling, its eyes fixed on the pair. With all the salt gone from the ground, absorbed into the monster's body, the boys saw skeletons and bones all around them.

"Aaaarrrrrggghh! You must die!" Waheel thundered, pounding his granite-like chest.

"Aaaaaaaaaaahhhhhh!" Pepper and Ormon screamed in unison, too frightened to even shoot.

"Run!" Pepper shouted, heading for the trees with Ormon in hot pursuit as Waheel galloped towards them, the ground shivering beneath his heavy feet.

Pepper turned and got off a shot, but missed.

"Water not save you this time," Waheel said.

"What's he mean *this* time?" Ormon screamed.

Pepper was too busy running for his life to reply. He'd almost made it to the tree line when he glanced over his shoulder to see the monster gaining on Ormon, who wasn't very fast. The monster had successfully separated the two and was now going after the weaker, slower boy.

Waheel lunged at Ormon, who barely dodged his razor-sharp claws, but made the mistake of running back toward the cliff, and certain death. Pepper was already in the forest. He could have easily saved himself, but he couldn't leave Ormon. He had to do something.

But what could he do?

Fear welled up inside Pepper when Ormon tripped and

fell with a sickening thud, his Super Soaker slipping from his hands and sliding just out of reach. Waheel was no more than a few feet away, advancing with lumbering steps and baring his teeth at Ormon.

"Now, boy will die!" Waheel bellowed, scraping his talons together.

"Please, don't kill me!" Ormon pleaded, rolling onto his back and desperately trying to scoot away, all the while moving perilously close to the cliff's edge. "I don't want to die!"

Ormon glanced over his shoulder and tried to decide what would be better; to be eaten alive by the Salt Monster or to fall several hundred feet to a painful end. Neither choice was appealing, but Ormon knew that without a miracle, the monster would make the decision for him.

An even more terrifying thought occurred to him: what if the monster just took a couple of bites out of him and decided to throw him over the edge, anyway? It was all too horrible to consider.

Just as Waheel moved in for the kill, Ormon heard Pepper's voice.

"Hey, ya big ugly monster, why don't you try picking on me?"

Behind Waheel, Pepper stood with his Super Soaker cocked. "That's right, I'm the one you want," Pepper crowed, as Waheel turned towards him – and away from the helpless Ormon.

His plan was working.

"You wanna eat somebody? Well, eat me!"

Waheel looked back and forth between the two boys, growled loudly and took another step toward Pepper.

"C'mon, I'm not gonna run from ya!" Pepper goaded.

As Waheel stalked Pepper, Ormon grabbed his Super Soaker and circled away from the cliff. Not taking his eyes from the big monster, Pepper motioned for Ormon to head for the trees. Waheel lunged at Pepper, who fired a stream of water, but missed.

Unafraid of the colorful water gun, Waheel advanced.

"You will make a nice dinner!" he declared, just as Pepper scored a direct hit on Waheel's taloned hand.

To Pepper's shock and surprise, the monster's hand disintegrated. "Aaaarrrrgggggghhhh!!!"

Waheel waved his stumpy hand in the wind. This time, however, it did not regenerate.

Ormon, who hadn't followed Pepper's order to hide, approached and fired a shot, taking off a chunk of the monster's arm.

"Yeah!" Pepper shouted gleefully, thrusting his fist in the air.

"What have you done to me?" Waheel cried, staring at his deformed, smoldering arm.

"It's called Toxic Rain," Pepper said, cocking his Soaker and moving in for the kill shot. "Hasta La Vista, Baby!"

Before he could pull the trigger, Ormon darted between Pepper and the monster. "Wait, Pepper!"

"What's wrong with you, Ormon? This thing tried to kill us!"

"I know," Ormon said, inching closer to the creature, who moaned in pain. "I think he's hurt. Look at him."

Ormon pointed to the bones scattered about.

"I'll bet his job's keeping people out of The Arch World."

"Or keeping them *in*," said Pepper.

"I think we melted him," Ormon said, moving closer

still and looking into Waheel's mournful eyes. "Hey, buddy, we didn't mean to hurt you. We were just looking for our friend."

"Boy get away," Waheel replied.

"You saw him?" Ormon asked in disbelief.

"Waheel not kill him," the monster said, pointing a sharp talon on his good hand toward The Lazantine Forest. "He go there."

Finally, Pepper lowered his weapon. The defeated Salt Monster wasn't a threat anymore. Besides, with him injured, Pepper figured he could take the beast out with a single blast from his holy water-fortified soaker.

Ormon rummaged through his backpack and pulled out a candy bar.

He edged toward Waheel and warily held it out.

"It's called chocolate," he said, motioning to his mouth to show Waheel that the gift was edible.

Ormon's heart skipped a beat when Waheel gently took the chocolate bar, the talons on his hand barely raking Ormon's sleeve. At that moment, Ormon was sure there would be no danger, for the creature could have easily ripped him to shreds had it so desired.

The boys watched as Waheel took a small bite.

"Uh, you shudda taken the wrapper off, Bookworm," Pepper said.

"I don't think it really matters much to him," Ormon said, as something resembling a smile crossed Waheel's face. "That's right, big guy, take another bite."

Waheel thrust the entire bar into his mouth. "Chocolate good," he said. "Really good."

Ormon smiled. "My dad says there's some good in everything." Ormon extended his hand to Waheel.

"Friends?" he said.

Waheel was confused by the gesture. It then occurred to Ormon that such a beast likely never had a friend. And, with all the bones lying about, Ormon was sure that the monster had probably eaten anyone who had tried to befriend him.

Ormon repeated the word, and watched in amazement as Waheel extended his stumpy hand for Ormon to shake.

"F-f-friiiieeennnddsss," Waheel stuttered.

As the boy and monster shook hand and stump, Pepper stole a glimpse at his map and saw Atlas' red heartbeat.

"Hate to break up the love affair, Bookworm, but we've gotta get going. He's this way," said Pepper, pointing to the forest and heading off.

Ormon took another candy bar from his pack and tossed it to Waheel, who munched happily while the boys disappeared into forest.

Having witnessed the devastation wreaked by his Super Soaker, Pepper cockily stormed through the brush ready to shoot at the slightest movement of a bush or tree. The Lazantine Forest was so dense that Ormon struggled to keep up.

"We have to be careful, Pepper," Ormon warned, "It's not like we're invincible just because the acid rain spray worked on that monster. There could be all kinds of dangerous stuff out here."

"You worry too much," Pepper replied. "We've prepared all our lives for this. 'Sides, our main job is to rescue Atlas, remember?"

"Yeah, but the enemy isn't supposed to hear you coming. That's part of the game, too. Remember how Atlas and I caught you in Mrs. Mapp's cottage?"

"But that turned out to be a good thing," Pepper said, sure of himself. "Look what happened with that. We got information when we found the maps, and that's how we knew where to search for Atlas' dad."

"Correction," Ormon said, "You *stole* the map, Pepper, just like you *stole* Neffer's holy water. Did you ever stop to think that he might actually need it for something?"

Pepper stopped and stared at Ormon angrily.

"Bookworm, that thing would have killed us if we didn't have the holy water. Would you rather be one of those skeletons with all the meat ripped off your bones?"

Ormon didn't know what to say. Even though the pilfered map and holy water had come in handy, Ormon didn't believe Pepper had a right to take what didn't belong to him.

But Pepper had different values when it came to these sorts of things. No, he didn't steal from the candy store or from old people or his father, but still, Ormon worried that someday Pepper's ways might get him into big trouble. Worse, he thought, Pepper would get them all into some dilemma that they might not so easily escape.

"Neffer will understand, just like Mrs. Mapp did," Pepper continued. "Now, can we worry about all this stuff later? We've got a job to do, and we're late. You said so yourself."

Ormon saw that it was a waste of time trying to convince Pepper of anything. He looked around and saw a clearing up ahead.

"Let's go over there and try to get our bearings," he said. "I feel like we're going around in circles."

The boys hiked into the clearing and took shelter under a tree. Pepper briefly examined the map, and then handed it to Ormon in a gesture of friendship. Pepper knew that he'd upset

Ormon and realized that they wouldn't get very far – or stay alive – if they fought with each other.

"Sorry, Bookworm," he said, giving Ormon a quick pat on the back.

"It's okay," Ormon replied, unfolding the map and trying to figure out the best course of action. Ormon searched for an easier path through The Lazantine Forest, but there was none. He knew that E'lum Village was straight ahead, but he couldn't tell how long it would take to get there.

"Next time we go to another world, remind me to bring a machete," he said, drawing a smile from Pepper, who pulled out a small pocketknife.

"That's not going to do it, Pepper," Ormon said. "We're going to need something a whole lot bigger than that to cut through this stuff."

Ormon had no idea that Sarah Mapp was watching their heartbeats at that very moment, trying to figure out how she could help them.

Suddenly, she bolted up as though struck by lightning and ran from the room. "That's it!" she said, to herself.

"Where are you going?" Jenny called after her.

"I've got an idea," Sarah shouted, on her way out the back door. Ahib looked up from his book with a perplexed expression.

"This doesn't make any sense," he said.

"What doesn't make any sense?" asked Jenny.

Ahib walked over carrying Ormon's book, *Mythological Curses from A-Z*, and showed Jenny a page with the heading: King Attanan Bushawri.

There was nothing else written on the page.

"It's strange," Ahib said, explaining, "This page on King Attanan Bushawri is the only blank page in the entire book."

Jenny couldn't begin to imagine what the blank page meant. Just then, Sarah rushed back into the living room, with several cans of paint in each hand. This caught Neffer's attention.

"What are you doing, Sarah?" he asked.

"I painted this map," she said, pulling out a paintbrush and mixing colors together on a palette. "So, maybe I can change it."

Neffer raised an ancient eyebrow. He didn't know if the plan would work, but he thought the idea sheer genius.

They all gathered around and watched in anticipation as Sarah dipped her brush into a light-brown color and made small strokes near the two slow- moving red heartbeats in The Lazantine Forest.

Ormon and Pepper grunted and groaned as they thrashed their way through the thicket of vines, trees and shrubbery. Suddenly, as if by magic, the forest parted like the Red Sea – a swath of brown earth replacing the disappearing trees as a clear path opened up before them.

"Whoa, dude, this is weird," Pepper said, with his mouth agape.

They had seen this kind of thing happen before - when the ugly World Below appeared on the map in Sarah's cottage.

Pepper unfurled his map and numbly watched as words materialized in black letters, both on the paper and upon the newly-constructed path: *"Boys, be careful!"*

"What is that?" Pepper asked, confused. But Ormon had already figured it out.

"Incredible, Mrs. Mapp," Ormon said, a huge smile spreading across his face. He turned to Pepper and added, "That's… divine intervention."

Pepper's expression told Ormon that he had no idea what Ormon was talking about. Ormon simply chuckled and headed off down the new path.

At Atlas' house, Neffer, Ahib, Jenny and Sarah watched the two red blips speed toward E'lum Village.

"Amazing," whispered Ahib.

Inspired, Sarah opened a can of white paint and spread generous dollops across the bottom of the canvas, obliterating the terrible World Below.

But the nasty image slowly reappeared, refusing to be erased. Sarah's shoulders slumped.

"I guess *that* was a little too much to hope for," she said.

Hidden among the rocks on Fossil Mountain, Boroom and Sharibu scanned the sky, finally seeing the small E'lum army approaching. "He brings them as promised," Sharibu snickered.

The fearsome duo crouched low to avoid being detected as the Skyriders drew closer. They saw Image, Freddy and Atlas on a lightboard out front, trailed by Ekim, who rode with an E'lum warrior.

"What is *he* doing with them?" Boroom said, eyeing the unexpected interloper. "This, the master will want to know."

The gargoyles slithered down the mountain and hustled back to The World Below.

Image was wary while guiding his Skyrider down to the base of the huge mountain. He did not see Boroom and Sharibu, but he sensed danger lurking. Having never been so close to The World Below, Image believed that this was the feeling that must always accompany the presence of evil.

The dark, blackened clouds over Fossil Mountain were

so thick that Image could just barely see the two suns and was unaware just how close The Arch World was to the convergence of the Novi. But he knew he was running out of time to rescue Vision and save the Arch World races.

When the craft landed softly on the hard ground, Atlas couldn't believe his eyes. Etched into the mountainside were five majestic faces, each with long regal beards and wearing the crowns of royalty.

The closest thing Atlas had ever seen to such a sight were the famous faces of the American presidents carved into Mount Rushmore.

"The Five Ancient Kings of Polema," Image explained. "They guard a door that leads to a shortcut into the city."

Atlas looked around, but did not see a door of any kind. "How do you get in?" he asked.

"You must ask their permission," Image replied.

Freddy Bearer, Ekim and several E'lum warriors gathered around, while Image directed several others to take up defensive positions in case of an attack. He was sure that Kibu was aware of the approaching E'lum army, and was quite disturbed by how uneventful their flight had been.

It was almost as though Kibu were *allowing* them safe passage.

Suddenly, their attentions were captured by slow movements of the kings' faces; they craned and stretched as if waking from a slumber.

Atlas stood mesmerized while Image and the other E'lum warriors bowed, their faces full of reverence.

Atlas felt his breath leave his body when the first king spoke in a booming voice.

"Why do you seek to avoid the Five Perils of Polema?" he asked.

Atlas whispered to Ekim, "What are the Five Perils of Polema?"

"They're tests of character, Atlas Mapp," Ekim said. "If you fail any one of them, you could easily be killed."

Atlas gulped.

"Yeah, Mr. Mapp," said Freddy, "but if they allow us to take this shortcut, we can skip all that."

Image stepped closer to the stone-faced kings. "It is for a noble cause, Dear Kings," he explained. "One son from The World Above seeks to save two fathers."

"Where is this son?" the king said, his eyes shifting among the group. Image nudged Atlas forward, whispering, "Time is precious."

Atlas took tentative steps toward the Fossil Wall.

The first king's gaze was so piercing that Atlas felt as though his body was being probed by an unseen force. Finally, the king spoke. "We will look into your heart."

Unsure if there were anything he was supposed to do that he wasn't doing, Atlas turned to Image, who simply nodded.

"Uh, okay," Atlas said to the Five Kings.

While the kings examined the nature of Atlas' heart, he was reminded of the time his parents took him to see Santa Claus at the mall when he was very young. Atlas would sit on Santa's lap and try hard to erase any bad thoughts from his mind (because he was sure that Santa knew everything), and only then would he reveal the gifts on his wish list.

Under the scrutiny of The Five Kings, Atlas tried to do the same thing.

He closed his eyes and went over a mental checklist. Was he kind? A good person? Were his motives pure? Atlas figured he was a good kid. He always tried to do right by others. He shared and neither lied nor cheated. He hoped the kings would see these qualities.

Atlas didn't know what criteria The Five Kings were looking for, and he couldn't remember doing anything that would give them reason to deny their request to use the shortcut to Polema. Still, for some reason, he was nervous and anxious.

He jerked to attention at the sound of grinding rock and looked up to see the heads of The Five Kings swiveling back and forth while they silently commiserated with each other. Like the E'lum, they also were telepathic and did not need to speak in order to be heard.

As one, The Five Kings looked off toward The Lazantine Forest and then fixed their eyes upon Atlas, ready to pronounce judgment.

"We see that you are honest," said the first king. "We see that you are courageous," said the second. "We see that you are loyal," said the third. "We see that you are selfless," continued the fourth.

There was an awkward pause.

Atlas had no idea what the kings were waiting for, but he quickly noticed that the fifth king's eyes were closed, as if he were napping. Before the silence became unbearable, the other four kings turned to face the fifth king.

"Well!" they demanded in unison, the power of their voices sending a small shower of rock and pebbles down from the mountaintop.

The fifth king stirred with a start and noticed the others glaring at him. "Oh, yes... I, uh... we see that you have a hero's vision," he said, finally.

"Thank you," Atlas said, turning to Freddy. "Is that good?"

"That's real good," Freddy said.

Image and the E'lum warriors smiled with relief. Not only had The Five Kings' approval saved them time, but it also spared them many dangers that lurked had they been denied permission to use the shortcut. At the very least, they would not risk death attempting to navigate their Skyriders over Fossil Mountain through the dense, dark clouds

Of course, going around the mountain might have meant battling other demons and spirits that had made pacts with Kibu to attack anyone who attempted to breach the outside walls surrounding the city of Polema. In exchange, Kibu protected them from the cleansing convergence by providing them sanctuary in the impenetrable darkness of The World Below.

Image gave thanks to The Five Kings, and the group heard a deafening rumble as Fossil Wall slid away, revealing a large tunnel.

"Be well on your journey, Atlas Mapp," The Five Kings said.

"Thank you," Atlas said, surprised that the kings knew his name.

"You must be a pretty special young feller," Freddy said. "The first time I tried to get through to Haven, I couldn't even pass the test."

"You've been to Haven?" Atlas asked, excited.

"Sure, Mr. Mapp," Freddy said, matter-of-factly. "It's way on the other side of Polema."

Before Atlas could ask another question, Image stepped on his Skyrider and said, "We must go. There is little time."

THIRTEEN
Reflect's Decision

Thanks to Sarah Mapp's quick thinking, Ormon and Pepper made quick time through The Lazantine Forest. But, as they got closer to E'lum Village, Ormon finally realized what had been bothering him.

"Do you notice anything strange about this forest, Pepper?"

Pepper stopped and looked around.

"Everything's strange about this forest. We're in a totally different world."

"That's not what I mean," Ormon said, staring intently into the trees on either side of the path created by Sarah's paint brush.

"I'm talking about *just* the forest. I mean, we practically live in a forest in Seattle and there's all kinds of stuff in there. Like, spooky sounds and animals and things. We've been in The Lazantine Forest for a while now, and we haven't really seen or heard anything. Have you ever been in a forest and not heard anything?"

When Ormon stopped talking, Pepper listened close. Other than a light, scratchy rustling of trees in the breeze, there was nary a sound.

"That is weird, Bookworm," Pepper said. "What do you think it means?"

"I don't know. It's just that when you consider that The Arch World is capable of supporting life, it just seems to me that there *should* be life here."

"Maybe that monster ate everything up," Pepper said, freaking himself out. "You saw all those skeletons on the ground. There were hundreds of them. Maybe there's more monsters just like him."

"I don't think so," Ormon said. "Of course, I don't know for sure, but he seemed like a pretty solitary creature. I figure there's got to be a reasonable explanation for this."

"Like what?"

"I dunno," Ormon replied, thoughtfully. "But whatever it is, I hope it doesn't put Atlas in danger. Let's get to E'lum Village. If there's a village, there's got to be people. Maybe somebody there can tell us something."

They hadn't walked very far when Ormon saw a huge black triangle in the sky, well above the trees. Pepper noticed it at the same time, and the boys crept wordlessly off the path back into the forest.

"What is that thing?" Pepper asked in a low voice.

Ormon shook his head and slowly moved forward and figured out that the triangle wasn't a spaceship, as he'd first suspected. Now, he could see that the object in the sky was the tip of an enormous black pyramid, and they were close enough to see shiny figures that looked like aliens at the base of the structure.

"Whoa!" he said, unable to tear his eyes away from the spectacle.

Pepper looked at his map and noticed that there was now a similar black pyramid right in the middle of the village they were searching for.

"According to this map," Pepper whispered, "E'lum Village is either right here or it's somewhere close. C'mon."

He moved past Ormon in a rush of excitement. Ormon

hurried to catch up, careful not to make too much noise lest they draw the attention of the pyramid's inhabitants. As they got closer, smaller transparent pyramids came into view.

"Those people look like they're from outer space," Pepper said. "We'd better be ready for anything, Bookworm. They might be hostile."

The boys checked their soakers to make sure they were prepared to fire if needed, then they observed groups of Mirror People milling about E'lum Village, some simply sitting, others talking in small groups, and some looking seriously up at the sky.

"Something's going on," Ormon said, following their gazes skyward. "They're waiting for something to happen."

Then the boys saw a startling and incredible sight.

Off in the distance, from their hiding place at the edge of the village, long caravans of very strange beings could be seen heading towards the large black pyramid.

Ormon and Pepper exchanged glances of wonder as they watched the members of The Arch World races enter E'lum Village, looking as though they were at the end of a long journey. Crude wagons and carts pulled by strange beasts were piled high with food and belongings, as if their owners had prepared for a long stay.

The boys marveled at the sight of mammals that resembled those from their own world, with only slight differences. One creature looked like a cross between a camel and a horse, with long strands of mane-like hair protruding from its belly. There were large Oxen-like animals, only with six legs.

Many of the beings in the caravan walked upright like humans, but others crawled on hands and feet like monkeys. One had large eyes, pointed ears and long whiskers like a cat's.

Curiously, the only beings that Pepper and Ormon saw who actually looked human were the reflective Mirror People.

For a long while, the boys observed the strange scene before them, too transfixed to speak. They were both enthralled and afraid at the same time, but it occurred to Ormon that they would have to do something soon.

Precious time was wasting, and, looking at the map, he could see that Atlas was moving further away.

Pepper was thinking the same thing. "Bookworm, we can't just stay here," he said. "Maybe we should circle around the village and track Atlas from there."

Ormon shook his head. "I think the best thing to do is to make contact and see what we can find out. Those shiny people seem to be friendly. I mean, we know Atlas was here last night, so it's likely that he stayed with them."

Pepper wasn't so sure.

His head danced with images of torture he'd seen in the movies and read about in comic books. He saw himself and Ormon being rotated on a spit over a hot fire by cannibals with voracious appetites, or whisked away to another planet against their will by hostile aliens. He tried to push the unsettling images from his mind, but they simply would not go away. Every scenario he imagined ended badly.

Pepper was still daydreaming of doom when he realized Ormon had made the decision for both of them. He'd stood up and walked back to the path, standing right out in the open, and made no effort to conceal himself as he headed straight for a group of Mirror People on the edge of the village.

Pepper quickly thought about the rules of their Toxic Soldier game and how Ormon was breaking every one of them by giving away their position. Unless they were surrendering, something Toxic Soldiers never did, Ormon was playing a

The Adventures of Atlas Mapp

dangerous game with both of their lives.

Still, Pepper couldn't allow Ormon to go alone. And he certainly didn't want to have to fend for himself in the seemingly uninhabited Lazantine Forest.

"Hey, wait for me!" Pepper whispered, leaping out of the trees and running to catch up to Ormon with his Super Soaker cocked and ready.

Suddenly, several of the reflective figures noticed them. Ormon shot a quick glance at Pepper and was horrified to see that Pepper was holding his gun in a menacing manner.

"Lower your weapon, Pepper!" he quietly commanded. "We need to show them that we come in peace."

"No way, Bookworm," Pepper replied defiantly. "We don't know anything about these… people. They could be dangerous."

"They don't know anything about us, either, Pepper," Ormon snapped. "Just put the gun down."

Reluctantly, Pepper obeyed. By now, at least twenty E'lum villagers had seen them. The looks of shock on their faces mirrored that of the boys, who inched closer, nonetheless. For a moment, there was complete silence.

And then, a young Mirror Girl young approached them.

"Are you from up there?" she asked, pointing to the sky. Ormon and Pepper exchanged glances.

"Dude, they speak English," Pepper said.

Ormon didn't reply. Instead, locked eye to eye with Reflect, he simply nodded several times.

"We are the E'lum," she said. "My name is Reflect. Welcome to our village."

Her warm smile immediately put the boys more at ease.

"We're looking for our friend," Ormon said, slowly, careful to make sure she understood. "His name is Atlas."

163

"So, you too have heartbeats?" she asked, with a giggle, drawing a curious look from Pepper. "May I see?"

Ormon remained as still as a stone, watching his distorted reflection in Reflect's skin as she placed a hand on his chest. After several moments, she smiled excitedly. "Yes, you are much like Atlas Mapp!"

Pepper and Ormon looked at each other again. "Do you know him?" Pepper asked.

"Yes. He is a friend of mine, too. He has gone to The World Below with a small army to help rescue my father, Vision."

Reflect could sense the pair's confusion.

"He is actually helping both of our fathers," she said. "You see, if he rescues my father from The World Below, he will help us save all of The Arch World races. Everyone you see before you have come to The Black Pyramid to escape the convergence of the Novi."

Reflect's explanation didn't help. The boys remained puzzled.

Who was her father and why would Atlas be trying to help him, Ormon wondered? Pepper was still stuck trying to figure out the convergence of the Arch World races thing.

Reflect had done the best she could to explain the situation to Atlas' friends, but did not realize that they didn't understand.

As Reflect spoke, Shine approached, wearing a look of concern. Without saying a word, the two communicated silently. Ormon quickly discerned that Reflect and the stout older man were using telepathy. Finally, she turned back to the boys and formally introduced them.

"Shine, this is Pepper and Ormon," she said. "They are friends of Atlas Mapp. They have come to help him."

"Hey, how'd you know our names?" Pepper asked.

Reflect smiled broadly. "Atlas Mapp told me of you. He said you were his best friends in The World Above and that he missed you very much."

"So, he's okay?" Ormon asked.

"For now," Reflect replied. "He is on a dangerous mission. There is a chance that he may not return. But he is our only chance to survive."

Ormon and Pepper swallowed hard in unison.

"He is very special, Ormon and Pepper. He is also very brave. I do not believe that any harm will befall him. I think he will fight Kibu and win."

"The evil spirit from The World Below?" Ormon said.

Reflect nodded. "There are many things that you would like to know," she said. "I am sure that this is all strange and unusual to you."

"You bet it is," Pepper said, gazing around.

"Well, to save time, I will tell the story directly to your mind," she said. "Just close your eyes and I will show you."

Pepper gave Ormon a look, only to see that Ormon's eyes were already closed. He wasn't sure it was the smartest thing to do, but he closed his eyes, too.

Suddenly, he heard Reflect's voice – only he couldn't actually hear it.

There was no sound coming from her lips. To be sure, he stole a quick glimpse and saw that her mouth wasn't moving. Still, her words penetrated his mind clearly.

Quickly, Reflect related the story of Kibu and the kidnapping of her father. She told them of the vision she had gotten of the boy from The World Above who could help rescue her father so that he could protect the vulnerable Arch World races from the convergence of the Novi.

"What exactly is that?" Ormon asked, with his thoughts.

Reflect explained how the two suns in the sky would come together whenever evil threatened to become stronger than good in The Arch World. When the suns converged, all the beings who could not find shelter like The Black Pyramid, or in The World Below, would be purged by the pure cleansing light created by this gigantic sun. This would restore a healthy balance to their world.

The E'lum could withstand the light, she said, thus believed it was their obligation to ensure that those around them would have a safe place to stay to survive the convergence.

Ormon and Pepper now understood when Reflect told them that her father was the only one who had the power to seal The Black Pyramid so that no light could penetrate it.

"So, without him, everyone will die," Ormon said, realizing why Atlas had decided to help.

"Yes," Reflect solemnly replied.

By now, many other E'lum had crowded around and listened as Ormon told Reflect telepathically about the map they had found and how Neffer and Ahib had discovered that an evil spirit from The World Below had used it to lure Atlas to him.

As Pepper listened to Ormon relate their story, he was glad to have his brainy friend there with him, for he wasn't so sure things would have worked out as well had he come alone. While it was true that he saved Ormon from the Salt Monster, Pepper realized that Ormon was much better at communicating, even with beings as strange as the Mirror People.

A feeling of calm overcame Pepper. He felt safe with

the E'lum and knew that Atlas was in good hands. Still, there was a sense of worry. Atlas had embarked on a dangerous mission and would be facing a deadly spirit. Pepper wondered, if the peoples of The Arch World couldn't fight Kibu, what chance did Atlas stand?

Finally, when Ormon had told Reflect and the other E'lum all that he knew, Pepper voiced his concern.

"Bookworm, if this Kibu guy was powerful enough to kidnap these people's leader and send the picture of the map to Atlas' mom in her sleep, then get him to come down here, he can do anything," Pepper said. "I mean, what can we do to stop him? And why do they think that Atlas can help?"

Ormon saw Pepper's point. Usually, at times like this, when Ormon didn't know what to say, he wouldn't say anything, but there was something special about these people and this place. If they believed that Atlas could help, Ormon thought, well, maybe he could.

"Pepper, I think we just have to trust them," he said. "I mean, at first you didn't think he made it here, and then you couldn't see how he could have gotten across The Monkey Bar Bridge, but he did it."

"He even got through The Lazantine Forest without help from his mom, so I think that says a lot about him. He's braver than we thought."

Pepper knew Ormon was right. For the E'lum, Atlas was a savior, and Pepper didn't have the right to take their hope away. But, he figured Atlas might have a better chance to survive if he had a few allies.

"Bookworm, we've got to get to The World Below," Pepper said. "I think Atlas needs us."

"Can you tell us how to get there?" Ormon asked.

"I can take you," Reflect said, drawing a disapproving

look from Shine.

The boys watched as the pair think-talked, almost as if they were arguing. For some reason, they couldn't hear this conversation. Ormon figured that they could control their telepathic messages so that they could not be overheard.

Reflect's eyebrows arched defiantly, her posture strong and sure. Finally, Shine slumped, realizing that he could not change her mind.

Reflect then spoke aloud so that everyone could hear. "Shine, if Atlas Mapp would go on a mission to save my father, I will go on a mission to save his," she declared. "Is this not what my father would do? And would you not do the same?"

Shine didn't reply. It was no use fighting the heir to the E'lum throne.

Without Image here to challenge her, Shine could not stop her. The stout fellow bowed to Reflect, who patted him tenderly on the head. She had never spoken to Shine in such a manner, and for that she was sorry, but she was sure he would someday understand.

Then Reflect walked over to the Sphere of Norova, climbed inside and was consumed with an energizing light. E'lum citizens stood in awe of their future leader, who stepped out with a bright aura surrounding her and produced a Skyrider with a wave of her hand.

"Cool!" Pepper and Ormon said together.

"We must go," Reflect said, motioning for the boys to climb aboard. Shine approached as the craft lifted up.

"Reflect, Image will not be happy," he said.

Reflect looked at Shine with conviction in her eyes.

"Shine, *I* will not be happy to see the people of The Arch World die if I do nothing to help them," she said.

With that, Reflect, Pepper and Ormon whizzed away.

FOURTEEN
Polema

A small jet airplane sliced through the nighttime sky. Written on the side in smart letters were the words, *Mapp Excavations.*

Inside, reclined on a cushy leather seat, Neffer slept fitfully. Open on a tray before him were books and letters that he had taken from Field Mapp's house, determined to find the source of the curse that held captive both a father and his young son.

Here, high in the sky, however, sleep finally overtook him.

Neffer didn't awaken when the plane shook violently from the turbulent skies, nor was he roused by booms of thunder or the crack of lightning that briefly illuminated the cabin.

So deeply unconscious was Neffer, in fact, that the old man did not even feel the gentle throbbing of the amulet hanging around his neck. It had begun to glow, once again alerting him that there was danger close to someone he loved somewhere in the universe.

At the same time, Atlas and the small E'lum army made their way through the tunnel deep inside Fossil Mountain. Their Skyriders illuminated the way as they glided towards the deserted city of Polema.

Despite the fact that no evil dwelled inside Fossil

Mountain, thanks to the mostly-watchful eyes of The Five Kings, Image thought it best that they proceed slowly, giving the E'lum more time to prepare for the perilous rescue mission before them.

Atlas studied their grim, noble faces and wondered what they were thinking. Were they afraid? Did they worry about death? Was it even possible to defeat Kibu in his own domain of The World Below?

Remembering that the E'lum could read minds, Atlas tried hard not to think of such terrible possibilities, but he couldn't stop his imagination from rambling. For Atlas, the strangest realization was that he was worried more for the E'lum than he was for himself.

In fact, Atlas was no longer afraid.

Other than his ordeal with the Salt Monster, his sojourn to this world had actually been quite pleasant. He'd seen many things with his own eyes that the average boy could never conjure, or only in the most fantastic of dreams. Luck, and it seemed, fate, had accompanied him each step of the way, leading Atlas to believe this was the way things were meant to be.

For a long while, he was lost in thought aboard the Skyrider, watching the jagged rock below as they passed over. Suddenly, he felt that this is what his father might be seeing at this moment, trapped in a mine with precious time running out.

Before Atlas could wonder more of his father's plight, the amulet around his neck began to glow, dimly at first, then brighter as the party moved through the belly of Fossil Mountain. Atlas closed his hand around the amulet to conceal its glare, and looked ahead in the distance, seeing a sliver of light as they advanced toward the end of the tunnel.

He was too late. Freddy had noticed his necklace.

"What's that you got there, Mr. Mapp?" he asked.

Freddy had been so quiet since they entered the tunnel that Atlas had almost forgotten that he was there.

"It's a magical amulet that protects me," Atlas said.

The amulet now glowed so intensely that Freddy saw the bones in Atlas' closed fist and the red blood coursing through the boy's hand.

Freddy looked alarmed.

"Well, you can't wear that thing in The World Below," he said. "That's like a flashing light telling Kibu we're here."

Atlas' face went pale. He clutched his amulet tighter. Even though he couldn't remember a time when it had actually protected him, he was comforted by the fact that Neffer and Ahib assured him that it would. Over time, his Agle amulet had become his security blanket. He didn't ever remove it, not even to bathe. The necklace was a part of him.

"You don't understand, Freddy," he pleaded. "I can't take it off."

Freddy shook his head.

"You have to, Mr. Mapp," he said. 'It's an evil place down there. Evil can smell evil and it can smell good, too. Give it to me and I'll hide it in a safe place. Don't worry, I'll give it back to you when we get out."

Atlas was flooded with fear. His knuckles were white. But Freddy clearly knew much more about these things than he did. He had no choice but to believe that what Freddy said was true.

Reluctantly, Atlas pulled the leather strap over his head and handed the amulet to Freddy. "Well, if you think it's best," he said.

"Of course it is," Freddy said, slipping the necklace into the pocket of his grimy overalls. "Trust me."

Atlas rubbed his chest where the amulet had been. He had grown so used to wearing it that he hadn't realized that he caressed it by habit. Now, without it, he felt naked and vulnerable.

"You won't have no problem wearing it when you get to Haven," Freddy explained. "That place is as pure as you can get."

Atlas' eyes lit up slightly at Freddy's mention of Haven. "But you've never been there, have you?" he asked.

Freddy shook his head. "No, Mr. Mapp, but I've heard a whole lot about it. I wanted to go because they say it's so nice and all, but I kinda like it around these parts. All that's missing is regular people."

"Well, regular people are a pretty big deal, Freddy," Atlas said.

"People aren't everything," Freddy replied, looking off.

The remark startled Atlas, but he didn't know what to say.

All his life, people had been the only things that mattered. He couldn't imagine life without his mother and father, or friends like Ormon and Pepper. What would a school be like without teachers, or a neighborhood without neighbors?

Freddy must have been in The Arch World for a very long time to forget just how important people were. It saddened Atlas that Freddy had forgotten.

Just then, Image's Skyrider cleared the mouth of the tunnel and Atlas turned around to see that the faces of The Five Kings were also etched into the rock of Fossil Mountain on this side. Ahead, he saw spires of a city beneath a gloomy sky.

There was no movement on its streets, no signs of life. It was almost as if the entire town had packed up and moved away. Though Atlas had no way of knowing this, it was exactly what had happened.

"This was once a beautiful and vibrant place," Image said. "But that was before the evil ones arrived."

Atlas and Freddy silently stared at the ruins, straining to see through the heavy fog that hung over the city. As they rose higher, Atlas saw a dark mass in the center of Polema, but couldn't make out what it was.

"That," said Image, "is the portal to The World Below."

Atlas turned to Freddy and shivered. "And you made it back from there?" he said, incredulous.

Freddy shrugged. "Just lucky, I guess."

The fleet sped up, flying quickly over Polema, then descending. They were headed towards a dark place where light seemed to shy away for no apparent reason.

The portal's pull was magnetic, and Atlas heard an insistent hum as Image landed before the wall of blackness with a pulsating center. This was a place where many who passed through never returned.

Image told them that this location was once a burial ground for the wicked. No one knew why or how, but, one day, darkness descended upon the spot and the portal sprang forth. Demons and spirits came into the city at night and made prisoners of Polema's citizens. When Kibu took residence here, the remaining inhabitants fled.

"There were great battles throughout The Arch World," Image said, "but a truce was negotiated and it was decided that the vile ones could remain here as long as they made no attempt to expand their territory."

"So they made a world of their own?" Atlas asked.

"Yes," Image replied. "Even the evil ones need a place to call home."

Atlas stared at the portal and felt like he had been here

before.

It seemed to reach out to them, imploring them to step through. Image approached first and touched the surface with a tentative hand.

Black goo quickly enveloped it. "Stay behind me," he said, and stepped through into the void.

Ekim followed along with several E'lum warriors, before Atlas and Freddy walked through, disappearing into The World Below.

Back at Atlas' home in Seattle, panic was setting in. Neffer was long gone, headed for Althanar. Ahib stayed behind to provide comfort and search for clues. Jenny sat with Sarah, who could not tear herself away from the map.

For hours, they had watched the red and gray heartbeats move from The Lazantine Forest to the city of Polema.

And then, both heartbeats disappeared.

Sarah covered her mouth. Jenny turned away. Ahib studied the map closely, making out a dark little spot where the heartbeats had been.

"He goes below, Mrs. Mapp," Ahib said, afraid of what that meant.

What Ahib, Sarah and Jenny had just witnessed did not go unnoticed by Neffer, who had finally awakened on the airplane in the middle of a ferocious thunderstorm.

He blinked several times to be sure his amulet was actually aglow, then unfurled a small map – seeing no sign of Atlas' heartbeat or the gray one.

Near Fossil Mountain, however, Neffer could see the bright red blips of Pepper and Ormon heading in the direction of Polema. He was angry with himself for falling asleep when there was so much work to do. But he also realized there was little he could accomplish while trapped on an airplane miles from anywhere.

Neffer clasped his amulet to his chest and said a prayer. "May God be with you, young Mapp."

He then busied himself with finding out more of the curse that was the source of all the bad happenings of the past several days.

Reflect talked with her two new friends as she guided her small Skyrider over The Lazantine Forest. Pepper was enthralled with the two suns in the sky, while Ormon was fascinated by the ground; watching still more caravans headed the other way toward The Black Pyramid.

"So, let me get this straight, Reflect," he said, "the convergence of the Novi cleanses The Arch World of all the evil things on the surface, and it can even kill *good* people if they don't take shelter?"

Reflect nodded.

"I don't understand that," Ormon said. "I mean, the good people haven't done anything wrong."

"I do not know why things are the way they are, friends of Atlas Mapp, but my father tells me that evil grows faster than good," she said.

"Makes sense to me," Pepper piped in. "You saw how fast The World Below grew on Mrs. Mapp's map, Bookworm. It took, like, seconds."

"Yeah, I guess you're right," Ormon said, thinking back to the frightening incident in Sarah's cottage, and suddenly remembering that they hadn't checked their own map in quite a while.

"Pepper, let me see that map."

Pepper handed the map to Ormon and could

immediately tell something was wrong from the way Ormon looked at it. Pepper scooted over for a glimpse and soon wore the same worried expression as Ormon.

"He's… he's gone!" Pepper said.

The boys went silent, each pondering Atlas' fate.

"He is not gone," Reflect said. "He is in The World Below now. I think that is why his heartbeat no longer shows up on your map. In the light of The Arch World, he was visible to you, but down there, no light can penetrate. Kibu uses the darkness as an ally. I believe he also uses it to keep my father prisoner."

"So, you've never been to The World Below, either?" Ormon asked. Reflect shook her head.

"Then how do you know how to get there?"

"It is simple, Ormon. I follow the Skyriders that went before me. They leave an energy trail that I can see."

Ormon and Pepper didn't see a trail of any sort. What they did see, however, chilled their blood. A short distance away was the imposing figure of Fossil Mountain. It was shrouded in a gloomy fog, and they were heading straight for it.

A cough echoed in the darkness as a single match flared. Field rose to his feet, unhurt, despite the violent secondary collapse. He quickly lit a torch and searched furiously for signs of life inside the considerably smaller mine. More rocks littered the mine floor and a thick, choking dust rained down onto his torch.

"Mahmoud! Habbibi! Denai! Are you all right?" Field cried out.

He heard nothing but the reverberation of his own voice, and then a hoarse cough came from the other side of the mine. "I am fine," Mahmoud said in a feeble voice.

Field moved as fast as he could over boulders and splintered wood to reach Mahmoud's side. Fallen rocks had trapped Mahmoud against the very wall where he had sought refuge.

"I'll have you free in a minute, Mahmoud," Field said, straining mightily to remove the debris that had nearly buried Mahmoud alive.

Field lifted stone after stone until he freed Mahmoud's arms and hands, then helped Mahmoud escape his makeshift tomb. Mahmoud stepped clear and they shared a teary hug, both thankful to be alive.

"What of the others?" Mahmoud said, cleaning his dusty spectacles and peering into the darkness.

"I am still here," they heard Denai say.

Somehow, despite tons of rock raining down all around his trapped and injured body, Denai had survived.

Field and Mahmoud clambered down to the floor of the mine and cleared away the coal and soot blanketing Denai's face. Despite his predicament and his condition, Denai found the strength to smile.

"What is it that they say, Professor? I have the lives of nine cats."

"Actually, you'd be a cat that has nine lives," Field said, opening a canteen and giving Denai a sip of water.

"Well, I prefer my way even better," Denai said. "That would mean I have eighty-one lives."

Suddenly, Denai's tone turned serious. "I suppose that those working above have fled the mine, Professor. I would think they would deem it too dangerous to continue searching."

Field averted his face as he spoke, not wanting Denai to see that he, too, was losing hope.

"They'll keep looking, Denai. I believe that and you have to believe it. We've never left a single man behind. And we never will."

There was silence as Field's words echoed in the air.

Mahmoud looked around, waiting for Habbibi's dissenting voice, but it never came.

Mahmoud moved slowly over the rocks and then he saw them – Habbibi's large shoes protruding from beneath several large boulders. Field followed Mahmoud's gaze to Habbibi's body, and could tell immediately that there was nothing they could do.

"Maybe we will join him soon," Mahmoud said in a resigned voice as he kneeled to pray for the angry fallen giant.

"Mahmoud, have faith," Field said, joining Mahmoud in prayer.

While Field quietly said kind and heartfelt words for Habbibi, a man who had tried to take his life only moments earlier, a series of strange thoughts came to him.

First, he remembered Denai asking how such a catastrophe had befallen them. The question resonated in Field's mind as he recounted how careful he and his engineers had been to make sure that the mine was secure.

He thought of the timing of the accident, and of how the mine chose to collapse at precisely the moment he decided to call Atlas with birthday wishes. All was fine before then, but Field suddenly found himself scrambling to escape a hail of rocks.

There was also Habbibi's admission that he had come on the expedition with the sole purpose of avenging his uncle's death.

Something deep inside told Field that all of these events were more than mere coincidence, although he couldn't find a connection. His thoughts made no sense, but he could not help but wonder if it had all been something more than just a cruel twist of fate.

Were there others like Habbibi who chose to work with him while concealing murderous intentions? Was this part of some sinister plan?

The most disturbing thought came with an image of Neffer, warning Field of some calamity just like this. Field recalled Neffer imploring him to be careful with a very serious look in his eyes.

Field felt confused and delirious. His mind was spinning, swirling with the thoughts of a madman. There was no reason or logic to them.

Field vigorously shook his head, knowing that if his confusion shone through, it would be impossible to keep up Mahmoud and Denai's morale.

A gurgling sound snapped Field back to the present. He could not see where it was coming from, but Mahmoud's cries made it clear there was danger.

"Professor Mapp, the water rises!"

Only then did Field realize that he was ankle-deep in water from an underground stream. He quickly deduced that the secondary collapse had created a larger fissure in the rock, allowing more water to flow into the mine.

Field's attention turned to Denai, who was still prone, but the heavy beam atop his body had shifted, making it possible to free him if they pulled at precisely the proper angle.

"Help me move Denai," Field said to Mahmoud. "I think we can get him out."

The two men steadied themselves and gently tugged at Denai's shoulders, careful to keep his face above the rising water. Denai grimaced in pain, but did not cry out as Field and

Mahmoud struggled to pull him to safety.

"I'm sorry, Denai," Field whispered. "Just remember that you are the cat with eighty-one lives. Okay?"

Denai nodded through clenched teeth, and, with one more tug, Field and Mahmoud pulled him from beneath the rubble and dragged him to higher ground.

Field, breathing heavily from all the exertion and the dwindling supply of fresh air, cradled Denai's head in his lap. Mahmoud leaned back against a rock wall and collapsed.

Denai, who had briefly blacked out from the intense pain, slowly regained consciousness and looked hopefully at Mahmoud's weary face. "Are we still alive?" he whispered.

Mahmoud, still fighting to catch his breath, swallowed hard. "Yes, boy," he said. "Barely, but still alive."

Sarah, Ahib and Jenny had been closely monitoring the map for any new developments. Three heartbeats ticked in Haven, and they felt agony at not knowing who was alive or dead. Worse, however, was not knowing what was happening to Atlas in the horrible World Below.

Jenny noticed the worry lines on her sister's forehead. Sarah had been in a constant state of agitation for days and had slept very little. Jenny knew that the strain was taking a dangerous toll.

Although Jenny was Sarah's little sister, she realized it was time to do something. She had to get Sarah away from this cursed map and convince her that nothing could be gained by continuing to watch it.

For all Jenny knew, everything they'd learned about the map was wrong. Sure, even she had seen The World Below materialize on the canvas right before her eyes, but, as Neffer explained, there were many things in this world that they could not possibly understand.

One thing Jenny understood with absolute certainty, however, was that Sarah was putting her health in serious peril by allowing her hopes to rise and fall over little blips on a map.

Suddenly, Jenny knew just what to do.

Without a word of warning, Jenny marched off to a bedroom and returned with a clean, white sheet. She gave Sarah a stubborn gaze, unfolded the sheet and prepared to cover the giant canvas with it.

Sarah was staring so intently at the two red blips near Fossil Mountain that she hadn't noticed Jenny standing there.

"Jen, what are you doing?" she cried in alarm.

"I'm doing what I should have been doing all along," Jenny said. "I'm taking care of you. You have to get some rest."

"I have to watch the map," Sarah pleaded.

"No, you don't," Jenny retorted. "Right now, Sarah, you don't know what's best for you. So, I'm going to do what's best for both of us."

Ahib, who had watched the scene from the dining room, came over and placed his hand on Sarah's shoulder.

"Your sister is right, Mrs. Mapp," he said softly. "You will drive yourself crazy sitting here staring at The Arch World. Atlas has the protection of Agle, the all-seeing Eagle. I am sure that no matter how much danger he faces no harm will come to him."

Sarah wanted to protest, but was too weak. Didn't Ahib and Jenny understand that it was *her* little boy all alone in The World Below, and *her* husband trapped – and maybe dead – in a mine in Althanar? Did they really comprehend what she was going through?

But somehow, Sarah knew that they understood. And she knew it was useless to fight. "Okay," she said, her voice trailing off. "Okay."

"Ahib and I will check on the hour," Jenny said. "If anything changes, we'll let you know. Okay, Sis?"

"It is really for the best, Mrs. Mapp," Ahib chimed in.

Sarah nodded and turned away as Jenny flipped the sheet over the canvas. What neither of them noticed was that the gray blip had returned – and was on a collision course with the two red blips speeding toward Fossil Mountain.

Ormon studied the threatening thunderclouds over the mountain while Pepper sat and watched Reflect's metallic hair blow in the breeze. She was a pretty girl, Pepper thought, even if she did look like a mirror. He wanted to tell her so, but had not been able to get up the nerve.

Watching Reflect, Pepper fantasized about what it would be like to show her off at school. He was already one of the most popular boys around, but having a girlfriend like Reflect would catapult him straight to the top.

Pepper never had trouble getting girls to like him. He had all the necessary features; he was taller than most of the other boys, slim and rugged-looking, and he had hair to die for. Usually, he didn't have to do anything to attract girls. Most times, he just showed up and watched the other contenders fall away.

He had only known Reflect for a little while, but was drawn to her. She was braver than any girl he knew back home. She could do really cool things, like fly a Skyrider, speak telepathically, and she was smart like Ormon.

But Pepper was irked by the fact that she didn't seem interested in him. This was quite a new experience. What needled him even more was the way Reflect talked incessantly about Atlas.

Pepper cringed with jealousy. From the moment he and Ormon met Reflect, it was *Atlas Mapp this, Atlas Mapp that, Atlas Mapp everything.*

He recalled Reflect saying how special Atlas was. She called him "The One." Pepper's personal favorite was when Reflect touched Ormon's chest and said, "So, you, too, are much like Atlas Mapp."

So, the guy has a heart, he thought. *Big deal. Everybody's got a heart.*

The way Pepper saw it, being older than Atlas meant that he, in fact, had a heart before Atlas did.

Pepper smiled, slyly, of course, as he formulated his plan. When all of this was over – provided they didn't get killed – he would invite Reflect back home and prove how much cooler he was than Atlas.

Atlas won't stand a chance, he reasoned, very satisfied with himself.

At that moment, Reflect turned to Pepper with a slight frown that made him nervous. She didn't speak, but Pepper heard her loud and clear.

"You are a nice boy, Pepper. I like you very much, both you and Ormon, but you will *never* be Atlas Mapp."

She smiled and resumed guiding the Skyrider toward the mountain. In an instant, Pepper's face became a mask of beet-red embarrassment. He was double-embarrassed, triple even, when he realized that she had heard every one of his devious thoughts.

His entire body flushed with shame as he struggled to hold in his thoughts. Pepper knew that whatever crossed his mind would only make him look cunning, or stupid. Pepper quickly glanced at Ormon and felt mildly better that he was unaware of what had just happened.

Reflect turned to him and smiled broadly, saying telepathically, "Don't worry, it is *our* secret."

Pepper buried his head in his hands.

Thanks to a strange sighting by Ormon, however, Pepper's embarrassment didn't last long. For what Ormon saw down on the mountain was a shock to everyone.

"Is that a *man*?" he asked, pressing his spectacles up tightly against the bridge of his nose so that he could focus more clearly.

Pepper saw the figure, too. Indeed, it was a man scrambling down a path leading to The Lazantine Forest.

But it was Reflect's reaction upon seeing the stranger that made Ormon and Pepper exchange glances for the umpteenth time.

"Freddy Bear???" she shrieked.

Reflect guided her Skyrider toward the man at a dizzying speed, seeming to forget that Ormon and Pepper were on board.

Reflect's shiny face was a mask of determination. Whoever the strange man was, Pepper thought, he'd better have a good explanation for the E'lum princess.

FIFTEEN
Freddy's Dead

Freddy Bearer's face went ashen when he saw Reflect's Skyrider bearing down upon him. He was even more shocked at seeing the two human boys on board with her. With nowhere to hide, Freddy simply stopped and waited for the trio to reach him.

Reflect brought the craft to a stop just above Freddy's head, ending a harrowing descent that left the petrified Pepper and Ormon wondering why they hadn't been tossed off onto the rocks of Fossil Mountain.

As he gathered his wits, Ormon figured that the fact that they were still alive had something to do with a gravity field around the craft when it was in flight, though Reflect had told him nothing of the sort.

Reflect fixed her angry stare on Freddy Bearer, ready to demand an explanation as to why he was not with the others. For a moment, Reflect feared asking, her mind conjuring all sorts of horrible events. Could there have been an ambush with Freddy the sole survivor? Had Image, overwhelmed, sent Freddy back to E'lum Village to gather reinforcements? A thousand possibilities ran through Reflect's mind.

"Freddy, what are you doing here?" she said, finally. "Where are the others?"

Freddy averted his eyes, obviously trying to think of an answer. "Uh, hey, Reflect," he mumbled, sidestepping her question.

"Where are you going?" Reflect demanded. "The World Below is the other way."

Freddy fidgeted.

Pepper and Ormon eyed the strange man suspiciously. They could tell that he was hiding something. But what? Who was he? Where did he come from, and why was Reflect so surprised to see him, they wondered?

Freddy grew increasingly nervous, stuffing his hands into his pockets and shifting his weight from one foot to the other.

Finally, he spoke. "Ah... well, Reflect," he said in a halting voice, "I guess I might as well just tell you the truth. Uh–"

Reflect's eyes narrowed. "Yes?" she said, placing her hands on her hips like a mother scolding a child.

Freddy opened his mouth to speak, but before he could, Pepper spotted something familiar. Very familiar, in fact.

"Hey mister, what's that around your neck?" Pepper asked, his tone full of accusation. "That looks like Atlas' necklace."

Freddy turned and tried to hide the necklace, but it was too late. Ormon had seen it, too.

"Freddy Bear, is it true that you wear the necklace of Atlas Mapp?" Reflect asked, confusion in her eyes.

Pepper aimed his Super Soaker. "You'd better start talking, Mister! This ain't no ordinary water in this here cannon!" Ormon raised his soaker, too, adding, "Yeah!"

The guilty look on Freddy's face told Reflect that he was not who she thought he was. She didn't know exactly what he had done, but something made her think of her father's decision to travel to the Valley of Fear alone, telling her he could not reveal the reason for his journey.

She remembered the mysterious message Vision had received, telling him that someone was in danger and desperately needed his help.

Ever since Reflect's mother's light had ceased to be, her father had doted on her, had shared everything with her, including his hopes for her to someday become a leader in The Arch World.

But this one time – the last time she saw him before he became Kibu's prisoner – Vision kept the purpose of his journey secret. She recalled the look in her father's eyes when he left for the Valley of Fear – a look that said he didn't know if he would see her or E'lum Village again.

Now, a queasy feeling in the pit of her stomach told Reflect that Freddy Bear, her friend, had led Vision into Kibu's clutches.

"You have betrayed us, Freddy Bear," she said, her eyes like fire. "It was you, wasn't it?"

"Reflect, you don't understand," Freddy stammered.

"Image said my father could only have been lured away from E'lum Village by someone he trusted," she said, raising her palm in Freddy's direction, a ball of blazing light swirling at its center.

Freddy's eyes widened. He had seen the power of the E'lum in combat and knew that even though Reflect was small in size, she could still blow him to smithereens.

Somehow, what hurt Freddy most was the look on Reflect's face. He had never seen her angry.

To Freddy, Reflect had always been an even-tempered and happy child, eager to learn ever more from him of The World Above.

But, with the two strange boys looking on, aiming strange, brightly-colored weapons at him, Freddy suddenly felt that he deserved whatever punishment Reflect decided.

Freddy had done the E'lum much harm, and he decided then that he would not die without telling Reflect the entire story.

"Reflect, I owed Kibu from a long, long time ago," Freddy began, his voice quivering. "It was a deal I wish I could take back, but I can't."

"What have you done with our friend?" interrupted Pepper.

"He went into The World below with Image and the others," Freddy said, lowering his head. "I swear."

"How'd you get his necklace, then?" Ormon asked, still wary of the stranger, despite his look of remorse.

"I just asked him for it. I told him Kibu would know we were coming if he wore it down there."

Freddy paused and looked at the necklace. It was no longer aglow as it had been when they neared the city of Polema. "That was the deal. Kibu wanted me to get the necklace off the kid and that's what I did."

Ormon and Pepper looked at each other, then to Reflect, who was contemplating shooting a powerful bolt of light into Freddy's chest.

Freddy's betrayal was the worst kind – a betrayal of trust.

Reflect had known him all of her life and had never seen anything in Freddy's character to prepare her for a moment like this.

He was special to Reflect and her people, this stranger from a world that the E'lum had not realized existed until he fell from the sky a long, long time ago.

Reflect was not alive when Freddy first arrived, but she knew his story well. According to Freddy, he had been sitting on a rock feeling sorry for himself, without a friend in the world, when the ground suddenly opened up beneath his very feet. Freddy claimed that a huge door appeared and he was sucked inside.

Freddy said he wandered The Arch World for days, somehow avoiding all of the perils and hidden dangers in The Lazantine Forest, The Valley of Fear, Polema and even The World Below. Eventually, he was found by some E'lum scouts who brought him to their village believing that Vision could help him find his way home.

But Freddy became comfortable in The Arch World and among the E'lum. He lived in their village for a while, and then set off to explore on his own. Vision and Image taught him many things to help him survive in The Arch World, and Freddy had learned well.

He would disappear for long periods of time, then return to visit the E'lum and regale them with fantastic stories of his travels. Reflect was much younger when she first saw this strange creature, who was unlike any other she had ever met, and she took a liking to him instantly.

For his part, Vision trusted Freddy enough to allow him to spend much time alone with his only child, and Freddy had become like a second father. When her mother's light went out, Freddy even said some kind words at the memorial.

He had been, as Reflect saw him, a good friend.

But now, as she pondering ending his life, an unsettling thought came to her – she had never killed anyone. Though Image had explained to her that killing was necessary in battle, Reflect was not in a battle at this moment, at least not with an enemy.

Instead, Reflect was battling herself.

She was fighting her sense of right and wrong. If she

were to blast Freddy Bear with light from the Sphere of Norova, she wondered what her father would think – if he were ever found.

Reflect's hand trembled. She knew that she would never be able to bring Freddy back. The ball of light in her hand flared, ready to fire upon her command. Pepper and Ormon watched in quiet fascination, having never before seen such a sight.

Then, slowly, Reflect lowered her hand and the light flickered out. A calm replaced her anger.

"I could take your life right now, Freddy Bear, but I will not," she said evenly. "Never again will you be welcome in E'lum Village, or share the kindness of my people. You are dead to us. I am sure my father will look favorably upon this decision."

The crestfallen Freddy said nothing.

"Goodbye, forever, Freddy Bear."

Silently, the Skyrider whisked off into the sky. Ormon and Pepper stared at the lone figure, who fell to his knees in anguish. Soon, he was indistinguishable from the rocks below.

"Who was that guy?" they asked in unison.

Reflect stared ahead. "He is no one," she said. "No one at all."

Reflect was nearly over the top of Fossil Mountain when she realized that she had lost her bearings. The emotional encounter with Freddy Bearer left her confused and she did not realize she was no longer following the light trail left by Image and the others. In a sense, she was flying blind.

She looked behind her and picked up the faint outline of the trail leading to the base of the mountain. In a flash, the Skyrider reversed its course and descended, with Ormon and Pepper holding on for dear life.

As they reduced speed, the boys saw the heads of The Five Kings carved into the rock.

"Why are we stopping here?" Pepper asked, seeing nothing but the solid rock of the mountain and the images of the kings.

"This is where the trail ends," said Reflect, looking for a sign as to where Image and the others had gone.

"There's nothing here," Ormon said.

Reflect shook her head.

"Image is a good navigator. He would not have come this way if there were nothing to be found."

She landed and they disembarked to take a closer look. As they searched, none of them noticed the watchful eyes of The Five Kings upon them. Ormon nearly jumped out of his skin when the first king spoke in a booming voice.

"Why do you seek to avoid the five perils of Polema?"

"Aaaaaaahhhhhhhh!!!!!" screamed Pepper and Ormon as the humungous kings stared with stony eyes. Reflect, however, was not afraid.

"We do not wish to avoid anything, kings of Fossil Mountain. We are looking for our friends and family who came this way," she said. "Their light trails end here. Do you know of them?"

The first king turned to the others.

"They say they do not wish to avoid the five perils of Polema. All who request passage seek to avoid the perils. How are we to believe them?"

Ormon stepped forward. "Excuse me, sir, but we don't know about any perils. We're trying to find our friend, and we'd really appreciate it if you can show us the way."

The second king raised his brows.

"So, you do not come seeking safe passage to Polema?"

Ormon shook his head. "No sir. We're not from around here."

"Shall we look into their hearts?" asked the third king.

Reflect grew impatient. "I am sorry, dear kings, but speaking in the most respectful way that I know how, I must tell you that we do not have time for this," she said. "We are on a mission of the utmost urgency and we will gladly face any perils before us if you can tell us how to get to The World Below."

"We will?" Pepper whispered to Ormon, with terror in his eyes.

The Five Kings were confused. Their heads swiveled noisily as they discussed the unusual request among themselves. Even the sleepy fifth king was wide-eyed now. For as long as they had protected the shortcut to Polema, there had never been a visitor who had not sought safe passage.

The kings regarded the unselfish visitors with wonder. Finally, it was the words of the fifth king that swayed the opinions of the others.

"There is no need to look into the hearts of those who seek no favor from us," he said, yawning softly. "Obviously, they are pure of heart. There is nothing more to question."

The others nodded in agreement.

"The shortcut is yours to take," said the first king. "Go, with our blessings, and pass safely through to Polema."

Fossil Mountain shuddered and shook as the rock wall slowly slid away, revealing a tunnel.

"Wow!" Pepper and Ormon exclaimed.

Once the wall fully opened, Reflect clearly saw the yellow vapor trail of light left by the E'lum warriors who had passed through earlier.

"It is this way," she said, motioning for Pepper and Ormon to climb back onto the luminescent light.

With the boys on board, Reflect guided the Skyrider upward to face The Five Kings and bowed delicately, saying, "Thank you, Kings."

"You are most welcome," they replied, their stony voices echoing in the children's ears as Reflect and her human friends zipped out of sight into the tunnel headed for the city of Polema.

SIXTEEN
Kibu's Castle

Sharibu was upset as he ambled along behind Boroom in the dark recesses of Kibu's castle. Ever since being chastised by Kibu, Sharibu had been bothered, and nothing Boroom did or said could lift his spirits.

The source of Sharibu's angst was that he desired to be among Kibu's most trusted servants. More than anything, Sharibu wanted to become his own gargoyle, breaking away from his big brother's shadow, to be powerful, feared and loathed – just like Boroom.

Sharibu also could not stand being left out of the loop. This was another thing that contributed to his sour mood.

"Obviously, Master Kibu does not trust us," Sharibu was saying, "Why did he not tell us of this 'backup plan' before?"

Boroom pressed a sharp fingertip to his lips.

"Stupid brother, Kibu does as he wishes," Boroom said. "It is not up to us to question him. Or do you so quickly forget?"

Sharibu's hand went to his still-tender chest. He suddenly remembered the intense pain he felt from Kibu's powerful blast.

"I was just thinking that with all the trouble we went through to get Ekim to bring them here, that Master Kibu could have told us," Sharibu said. "Have we not proved our devotion enough?"

Boroom shook his head. He knew there were many things Sharibu would never understand, and this is why he did all he could to protect him. Boroom made it his business to stay by his brother's side. He worried constantly that Sharibu would someday find himself in some kind of trouble that he could not escape.

"He has told us all that we need to know," Boroom said firmly. "We must prepare to kill the E'lum warriors."

"Yes, yes," Sharibu said. "That should be fun."

Boroom heard Sharibu's slimy snicker. Killing always made his little brother happy, precisely the reason he was not to be trusted. Boroom was sure that had he not been in The Lazantine Forest on the night the E'lum found Atlas Mapp, Sharibu would have torn the strange boy to shreds.

Boroom could not have saved Sharibu from Kibu's wrath had that happened. For better or worse, Boroom would be his brother's keeper for as long as they lived.

Simply put, Sharibu could not survive in The World Below without him. "Be patient, Sharibu, we will be rewarded," Boroom said. "When Kibu has the boy he has so long desired, we will get all that we deserve."

At that moment, Atlas Mapp was not far away. The progress of the approaching E'lum army was steady. Soon, war would come to The World Below.

While Image and the E'lum warriors advanced in a defensive formation, with fighters at the front and rear, Ekim waddled alongside Atlas on a familiar path riddled with ugly, snake-like vines.

Every once in a while, an E'lum fighter would fire a blast of light from a palm or staff, forcing the vines to retreat. But, so far, they had faced no other threat.

"I am told you have a map used to find The Arch World," Ekim said to Atlas. "Is this true?"

"My mom painted it," Atlas said, his heart pounding now that he was in the bowels of The World Below.

"Interesting," Ekim replied. "A map showing the way into The Arch World must also show the way out?"

"I guess. I mean, that makes sense, but I really haven't had to use it much since I've been here. I figure after we rescue Vision, it'll take me to Haven."

Ekim's eyes widened. He stared at Atlas, as if the map could be of great use to him. Atlas didn't notice Ekim's hungry gaze, so focused was he on watching for danger from the vines in The Emaciated Forest.

But Ekim was insistent. "May I see this ma-"

"Quiet!" Image commanded. "There is something here."

Image and the others crouched, poised for an attack. Image, sensing imminent danger, silently pulled out a light sword. Although he had never been to The World Below, his intuition was keen. Image knew that whenever things grew too quiet, this was precisely the time the enemy would strike.

It happened in a blur – spindly vines shooting out like Octopus tentacles from every direction, powerfully taking hold of E'lum warriors, wrapping themselves around their metallic bodies like pythons.

Before Atlas could run, a thick, slimy vine circled his waist and yanked him towards the twisted and diseased trees.

"AAAAhhhhhhh!" he screamed. "Image! Help!"

Ekim pulled a sharp dagger from his loincloth and leaped upon the vine, hacking away, but it refused to let Atlas go.

Image spun and shot a bolt of light from his hand into

the vine. It instantly loosened its grip, nearly allowing Atlas to wriggle free. Image finished off the vine with a quick and sure swipe from his light sword, and caught Atlas before he fell to the ground.

"Stay close to me!" Image commanded, as he fought to save the lives of other imperiled E'lum warriors.

The scene was frantic. All around, Atlas saw E'lum fighters in the midst of battle with an enemy that seemed to have a million arms. No sooner did a warrior slice through one vine than another would take its place.

Explosions of light illuminated the melee.

There were dull E'lum carcasses with the light sucked out of them. The vines were on a feeding frenzy, both protecting the path to Kibu's castle and gorging at the same time.

Atlas watched the brave E'lum warriors and tried to figure out how he could assist them. Suddenly, he remembered the Super Soaker dangling from his backpack. He reached for it, but just as quickly figured that even the acid rain spray would not help much here.

All over the path, vines lay twisted, broken and smoldering. Several lifeless E'lum warriors lay splayed there, also. Atlas felt that the tide was turning. The vines were winning.

It was then that he spied the source of the vine's strength, something that Image was too busy brawling to notice. Atlas saw that the vines were attached to thick trunks set further back in the forest.

If the E'lum attacked the trees themselves, Atlas thought, the vines would have to retreat.

"Image, shoot there!" Atlas shouted, dodging several vines trying to grab him. Image never turned to face Atlas, but instantly knew what the boy was talking about by reading his thoughts.

"Yes, we must attack the root of this heinous tree," Image said, relaying the message to the other E'lum.

From the palm of his hand, Image unleashed a great ball of light, engulfing the trees in white-hot flame. Instantly, the vines recoiled, shrinking back into the darkness. In seconds, all the vines were gone except for the jagged, disembodied pieces sliced off by the fighters.

The fierce confrontation ended as quickly as it started.

It was quiet now, except for the crackle of small fires and whimpering sounds from the forest, where the deadly vines nursed their wounds. They gave off an overwhelming, acrid smell, like that of burning flesh.

"Those vines did not attack us of their own accord, they were simply doing Kibu's bidding," Image said. "Our approach will not be a surprise. He is aware that we are here."

Atlas watched as Image tended to the dead and wounded.

Image bent over a dying E'lum warrior and whispered something that sounded like a prayer. He squeezed the warrior's hand and closed his eyes. The light of their bodies merged, and then the warrior's glow faded away.

Atlas recalled Reflect's story of when her mother's light ceased to be when she was just a child. For the Mirror People, he figured, this was death.

Atlas had seen many skeletons and decomposed bodies on excavations with his father, but he had never actually seen anyone die.

Seven E'lum warriors had fallen, and Image and those remaining solemnly placed their bodies together side by side. Image waved his light staff over them and said, "I commit these souls to Norova."

The bodies took on a bluish glow and disappeared. Image turned and could see questions in Atlas' eyes. "Are those men gone forever?" Atlas asked.

"For now," Image said. "We will see them again."

"But where did they go?"

Image pointed skyward. Atlas didn't know if that meant the souls had returned to The Arch World or E'lum Village; he had so many questions, but now did not seem the time to ask. He was also worried about Image, but didn't know what to say.

Image heard his thoughts.

"Do not worry. I am fine, Atlas Mapp," he said. "This is the way of war. I have seen much like it before."

"What do we do now that Kibu knows we're coming?" Atlas asked.

Gathering his fighters, Image told Atlas, "We will continue on. Kibu expects us – and we will not disappoint."

The party continued for a distance and stopped just short of a clearing. In the hazy moonlight, an ominous structure made of rock, mortar, and wood came into view. At the four corners of the building, turrets rose into the sky. Inside their windows, Atlas saw gargoyle sentries on the lookout for intruders.

He did not need Image or Freddy to tell him about this place. From the smell of danger in the air, Atlas knew that this was Kibu's castle.

In the shadows, Atlas saw the deformed shapes of gargoyles lurking near the entrance, and guard dogs resembling overgrown wolves straining against their heavy chains.

Crouched in the brush beside Image, Atlas wondered what was going through his mind. He couldn't see how they could possibly penetrate Kibu's defenses. There simply weren't enough warriors to fight off Kibu's guards. And, other than Toxic Soldiers, Atlas knew nothing about war.

But Toxic Soldiers was just a game. There were no real enemies. It was just three friends imagining what it would be like to be at war. No one got hurt, other than the time Pepper fell out of a tree he'd climbed to try to surprise Atlas and Ormon. Plus, at the end, they were all still friends.

The thought made Atlas look at his Super Soaker, and he momentarily considered leaving it there in the brush. What good could it possibly do here in The World Below? Deep inside, he knew there was no real acid rain spray. It was only pretend. He was smart enough to realize that it had only worked on the Salt Monster because, well, he was made of salt.

Looking at Kibu's castle, Atlas knew *this* was real. He'd watched E'lum warriors trained to fight very hard in actual battle lose their lives. And there was a possibility that Atlas would die, too.

Atlas' thoughts were interrupted when Ekim waddled up. "There's a back entrance to the dungeon, Image," the Byab whispered. "Some of my people who were kept prisoner here say Kibu has a windowless room there."

"That must be where he keeps Vision," Image replied.

"We should alter our plan, Image," said an E'lum warrior.

But Image wouldn't be deterred. He had to attack now or risk losing everything.

"There is no time for planning," he said firmly. "The convergence does not wait. Ekim, show the way."

Concealed by overgrown weeds and poison foliage, Ekim circled around the clearing to the rear of Kibu's castle. Atlas, with his heart pounding almost loud enough for him to hear it, stayed very close to Image and the E'lum warriors.

They were so careful to hide their movements that none of them noticed a pair of evil red eyes peering down from inside the castle.

Kibu, as shrewd as he was demonic, was allowing the E'lum to approach. He had instructed his guards to act as though nothing was amiss, and planned to capture the E'lum and Atlas, his prize, only after they had gained entry to his lair.

The shapeless form of Kibu grinned as he saw that his ploy was working. From the beginning, he had anticipated that with the convergence imminent, the E'lum would be forced to press forward with their attack, even at their own peril.

Like Kibu, deep inside the bowels of the fortress, Vision also knew that his people were near, but he was powerless to warn them. He felt the light of their presence and it lifted his spirits, though he was much too weak to communicate with them, much less fight alongside them.

"They come for me," he said, struggling to stand in his dark prison cell, before slumping back to the floor.

Outside, Image eyed the unguarded back door of the castle suspiciously. He had been in enough battles to know that entry to a place such as this always came with a price. Still, the enemy was nowhere to be seen and he knew they were running out of time.

"It's got to be a trap, Image," Atlas whispered. "Kibu is probably waiting for us to go inside and that's when he'll attack us."

"I am well aware of that, Atlas Mapp, but he leaves us little choice," Image replied. "Without Vision, The Black Pyramid cannot be sealed. This is a chance we must take."

Atlas reached down to caress his amulet, only then remembering that it was gone. He thought of Freddy Bearer's promise that he would return the medallion once Atlas emerged from The World Below.

Where was Freddy, he wondered? Only now did he notice that Freddy had vanished shortly after they entered The World Below. Now, Atlas wished that he had refused Freddy's request. He felt powerless and vulnerable without his necklace.

Image sensed the boy's dread and gently squeezed his hand. "Do not fear, Atlas Mapp," he said, "I will protect you with my life." Image nodded in the direction of the other E'lum warriors who stood ready for battle, and added, "We all will."

Atlas was very relieved at knowing that he was not alone. He thought of his mother back home, hoping that she wasn't worried, and of his father in Haven. He then thought of Ormon and Pepper, wondering if they would actually come for him, and silently forgiving them if they had not. He knew that such a journey was a lot to ask of anyone, even his best friends.

Then, mustering all of his courage, Atlas looked squarely into Image's eyes and said, "I guess we better go inside. Kibu's waiting."

SEVENTEEN
A millionpieces

As Atlas and the E'lum warriors prepared to enter the innermost reaches of Kibu's castle, they had no idea that Pepper, Ormon and Reflect were at the portal, simultaneously preparing to enter The World Below.

The three stood anxiously staring at the portal. It pulsated, burped and gurgled, turning various shades of gray and black. They were only sure that this was the way because the vapor trail from the E'lum warriors' Skyriders had ended here.

Ormon studied the portal before finally deciding to test it with a delicate touch. Reflect and Pepper watched as Ormon brushed the surface with a fingertip, then stuck in his entire hand. It was covered in black ooze when he pulled it out.

"It's like a Stargate with goo," Ormon concluded, watching the substance drip off his hand onto the ground.

Reflect stepped in front of the boys and said, "If you are afraid, then I will go in alone. There is not much time."

Before they could protest, Reflect disappeared into the portal. It swallowed her shiny body with a slurp.

Pepper hesitated, then flashed a nervous smile, saying, "Well, if a girl can do it, I guess I can, too."

Pepper followed Reflect inside, leaving Ormon alone. It took Ormon only one quick look around at the deserted city of Polema before he lumbered through the portal as fast as he could.

Unlike their descent into The Arch World, though, the boys did not find themselves spinning and falling weightlessly through space. Instead, they stood on thick, slimy steps that led down into an inky darkness.

In the sky was a wretched-looking, crescent-shaped moon that cast almost no light, but was just bright enough for them to see a path at the bottom, which wound through a forest thick with spindly trees and vines.

"Now, we're *really* not in Kansas anymore," Pepper whispered.

"I'll say," replied Ormon, carefully following Pepper and Reflect down the steps. "This place looks worse than it did on Atlas' mom's map."

Reflect was oddly silent as she walked, determined and with purpose, almost as if she'd been here before. What the boys didn't know was that she could sense that there had been a great battle not long ago.

"Several E'lum have died here," she said. "I can see the essence of their souls ahead in the forest. Image is not among them."

"Died?" blurted Pepper.

"What about Atlas?" said Ormon.

"If Image lives, so does Atlas Mapp," Reflect said. "Image would sacrifice his life before he allowed harm to come to your friend."

Reflect's words comforted Pepper, but did not make him any less afraid as they descended into the thick, hazy fog. The boys got goosebumps as they inched along the perilous winding path towards Kibu's castle.

Unlike The Lazantine Forest, there were sounds here, the creaking and swaying of infected tree limbs and spiny vines smoothly slithering along the ground. And like Image before her, Reflect sensed the imminent danger.

"Stay close to me," she said, pulling out a small light sword and readying her palm to fire at will.

Pepper and Ormon cocked their Super Soakers and slowly advanced behind Reflect, each actually hoping that there would be no trouble. Down here in The World Below, the enemy could be anything, could come from anywhere and at any moment.

"Something's burning," Ormon said, right before they came upon acrid, small fires still raging from the earlier battle.

Suddenly, there was a flash of light and a crash. Reflect rushed ahead while Pepper and Ormon frightfully stood their ground. Lying on the path was an injured E'lum warrior who had fallen from the trees. He was in great pain and moaning softly. Reflect knelt over him.

"Where are the others?" she asked, then listened as the warrior spoke to her without words. He was clearly trying to warn her.

"No, I cannot go home, courageous one," Reflect said aloud. "I must find my father. Where is he? Tell me!"

"In the dungeon," the warrior murmured. "They fight for him."

There was a flash as the warrior's entire body illuminated, turned blue, dimmed, then flickered out. The boys stood by silently as Reflect tenderly stroked the warrior's face, saying goodbye. Then, he disappeared.

When Reflect finally stood, her jaw was set and her eyes were clear. "I told you this would be dangerous, friends of Atlas Mapp," she said. "I will not blame you if you wish to turn back."

This time, Pepper didn't look to Ormon. He knew what to say. "We're going with you, Reflect," he said. "We came here on a mission to find Atlas and bring him home. We made a promise. And if Atlas doesn't make it home," he said, pausing, "well, I guess we won't either."

Deep inside Kibu's castle, Atlas, Image and the E'lum warriors navigated treacherous stairs and a series of musty corridors, with Ekim leading the way.

Ekim stopped at a pair of tunnels, one going right, and the other left. "It is as described," he said. "This way."

The group silently walked through the left tunnel, coming upon a large room, their footsteps echoing softly off the stone floor. It was dark inside and difficult to see, but suddenly, torchlight filled the room – and gargoyles pounced from every direction.

"If they resist, kill them!" commanded a large goyle brandishing a large wooden club with sharp steel spikes protruding from it.

Swiftly, the E'lum warriors formed a combat circle to protect Atlas and Ekim. Flashes of light filled the room as the warriors blasted at the surprisingly fast beasts advancing upon them.

The clash was fierce, and in the middle of it all, Image was a sight to behold. He wielded his light sword like a master, slicing the first goyle in half with one easy swing. Another was dispatched with the blast of light from his palm. The gargoyles attacked so quickly that the circle around Atlas and Ekim disintegrated, leaving the pair exposed and vulnerable.

Image fought with an eye on Atlas, who had picked up the sword of a fallen warrior and swung wildly to keep several goyles at bay.

Ekim, jabbing the ankles of his attackers with his baby-sized dagger, spied an open doorway and yanked Atlas toward it. "Come, Atlas Mapp! This way," he yelled.

Atlas didn't want to leave Image and the others, but he realized there wasn't much he could do to help and ran through the doorway behind Ekim.

The instant Atlas entered the room, his heart nearly stopped.

Ekim stood several feet away, smiling at Atlas and no longer looking for a place to escape. The expression on his face told Atlas that this had been Ekim's plan all along, to lure him here. For some reason, the room was vaguely familiar, but Atlas didn't immediately know why.

Before Atlas could speak, he heard a strange whooshing sound and darkness enveloped him. Atlas ran to the wall and grabbed a torch from its holder – now realizing that he *had* seen this place before. It wasn't a room. It was a cave with smooth, hard rock walls. In fact, it was *the* cave from his nightmare nearly a week earlier.

Atlas sneered at the little Byab.

"You lied to us, Ekim," he said, with anger and confusion in his voice. "You're working for Kibu, aren't you?"

"I didn't lie to you, Atlas Mapp," Ekim said. "I said that I could show you the way – and I have. You *are* here."

Atlas didn't see anyone else in the cave, but he sensed that he and Ekim were not alone. Then he heard a chilling, low voice, and saw red glowering eyes flickering in the darkness.

"Yes, *finally*, you are here, my son," said the voice. "Come to me!"

Atlas was too petrified to scream as the shapeless black form began to materialize into something almost solid.

"Get away from me," he whispered, slicing the air with his torch in hopes that the light would keep the demon away.

But Kibu only came closer.

"I have waited a long time for a son of my own," Kibu said. "One thousand and ten years of waiting for this moment."

Atlas breathed heavily, his fear threatening to paralyze him. Again, he swung his torch as Kibu crept closer, avoiding the torchlight.

"Get away from me!" he screamed. "I'm not your son. Dad! Daaaadddddd!!! Immmaaaaaggggeeeee!!!!!"

"Image cannot help you," Kibu replied. "Only *you* can help yourself. Agree to be my son."

"No way!" Atlas yelled. "Immmmaaaaggggeeee!!!"

At that moment, a burst of bright light filled the room. It was Image. Kibu instantly shrank back into the shadows.

"Don't fight a child, Kibu," Image said calmly. "Fight me!"

Image contorted his body into a large mirror, flashing pictures at Kibu that were so frightening and horrible Atlas could not bear to look.

A cold wind filled the room and shadows began to overwhelm the light on the walls emanating from Image's body.

"Do you think you can frighten me?" Kibu taunted.

Image's body trembled. He was expending a tremendous amount of energy sending out light from the Sphere of Norova to battle Kibu's corrosive dark power.

Atlas uncovered his eyes and saw that Image was wavering, trembling. "Image, what's wrong?" he cried.

Image tried another tactic, displaying images of love, peace, harmony, togetherness, but to no avail. He quivered and shook violently as he struggled to hold back the demonic Kibu.

"He...has...no...fears," Image said, straining mightily.

Before Atlas' terrified eyes, Image's body began to crack just like glass, or a mirror. Small pieces of the E'lum warrior fell to the floor. The light inside the room dimmed.

Image looked into Atlas' eyes and struggled to say something, but Atlas could not make out what it was.

Then Atlas heard Kibu's cold voice. "Let me end your misery," he said.

"Run, Image!" Atlas screamed. "Run!"

A red ball of flame erupted from nowhere into Image's body. Atlas screamed again, but made no sound. Time stood still.

There was a brilliant explosion of light – and Image shattered into a million pieces.

Atlas reached out to Image, crying, "Noooooo," his voice echoing throughout Kibu's castle and beyond.

It was too late. Image was gone.

Not far from the castle, Pepper, Ormon and Reflect cocked their ears.

They had heard a scream, but couldn't tell where it came from. "What was that?" Pepper asked, not really wanting an answer.

"It sounds like somebody's in trouble," Ormon replied.

Reflect's knees buckled. She held her stomach as if ill.

Ormon ran over and knelt beside her. "What's wrong, Reflect?"

"Image," she said with small droplets of mirror tears in her eyes. "He is no more."

"What do you mean?" Pepper asked.

"We are all connected," she explained. "I sensed that his spirit was under a great strain, and now I can no longer feel him."

Ormon suddenly understood how Reflect knew that

E'lum warriors had fallen in battle. Her connection to her people was similar to what he felt for his family and friends, only much stronger. His next thought was of Atlas, for if Image had indeed been protecting his friend, this news meant that Atlas was now alone in Kibu's castle.

Ormon bristled at the thought.

As he helped Reflect to her feet, a sound in the darkness startled them.

"Watch out!" Reflect cried, raising her hand and shooting a fireball of light mere inches past Ormon's face into the body of a large, slimy creature that leapt out from The Emaciated Forest. It was a gargoyle.

"Aaaaaaaahhhhhhh!" screamed Pepper and Ormon as the energy ball incinerated the monster.

"Get them!" shouted another goyle with gleaming, serrated teeth and claws of sharpened ivory. Pepper and Ormon then saw at least a dozen more of the creatures stalking them with very bad intentions.

"Stay with me!" Reflect commanded.

"I'm not going anywhere," Ormon said.

A bolt of lightning flashed from the sun crown upon Reflect's head, making quick work of a pair of ferocious goyles. While she did all the work, the duo was temporarily benumbed by terror, but that changed when a dangerously close swipe by another goyle forced them to action.

"Use the acid rain spray!" Pepper called to Ormon as he unleashed a jet stream of holy water from his soaker into one of the beasts, melting its insides. The stunned monster gaped at the hole in its belly and toppled over.

"Whoa, Dude, did ya see that?" Pepper yelled.

"Yeah," Ormon screamed, "but don't congratulate yourself yet, Pepper, there's a whole lot more where that guy came from. Keep shooting if you wanna stay alive."

The twosome stood back to back, spraying lethal holy water while Reflect dispatched the enemy with fire and light from the Sphere of Norova.

Suddenly, to Ormon's horror, the demon that he thought was vanquished by Pepper leapt back to its feet.

"Foolish being!" the gloating goyle said, as it inched towards Ormon with slobber dribbling from its lips.

"Pepper, he's not dead! The acid rain spray didn't work," Ormon cried.

Pepper fired off another frantic shot and hit the goyle right between the eyes, instantly obliterating its head. This time, the goyle didn't get up.

"Shoot 'em in the head, just like in the movies," Pepper said coolly.

"Remind me to thank you when we get back home," Ormon said, whirling to face the other goyles and blasting away at their vulnerable little noggins. Soon, the fracas was over and the floor of The Emaciated Forest was littered with the bodies of dead gargoyles.

Reflect, Pepper and Ormon were exhausted from the fight, but energized to have beaten such a formidable enemy.

"You are fierce warriors, friends of Atlas," Reflect said. "You have great courage. I could not have defeated them all alone."

"I wouldn't exactly call it courage, Reflect," Ormon replied, "but there's no way we could have done it without you."

"Yeah," added Pepper, "I'm glad we've got each other."

As the boys shared a victorious smile, Reflect reminded them, "We have only won a small battle here. There is still a war to be fought."

Ormon and Pepper nodded and scampered down the path behind her. Before long, they came to the clearing and saw Kibu's castle. "This place needs a paint job," Pepper said.

"I get the feeling that wouldn't help much," Ormon replied. "Remember Mrs. Mapp's painting?"

"There is no time for talk," Reflect insisted, heading off for the castle. "I must find this dungeon."

Ormon grabbed her by the arm. "Wait, Reflect!" he whispered. "You saw what happened back there in the forest. Kibu's guards were waiting. If we don't make a plan, we don't stand a chance."

Reflect looked anxiously towards the castle and turned to the boys. "Yes," she said, "A plan would be wise."

They took cover in the brush and began brainstorming a way to outsmart the Dark Lord of The World Below. Their mission would be much more difficult than they'd anticipated; not only did they have to help rescue Vision, but they also had to try to save Atlas at the same time. Moreover, with Image gone, they'd have to do it all by themselves.

By now, Neffer had arrived in Althanar.

Under a blazing sun, he rode in a truck down a dusty road with several Arab men wearing metal hardhats. The men looked skeptical.

"I do not mean to question, Neffer, but how can you be so sure that they are alive?" asked one.

"It is more than even I understand," Neffer replied, "but our priority is to get them out as soon as possible. We can figure out how they survived later."

The vehicle pulled to a stop before the mine. Workers were scattered about, lounging lazily in the shade. They snapped to attention at the sight of Neffer, who walked to the boulder-strewn entrance of the mine and kneeled in prayer. The men watched the ancient old man with reverence.

Neffer turned to them wearing a very serious look.

"I know you are fearful, but you must cast your fears aside," he said in a strong, clear voice. "There is work to be done here. Inside this mine are men who have families, who have been like brothers and fathers to you over many years. Three of the four are alive."

Whispers knifed through the gathering of workers.

"The Goddess Mariah herself has told me so. I do not dispute her words," Neffer said, drawing even more gasps of surprise from those in attendance. "There is little time. Let us begin."

Neffer saw reluctance in the men's faces. They were dirty, sweaty and their bodies were tired from working around the clock since the first collapse. Though it was dangerous to continue searching, Neffer knew that many of the workers were believers in gods. Now, he had to find a way to appeal to their belief in miracles.

So, Neffer hiked up his purple robes and bent down, lifting a small rock and tossing it to the side. Then, he repeated the process, picking up stone after stone until he had created a small pile.

The men, most of who were many years younger, exchanged glances. Despite their fear and exhaustion, watching a man Neffer's age doing young men's work made them feel very guilty.

One by one, the men joined in, until soon there was an army working beside Neffer. They attacked the mine with rakes, pick axes, shovels - and even bare hands - grunting and groaning in the heat. Neffer toiled with them until a young man pulled him away and offered a sip of water.

"You have earned the right to watch others work, Dear Neffer," he said. "If the Goddess Mariah says that three still live, we will not stop until we find them."

Neffer slumped in the shade and smiled, too tired to do more than that.

Back in the cave in The World Below, Kibu watched Atlas mournfully pick up large shards of Image's shattered body and carefully place them into his backpack. He was a mean spirit, but still, Kibu felt a hint of compassion watching the boy.

Atlas ignored Kibu as he worked. His heart was hurting so much that he wasn't even afraid anymore. He'd seen so much pain and suffering over the past several hours that he was now nearly immune to fear.

In fact, everything that Atlas had experienced since landing in The Arch World had changed something inside him. All that he had overcome, from his treacherous trip across the Monkey Bar Bridge, to his narrow escape from the Salt Monster, his night alone in The Lazantine Forest and the fight against the gargoyles in the Emaciated Forest, had transformed him.

Quite possibly, his trials had made him stronger.

Now, as he collected the remains of his new friend, Image, Atlas was almost indifferent to the master of this world. He was also resigning himself to making a deal with the devil of The World Below.

"How do I know you'll let my dad go if I do what you want?" Atlas asked without looking at Kibu.

"Because I am a spirit of my word, Atlas Mapp," Kibu replied. "I could have taken you long before this moment, but I did not. Do you not trust me?"

Atlas looked into Kibu's glowing red eyes. He did not reply, but he was sure that Kibu knew his answer.

Outside the castle, Ormon and Pepper's plan was underway.

Casually, they strolled right out into the open before the gargoyles and ghouls guarding the castle. Ormon was even whistling, despite the fact his knees were knocking beneath his fatigues. He knew *that* would get their attention.

The devilish dogs howled and tugged hungrily against the chains that tethered them close to the castle's entrance. The boys' strategy to lure their enemies to themselves was working.

Two menacing gargoyles charged out to greet them, Boroom and Sharibu. They swooped down with fangs bared and talons ready. Several other gargoyles left their posts to gawk at this encounter, which they were sure spelled doom for the helpless outsiders.

Ormon and Pepper somehow resisted their urges to run back to the portal to The Arch World as fast as they could. They didn't budge an inch.

"These two obviously have a death wish, brother," Boroom thundered. Sharibu snickered. "Which one should we devour first?"

Out of the corner of his eye, Ormon watched as Reflect snuck toward the castle while they preoccupied the guards.

"Look guys, uh – whatever you are – we don't want any trouble," he said. "Just let us get our friend, Atlas, and everything will be okay."

Boroom roared angrily. His wanted to rip the boys limb from limb and eat one's heart while the other watched, but he was forbidden to make a move without Kibu's consent.

Ormon counted on this when he devised the plan to get Reflect inside the castle. Pepper thought it was a crazy gamble, but everything else Ormon had done since they left home had worked out, so he went along with it.

Boroom shuffled close, baring his teeth and snorting hot, smelly breath into Ormon's face.

"Surely you jest, standing here in the face of death," he snarled.

"Dude, he is *so* serious," Pepper said, turning his nose up at the horrible odor coming from the goyles. "We can do this the easy way, or we can do it the hard way. It's up to you."

The gargoyles looked at each other and laughed demonically. Surely, these intruders were insane, they thought. Never in all the time they had kept watch over Kibu's castle had such a ridiculous thing ever occurred.

All those in The Arch World and beyond knew that to trespass in The World Below meant a painful and certain demise. Had these creatures not heard?

"I would enjoy eating your still-beating hearts," Boroom said in a hoarse whisper, "but Master Kibu might have use for you."

With that, he grabbed Ormon by the back of his shirt while Sharibu snatched Pepper, and they dragged the boys inside to see their master.

EIGHTEEN
Kibu's Deal

Atlas sat pondering Kibu's deal. It was simple: if he
agreed to remain in The World Below as Kibu's son, his father,
Field, would be released.

Still, it didn't make sense to Atlas. He didn't
understand why Kibu had chosen *his* father or how he had
come to believe that Atlas was destined to become his son from
the day that he was born. But what choice did he have?

Kibu was all-powerful and could not be defeated.

Atlas reasoned that if Kibu had the power to cause the
mine collapse in Althanar that imprisoned his father, that he
could also easily take Field Mapp's life. Atlas couldn't bear the
idea.

"Well, at least mom and dad will have each other," he
thought, burying his head in his hands.

At that moment, Boroom and Sharibu walked into
Kibu's cave - dragging Pepper and Ormon. At first, the boys
were so riveted by the sight of the black shapeless figure with
pulsing red eyes that they did not notice Atlas, who sat against
a wall mired in deep contemplation.

"Master Kibu, we have something for you," Boroom
said, tossing Pepper to the floor. "These are friends of the boy."

Pepper, Ormon and Atlas' eyes met simultaneously.
"Atlas!" the pair cried, overcome with joy, despite their dire
circumstance.

The threesome rushed into each other's arms, hugging

and backslapping as if years had passed since they last met.

"I can't believe you guys really came!" Atlas said.

"Toxic Soldiers don't ever leave anyone behind," Pepper said with his trademark sly smile.

"That's right," Ormon added, "All for one and one for all."

"Thanks, guys," Atlas said, his thoughts quickly turning to home.

"How's my mom? Is she okay?"

"Well, considering that her husband is trapped in a mine and her kid's off fighting gargoyles and demons in another world, I'd say she's holding up pretty well," Pepper said.

Atlas managed a smile.

"I'm glad you guys are alright," he said. "I really feel bad about getting you involved in all of this. I don't know if I would have been brave enough to come if things were the other way around."

"Sure you would, Atlas," Ormon said. "You've never let us down."

Kibu had seen enough pleasantries. He also could not abide watching the affection Atlas displayed for his friends from The World Above.

"I will leave you to make your decision, Atlas Mapp," he said, and flew out of the room with a whoosh, leaving Boroom and Sharibu to stand guard.

"What decision?" Ormon asked, when Kibu was gone.

"He wants to take my soul in exchange for setting my dad free."

"No way, Dude," Pepper exclaimed. "You can't do that!"

"So, he's responsible for all of this?" Ormon asked.

Atlas nodded.

"I knew it was more than a coincidence," Ormon said.

"What are you gonna do?" Pepper asked.

Atlas hung his head for a long moment, then said softly, "I don't know."

Truthfully, however, Atlas had already made up his mind. He just didn't have the heart to tell Pepper and Ormon. He didn't think they would understand that if he didn't agree to Kibu's deal, his father would die.

"Guys," Atlas said finally, "I really don't have a choice."

Ormon checked to make sure that Boroom and Sharibu weren't listening, then whispered, "Don't give up, Atlas. We've got a plan."

Atlas raised his eyebrows.

"That's right," Pepper said. "Toxic Soldiers always have a plan."

Atlas was torn. He was very happy to have his friends beside him, but he was also growing despondent over his impending decision.

At any time, Kibu would return to the cave and demand an answer. He felt trapped. Anything other than agreeing to Kibu's arrangement would result in tragedy.

Ormon and Pepper, he thought, did not have a plan to deal with that.

What Atlas didn't know was at that very moment, couldn't, actually, was that several E'lum warriors were still battling gargoyles elsewhere in the castle – and that a very determined Reflect was on her way to help.

NINETEEN
Old Friends

With her light sword drawn, Reflect padded down the large stone steps towards the sounds of battle. She sensed that most of the E'lum warriors had fallen at the hands of Kibu's legion of demons, but that others still bravely fought on.

At the bottom of the stairs, she silently crept along in the dark, stopping to peer down a long corridor. At the end was a barricaded door.

"He is there!" she said to herself, just as an E'lum warrior bolted out into the hallway. The soldier was stunned to see Reflect standing there, but snapped to attention when she commanded, "My father is behind that door. Help me."

"Yes, Princess," he replied, and sprinted down the hall with Reflect in tow. She stood by anxiously with her light sword at the ready while the warrior struggled with all his might to lift the steel bar from entrance.

Reflect did not know what she would see inside and quickly recited an ancient E'lum prayer before the door was pulled open.

To her amazement, Vision stood before her, weak and haggard, but nonetheless alive.

"Father!" Reflect cried, rushing into Vision's arms with such force that she nearly knocked him over. "I knew you were alive. I just knew it."

As the two shared a long hug, Reflect's light energized her father, who instantly felt a surge of strength.

"Reflect, you were brave to come here, but you should not have," Vision said. "Where is Image?"

"He is no more," Reflect said, realizing that having been kept imprisoned in darkness for so long, her father had been unable to feel Image's passing.

Alarm crossed Vision's face. He wondered what else he had missed. "Has the convergence happened?" he asked, fearing the worst.

"It is close, father," Reflect replied. "I know we must go, but first, there is a boy from The World Above that we must rescue."

"We cannot wait, little one," the E'lum warrior protested, then addressed his king. "Vision, we must leave immediately. Our numbers are low and we cannot hold off the evil ones much longer."

"But Atlas Mapp helped us," Reflect implored. "We can't just leave him here. His friends helped me get inside the castle. What of them, father?"

Vision was torn as he gazed into his daughter's pleading eyes. Many times he had explained to her that life sometimes required making difficult decisions. This, he knew, was one of those times.

"I know of this boy," Vision said, stroking Reflect's face tenderly, "but one life is not worth the many that will be lost if I do not return to seal The Black Pyramid."

"But, Father-"

"Reflect, we must leave now," he said, softly, but in a firm voice. Sadly, Reflect bowed her head and nodded. She could not disobey.

Vision took her by the hand and hurried down the corridor, where they were joined by more retreating E'lum warriors. Together, they hurried up the stairs towards freedom.

As Vision and Reflect headed for E'lum Village, Pepper and Ormon were growing nervous that she had not yet come for them.

"Something's wrong, Bookworm," Pepper warned. "I can feel it. Reflect and the others should have been here by now."

Ormon was thinking the same thing.

"I know, Pepper, but we don't have a choice," he said. "All we can do is wait for them."

Suddenly, there was a commotion outside the cave as several gargoyles burst inside the room to inform Kibu of Vision's escape. When Kibu entered the room, they shrank in shameful failure, but the evil apparition did not care that Vision had been freed.

"Let him go," he said. "I have what I want. And soon, I will have *everything* that I have ever wanted."

"But, Sire-" one of the goyles protested.

"Leave!" Kibu commanded. "I have pressing matters to attend to."

The goyles slunk off into the darkness. Kibu retreated with a satisfied smile.

Now free from Kibu's castle, Vision, Reflect, and what remained of the small army of E'lum warriors, sped away through The Emaciated Forest on their Skyriders. In no time, they burst through the portal back into The Arch World and headed for home.

As they rose into the sky over Fossil Mountain, Vision warily regarded the two suns in the sky; they had moved closer together than ever.

With a grim expression, he accelerated towards The Black Pyramid. At his side, Reflect wore the saddest expression her father had ever seen.

She took a final glance backwards at the portal and wondered what would become of Atlas, Ormon and Pepper, what dangers they faced at Kibu's hands, and whether he would take their lives.

She thought of how brave they had been to help her rescue her father, and feared that she would never have the chance to repay them. For Reflect, this was the saddest regret of all.

Vision gazed at his daughter. The memory of her had gotten him through the many days and nights that he was held captive in Kibu's castle. He dreamt of the moment he would see her again and hold her in his arms, but this was nothing like the dream. The moment had come, yet he had no words to console her.

So, Vision focused on the task at hand: getting to The Black Pyramid in time to seal it before the convergence.

And, while Vision hurried to save the Arch World races, a world away, another rescue was in motion.

Under Neffer's watchful eye, workers at the mine in Althanar had made considerable progress clearing the rubble from the entrance. They had been inspired by Neffer's words and the knowledge that the Goddess Mariah herself had told the old man that three men were still alive. Now, they worked without regard for their personal safety and without fear.

It felt like a tomb down below, where Field and Mahmoud anxiously watched the water climb higher, hungrily lapping at their feet. Their hope was waning, for they knew it was just a matter of time before the entire area was engulfed. They had to be rescued very soon.

Field heard it first, a faint *rat-a-tat*.

He cocked his ears and listened closely, but because of the sound of gurgling water, he couldn't be sure.

A pick axe maybe?

After listening intently for several more moments, he was certain that the sounds meant a renewed effort was underway to get them out. Mahmoud heard it, too. The look of despair faded from his face as he jumped to his feet.

"Oh, such sweet sounds, Professor," he said. "You were right all along. You said they would come."

Field didn't reply. He scanned the water for Habbibi's body, but it was now completely submerged. Although he had done all that he could to avoid a confrontation with the lumbering giant, he felt remorse that Habbibi was not alive to be rescued. He was pondering what more he could have done when Mahmoud grabbed a metal pipe and started banging it on the rocks.

"We're here! We're alive!" he shouted with glee, oblivious to the fact that his actions could trigger another collapse in the fragile mine.

"Be careful, Mahmoud," Field warned, "They know we're here."

"I am sorry, Professor Mapp," Mahmoud said, feeling foolish. "I guess I was simply overcome by the moment. It would be quite a shame if I were responsible for our demise with help so near."

Mahmoud sat back down, his expression serene. "Yes, yes, Professor, you were right," he said. "If only Habbibi had listened....".

"No, Mahmoud," Field said. "*We* were right."

Neffer and the rescuers had heard Mahmoud banging the pipe and his elated cries. Cheers erupted among the workers, who doubled their efforts to reach the trapped men.

Neffer, exhausted, sat and looked toward the heavens. "Thank you, Goddess Mariah," he whispered. "Thank you."

Sarah nearly collapsed with relief when Neffer called by satellite phone to tell her that Field's rescue was close at hand. She thanked Neffer profusely and relayed the hopeful news to Jenny and Ahib. Now, they could only wait to find out for certain if Field was among the survivors. Sarah grew nervous once again.

"It is not exactly the news we would like to hear, Mrs. Mapp, but it is better than no news," Ahib said, trying to make her feel better.

Sarah glanced over at the covered map on the easel and nodded several times, then buried her face in Ahib and Jenny's comforting embrace.

Back in Kibu's castle, the evil spirit silently floated about the room, allowing Atlas more time to make his decision. Pepper, Ormon and Atlas sat against the wall, their hope fading with each passing moment.

While Atlas gathered his thoughts, Pepper and Ormon stared at the curious creature in a loincloth with the face of an old man.

"Dude, that's one ugly kid," Pepper whispered.

"I'll say," Ormon replied.

Then both were frightened into silence by Kibu's terrifying voice. "Have you decided?" he asked Atlas.

Atlas didn't reply. He had no idea that his father was close to being rescued by the workers in Althanar. He also didn't think that Kibu would allow him to leave if he refused the offer. The way Atlas saw it, he was trapped. The whole scenario was like a trick question; whatever he decided, he would lose.

He didn't understand what it would mean for him to give his soul to Kibu, but he figured that it had to be just like death. How else could he be transformed into a spirit like Kibu? Weren't spirits once real, live people? Atlas contemplated being forced to spend the rest of time trapped in The World Below. It would be a miserable existence.

But Atlas could also envision his mother and father together again, and this thought made him happy. Though they would have their son no longer, at least they would have each other, and maybe they could even have another child. Maybe a little sister.

He had so many conflicting thoughts and not much time to think them. Right now, Sarah Mapp was alone. Atlas loved her very, very much, and could not bear to think of her living out her final days this way.

As he gathered the courage to tell Kibu of his decision, Atlas sensed that he had some power in the matter that he could use against his captor. He would not give in without getting something in return.

"I have decided," he said in a calm voice.

"And?" Kibu replied, arching his filmy brows.

"Let my father go and I'll do it," Atlas said, to the collective horror of Pepper and Ormon, who watched him with pleading eyes.

"As you wish," Kibu said, gesturing skyward.

At that moment, the workers in Althanar felt the ground tremble. They fled, fearing another collapse. From the glow of his amulet, however, Neffer knew there was something else afoot here. His suspicions were confirmed when several massive rocks blocking the mine entrance suddenly levitated and moved aside, clearing the way.

From a safe distance, the workers gawked in awe, feeling as though they were witnessing a miracle. Many gave thanks to the Goddess Mariah.

Neffer approached the entrance with trepidation, feeling that somewhere in The World Below, Kibu had gotten his wish. From what the Goddess Mariah had told he and Ahib, the old man knew that Atlas had made the choice to sacrifice his soul for the life of Field Mapp.

Neffer called down into the darkness. "Field, are you all right?"

"Neffer, is that you?" came Field's faint reply.

"It is I, old friend," Neffer said with a bittersweet smile.

"In that case," Field called, "I've never been better."

Mahmoud faced Field, looking relieved, but also quite serious. "Professor Mapp, I announce my official retirement," he said, "commencing with the moment my feet touch solid ground."

Field smiled wistfully. Mahmoud had been with him on numerous expeditions and was a valuable ally. His intelligence and knowledge of ancient artifacts was second to none. But Field understood that this brush with death had been a harrowing experience for Mahmoud and that it would be useless to try talking him into staying on.

"Well, then," he said, "I regretfully accept your decision to retire, Mahmoud – commencing with the moment we are safe and sound."

As they shared a hug, Denai regained consciousness.

"Professor, now that you have kept your promise to me, I must keep the one I made to you," he said in a thin voice.

"When we get out of here, then we can talk," Field said.

"No, no," Denai persisted, "I have already waited much too long. I am sure this is something you will want to know."

TWENTY
A Very Big Mistake

Atlas stared into Kibu's red eyes, waiting for something to happen.

The evil spirit had finished his grand gesture, but Atlas did not feel any different than before Kibu claimed to have released Field Mapp and the others from their prison inside the collapsed mine.

Pepper and Ormon, who had expected Atlas to be turned into a ghost, were baffled. Maybe Kibu taking their pal's soul wasn't as bad as they'd feared. Maybe there really was a way out of this.

But Atlas knew there was more to come. He was sure that if things were as simple as they appeared, Kibu would not have waited one thousand and ten years to initiate his plan.

"How do I know that you let my dad go?" he asked, finally.

"There is no gain in deceit, my son," Kibu said. "Your father has been freed. Now, it is time."

Pepper and Ormon's hearts beat in double-time as they awaited Kibu's next move. It was then that Ekim spoke.

"If you will, Kibu, there is the small matter of my reward," he said.

"What is your desire?" Kibu said.

"The map that the boy used to enter The Arch World," Ekim replied without hesitation, drawing quizzical stares from Atlas, Ormon and Pepper.

"And what would you do with this map?"

"I wish to flee to The World Above."

"Yes," Kibu said, "To cheat death and fate."

"So that's why he was so curious about the map," Atlas thought, remembering Freddy Bearer's explanation that Ekim's life cycle would end when the two suns came together.

In Atlas' world, however, Ekim believed he could live forever, or at least not be forced to live knowing when his life was going to end.

Atlas thought of the map in his back pocket. He simply couldn't give it to a creature like Ekim, who didn't understand what life was like in Atlas' world. At most, Atlas figured, Ekim would be a circus curiosity. And without family or friends, how could he survive?

Before Atlas could figure out what to do, Kibu turned to him. "Give him the map," Kibu said firmly.

Atlas froze. Ekim waited, with stubby fingers outstretched.

"He... he doesn't have it," Ormon blurted, drawing a bewildered look from Atlas. "Give him the map, Pepper."

For several seconds, Pepper was just as confused as Atlas, but then he realized Ormon's plan. Since the maps *were* different – theirs didn't have The Monkey Bar Bridge on it, as did Atlas' – Ormon believed that Ekim wouldn't be able to use it. He would remain in The Arch World, where he belonged.

Pepper handed his map to Ekim, who snatched it greedily.

"I don't know what good it'll do you – unless you go to New York," Pepper said, adding, "That's the only place you'll fit in."

Ekim looked at Pepper with a jagged smile.

"New York? I like the sound of that," he said. "New

York it will be."

Pepper gave Atlas a reassuring glance and the boys watched Ekim happily waddle out of the cave.

"And now," Kibu said, "I shall have my prize!"

"Uh, excuse me, Mister Kibu," Ormon said nervously, "Can't we work something out here?"

"Silence!" Kibu thundered, lifting the boys off their feet with a wave of his hand.

Pepper and Ormon hung in thin air, afraid to speak, lest Kibu hurl them to the floor like rag dolls. They floated across the room, where Kibu's magic stuck them against the cave wall, unable to move.

"You two will interrupt me no more," Kibu said.

"Don't hurt them, Kibu!" Atlas cried. "This is between you and me. If you want my soul, you have to promise to let them go."

Kibu paused, admiring Atlas' courage and devotion to his friends. "You are right, Atlas Mapp," he said. "I will set them free when you and I have completed our, shall we say, transaction."

Unable to do anything else, Ormon and Pepper looked on in dread. Their muscles were frozen and they could only move their eyes. As Kibu prepared to do some unimaginably dastardly deed to Atlas, they were helpless to intervene.

"Okay," Atlas said, uneasily.

"Good. Let us proceed," Kibu replied, shooting a blast of red light straight into Atlas' chest.

Atlas writhed in pain. He tried to resist, but saw, and felt, a bright blue light being slowly extracted from his body.

It was his soul.

Atlas struggled mightily, mustering just enough energy to shout, "Wait! Wait!"

Puzzled, Kibu halted his soul-stealing assault. "Why do you wish this delay?"

Clutching his chest in angst, Atlas stood and faced Kibu.

"My friends ... told me that all this stuff ... has something to do with a curse on the diamonds of King Attanan Bushawri," he said, struggling to breathe.

"Yes?" Kibu replied.

"So, if you're going to take my soul, I think you owe it to me to explain everything. I mean, what does it have to do with you?"

Kibu's laugh was deep and sinister. He realized that he held all the cards. Indeed, what would a few more moments matter when he had waited so long for this one? And, he *did* want Atlas to be happy living as his son in The World Below when this was all over. For eternity.

"An explanation, then, is in order," he said. "I will tell you what you wish to know."

In Althanar, Field's life-and-death struggle was over. He was now free from the mine and sat in the shade of a palm grove alongside Mahmoud and Denai, who lay on a stretcher being tended to by a doctor.

The three had just listened to a fantastical story told by Neffer of the curse that had caused their hardships and which now threatened the life of Atlas and his two friends.

The tale was difficult for Field to believe, but even he had thought strange all the coincidental occurrences in the moments before the mine collapse. Still, his rational mind would not stop questioning the curse.

"How can this be?" said Field, who until now had believed that Atlas was safe at home with Sarah.

Denai answered instead. "Professor Mapp, what Neffer says is true," he said. "Please allow a regretful man to make his peace."

Mahmoud moved closer, very interested to hear the story that Denai had been eager to tell hours earlier.

"Go on, Denai," Neffer coaxed gently.

Denai cleared his throat. He was thankful for all that Field had done to keep him alive, and this made it very difficult for him to reveal the secret had had harbored for so many years.

"I owe you greatly for allowing me to work with you after my brother, Ada, stole the Diamonds of Bushawri," Denai began, his eyes downcast.

"What Ada did had nothing to do with you, Denai," Field said. "You were only fourteen years old."

"Still, I knew of the curse long before," Denai replied, his words becoming of great interest to Neffer. "Professor, it was no accident that the map which led you to the Diamonds of Bushawri found its way into your possession. My brother sent it."

"Ada?" Field asked, with a look of surprise.

"Yes. He knew of the curse. That is why he allowed *you* to uncover the diamonds. Ada had already discovered their location."

"So that the curse would fall on the professor instead of Ada?" Neffer interjected, unraveling the plot in his mind.

As Denai spoke, Field's heartbeat quickened. Droplets of sweat formed at his temples. He saw himself back inside the cramped tunnel, unearthing the very diamonds that his father had lost his life searching for.

Ten years had passed since that day when he experienced the dual joy of discovering a treasure many thought was little more than a myth, and seeing his newborn son, Atlas, for the first time.

Denai's account forced Field to revisit a time he had not allowed himself to think much about since Ahib discovered that Ada stole the precious diamonds. For some reason, Field tried to convince himself that Ada was not a thief, despite the fact that he was never heard from again.

Now, a decade later, Ada's younger brother was confessing the horrible truth: Ada had joined that long-ago expedition with the sole intention of stealing the diamonds.

While Field struggled with his emotions, Neffer, however, was not surprised. He had known Ada's family for a long time and always believed that Ada was a bad seed. There was something in Ada's eyes, even as a child, that Neffer noticed, but he was never able to put a finger on it.

Ada had gotten into minor troubles like most young boys, but that was not what concerned Neffer; what bothered the old man most was how Ada would go to extreme lengths to avoid hard work and responsibility.

In a way, Neffer also held himself responsible for the theft because he was the one who recommended Ada for the expedition in hopes that it would help the young man turn his life around. And, until the day the Diamonds of Bushawri and Ada went missing, Neffer had not regretted his decision.

As Denai revealed more, Neffer realized that Ada had hoodwinked him, too.

"I remained by your side all these years to try to protect you," Denai explained. "I hoped to restore my family's honor. I knew the curse would come for you someday, but not how or when."

Word of Denai's story spread around the camp and many of the rescue workers gathered around to listen in.

"Tell us of the curse," Neffer implored gently.

Denai sighed as he prepared to relieve himself of a heavy burden that he had been carrying for a very long time.

"It began a thousand years ago…"

At the precise moment that Denai began to tell the story of the ancient curse, a wind whipped through the Mapp house, drawing the attention of Ahib, Sarah and Jenny, who sat watching the now-uncovered map.

To their astonishment, on the table in the dining room, Ahib's book flipped open, and the pages turned by themselves.

"The book!" Ahib cried, rushing over with Sarah and Jenny close behind. Before their disbelieving eyes, the book of curses filled with demons and spirits stopped at a page that was empty – except for the heading, King Attanan Bushawri. Suddenly, letters and words materialized.

The words appeared at the exact moments they fell from Denai's lips.

"…A thousand years ago," the incredulous Ahib excitedly read along.

Even more incredibly, deep in The World Below, Kibu was telling the same tale: *"…lived the aging ruler of Barumba, the powerful King Attanan Bushawri… Facing his mortality and certain death, the king desired nothing more than to sire a son – an heir."*

Stuck to the wall of Kibu's cave, Ormon and Pepper craned their necks to share a knowing glance. Finally, they were learning exactly why all of these strange events had happened to them over the past several days.

In Althanar, Field listened as Denai spoke, still not fully able to believe his ears, although deep down he knew the story was true.

Together, Denai, Kibu and Ahib related the story.

"For the woman who would bear the king a son, her reward would be a collection of the most glorious diamonds and jewels the world had ever seen. For ten years he tried, marrying one hundred women who produced one hundred daughters."

At the same moment that Denai paused to allow Neffer to dab speckles of water on his parched lips, Kibu paused, as if remembering this tale that had not been told for more than a thousand years – and the words stopped appearing on the pages of Ahib's book.

"What is happening here?" Ahib cried, fearing that the book would reveal no more. "Is this all?"

To his relief, the words in the book once again appeared, just as Denai and Kibu resumed telling the story. Ahib read on.

"Bitter, frail and frustrated, the king made a deal with the devil and buried the diamonds with this proclamation: He who one day possesses the Diamonds of Bushawri will in ten years forfeit his first-born son – a curse delayed for each year the king had tried to sire a son of his own blood."

Field and Neffer exchanged glances.

In Kibu's cave, Atlas did the same with Ormon and Pepper. Around the dining room table, Ahib, Sarah and Jenny locked eyes.

"In exchange, the devil made the king a servant and gave him a new name..."

In Althanar, Field, Neffer and the workers watched as Denai mouthed the word.

At the Mapp home, Sarah, Ahib and Jenny watched in shock as the word materialized.

Down in The World Below, Atlas, Pepper and Ormon's mouths fell open as the evil spirit magically transformed into an old man in royal robes – who completed the sentence.

"Kibu."

Neffer was astounded.

Sarah, Jenny and Ahib were speechless.

Atlas, Ormon and Pepper, gazing upon the rather mortal figure of King Attanan Bushawri - wearing his human form - were in disbelief.

"King Bushawri... Kibu," Atlas said, repeating the words over and over, finally putting it all together. "So that's why your name seemed so familiar. I've heard the story of the Diamonds of Bushawri all of my life. You're here because you made a pact with the devil."

"Yes," the old man replied. "I am King Attanan Bushawri. And now that you know all, it is time to fulfill my destiny. *Our* destiny."

He lifted a gnarly hand to resume extracting Atlas' soul, but was stopped by Atlas' sudden protest.

"Hold on, King, uh... Kibu," Atlas pleaded, his face cloaked in confusion as he turned the details of Kibu's story over in his mind. He knew the story of his father finding the Diamonds of Bushawri well and recalled asking him to retell it again and again when he was a small boy.

But as Atlas thought of that tale now, along with the unbelievable story Kibu had just told, he couldn't help but feel that something was *wrong*. As hard as he tried to figure out what bothered him about it, Atlas couldn't put his finger on it – and Kibu was growing impatient.

"I have told you what you wanted to know, Atlas Mapp," he said with bubbling annoyance. "There can be no further delay."

Suddenly, Atlas figured it out. As clear as day, he realized what was wrong with Kibu's story; the trouble would be getting Kibu to believe him.

"You've got the wrong kid, King Bushawri," he said. "You made a mistake."

A look of befuddlement crossed the king's face. "What is this trickery?" he demanded.

Pepper and Ormon didn't understand what Atlas was getting at, either. "It's not a trick," Atlas replied. "You made up the curse yourself."

"So???"

"Well," Atlas explained, "Your curse says that whoever *possesses* the diamonds has to forfeit his first-born son. Right?"

Atlas paused to make sure that the king understood his point. "Yes. That first-born son is you, Atlas Mapp," Kibu said.

"No, it's not," Atlas argued. "See, my father *never possessed* the diamonds. He only *found* them. Ada, a man who worked for my dad, stole them that very same day."

From the cave wall, Pepper and Ormon simultaneously uttered, "Whoa!"

For what seemed an eternity, Atlas watched the brittle old man pace silently, a mixture of confusion and pain in his face. Slowly, it dawned on the ancient king that the boy *was* right.

"How could I have been mistaken?" he said aloud to himself. "No! No! No!"

As Kibu struggled with his emotions, a cold wind blew through the cave, nearly causing the torches on the wall to flare out. The flames rose higher as Kibu became angrier.

Somehow, seeing King Attanan Bushawri as he looked more than one thousand years ago, weak, fragile and nearing his end, Atlas felt pity.

Although Atlas was just ten years old, he imagined a thousand years to be a long time to wait for something. And though his discovery was ruining the king's plan – and could save Atlas from spending the rest of time in The World Below – he still felt a bit of sadness and compassion.

Atlas knew that if honor meant anything, Kibu had to let him go. "I'm sorry, King Bushawri," Atlas said. "It's true. You made a mistake."

"A very big mistake," Ormon chimed in, as he and Pepper suddenly slid down the cave wall to their feet, released from the spirit's grip.

Just then, the old man whirled to face Atlas with rage in his eyes. "I refuse to believe it!" he declared. "My destiny must be fulfilled!"

Obviously, the truth meant nothing to Kibu. Even after realizing his error, in his madness, Kibu would not allow Atlas to leave The World Below. Kibu *would* have the son he had desired all of these years.

"But… you said you were a spirit of your word!" Atlas pleaded. Kibu's face softened into an expression that was, well, almost kind.

He reached out and touched Atlas' face, stroking his cheek with cracked fingernails.

"From afar, I have watched you since the day you were born," he said. "You were such a beautiful little boy, smart, intelligent and strong, the kind of boy who would make a wonderful king."

"But I don't want to be a king."

"No," Kibu said softly, "but you do want a father, and you have always wanted a father."

Tears formed at the rims of Atlas' eyes as Kibu spoke.

"I have seen you cry in the night when you are alone," Kibu continued, "and he - Field Mapp, the great explorer - was nowhere to be found."

Ormon and Pepper looked at each other. Over the years, they had also noticed Atlas' depressed moods when his father was away for long periods of time. Still, they didn't like seeing Kibu manipulate their friend.

"Mr. Kibu," Pepper said, "That is, like, soooo uncool."

"That may be," Kibu said without taking his eyes off of Atlas, "but it is also true. All of your life, Atlas, you have wanted a father who would be there for you; a father who would never allow harm to come to you; a father less concerned with material riches and treasure hunts than in spending time with the ones he loves.

"All of your life, you have desired a father who *wants* to be a father," Kibu said. "Atlas, I *am* that father."

Atlas was silent for several moments, and then he wiped away the tears and glared angrily at the old man.

"My dad is a good person," he said through quivering lips. "He loves me and my mom and he cares about other people. Before I came here, I didn't really understand that the reason he was away all that time was because he's responsible for a whole lot of people. Now I know that it doesn't mean he didn't love me or want to be with me."

Ormon and Pepper watched as Atlas spoke through clenched teeth, clearly upset by Kibu's ploy.

"More than anything, King Bushawri, or whatever you call yourself, my father is an honorable man. He doesn't take what doesn't belong to him.

"He's earned the right to be a father. Someone like you might make a good father for somebody else, but you could *never* be my father. *Ever!*"

Kibu was stung by Atlas' words and turned away.

For a long while, silence filled the room. Kibu was thinking. He had tried everything to persuade the boy to give his soul of his own will, but nothing had worked. When Kibu finally turned back to face Atlas, his eyes were again evil and red. Kibu had decided that he would not be denied.

Atlas cowered, knowing there was nothing else he could do. Kibu firmly fixed his gaze upon Atlas.

"Your contempt for me will fade in time, young one," he said, raising his bony hand. "But now, my destiny will be-" *Bbbooooommmmmmmm!!!*

Kibu never saw it coming. From the entrance to his cave came an explosion of bright, white light. The bolt hit Kibu in the chest and sent him crashing to the floor. He was dazed.

When Atlas turned, Freddy Bearer stood there beside an E'lum warrior. Freddy tossed Atlas his glowing amulet of Agle the Eagle.

"Let's get out of here kids," Freddy said. "Kibu's gonna be madder than a rattlesnake when that light blast wears off!"

For a brief moment, none of the boys could move. But then they saw King Bushawri transforming, losing his human form and changing back into the shapeless creature loathed and feared throughout both The Arch World and The World Below.

"Come on!" Freddy commanded. "We ain't got much time 'til he turns back."

The boys hustled out behind Freddy and the E'lum warrior.

Despite the fact that Freddy had just saved them, Pepper remained unsure about which side the gangly stranger was on. "Hey, mister, I thought-"

"Just run! I'll explain later," Freddy replied.

The group raced through dimly-lit corridors and up the stone stairs toward a door leading out of Kibu's castle. As they neared the exit, Kibu's bloodcurdling scream filled the air.

"Aaaarrrrrgggghhhhh! Freddy Bearer," he declared,

"You are mine!"

Atlas' heart skipped a beat. He had witnessed firsthand Kibu's deadly power and feared that there was no way they could make it to the portal out of The World Below before Kibu caught up to them.

As he ran, Atlas' mind churned. He was hyperaware of everything around him. He could feel the wind rushing past his face and heard the slightest of sounds, each one sending shivers up and down his spine.

As they neared the door leading from the castle, Atlas' amulet gave off a red glow, something he had never seen before. But Atlas could not stop to consider it. At this moment, all he could do was pray that he and his friends would escape this place and make it safely back home.

TWENTY-ONE
Agle's Swift Sword

Field stared out the window at the rugged terrain of Althanar for the last time as the small plane gracefully took to the sky. No, he had not found the treasure he'd come hunting for, but his life-threatening experience in the mine had shown Field that he'd been forsaking his precious family while searching the globe for precious relics.

Field looked at the little map Neffer gave him and tried to imagine what Atlas and his friends were going through. Because the boys were still in The World Below, Neffer had explained, there were no little red blips to indicate whether they were alive or dead.

Field stared at the piece of paper and waited.

"This would never have happened had I just been there," he said softly, his voice full of remorse. "I should have listened to you, Neffer."

"Even your father did not believe in such things in his youth," Neffer replied. "You cannot blame yourself for Atlas' predicament. All you can do is hope that you have prepared him for a time like this."

Neffer patted Field's hand. "I believe that you have."

As Field and Neffer jetted through the sky toward Seattle, Atlas, Pepper, Ormon, Freddy and the E'lum warrior ran for their lives in The World Below. Now, they were outside Kibu's Castle, headed for The Emaciated Forest and the portal back to The Arch World.

Not far away, Kibu's screams of fury resonated in the air, heightening their fear.

Atlas was tiring. He was weighed down from his heavy backpack, filled with the shattered pieces of Image's body. He slowed and turned, only to see that Freddy Bearer was also laboring – and he was startled to see a dim light emanating from Freddy's chest.

"Freddy, you're glowing!" Atlas said, stopping in his tracks.

Freddy plodded several more steps, and then stumbled to the ground as the strange, gray light began to envelop his entire body.

"Pepper, Ormon, wait up! Something's wrong with Freddy!"

Atlas took off his pack and kneeled over the stricken Freddy, whose body was transforming into something ghostly.

"Freddy, are you OK?"

Freddy tried to speak, but had lost his voice.

With Freddy in peril, Pepper and Ormon took up defensive positions with their Super Soakers cocked and ready. Behind them, Pepper saw legions of gargoyles closing in.

"Atlas, let's leave this guy," he said anxiously. "We've got to get to The Black Pyramid. Besides, he was working for Kibu."

Atlas shook his head. "We can't leave him, Pepper. He saved us."

Pepper knew Atlas was right. Still, he looked to Ormon for a second opinion, but Ormon was too busy gasping for air to be of much help.

Ormon was locked in concentration as he stared at the rapidly aging Freddy, who was taking on the look of a faded old postcard. Ormon recognized the color now brightly shining from the mountain man's body.

"Freddy was the gray blip on the map with Atlas, Pepper!" he exclaimed. "His heartbeat wasn't red like the others."

Pepper scratched his head. Ormon's theory *did* make sense. "Maybe Kibu took his soul like he tried to do with Atlas," Pepper said.

Freddy's voice had returned, but was merely a whisper. Atlas had to lean close to his face to hear.

"Freddy, tell me what's happening to you. Maybe I can help."

"There ain't nothing you can do, Mr. Mapp," Freddy said, with a shake of his head. "Kibu's taking back what I owed him, that's all."

"But I don't understand. What do you mean?"

"Well, when I tol' you 'bout how I got here, I didn't tell you the whole story," Freddy began. "See, I wasn't by myself that day. I had my l'il baby boy with me. Colin was just three months old…"

Pepper, Ormon and Atlas looked at each other with raised brows as Freddy talked on.

"My wife had died and I didn't know nothing 'bout raising no infant. That's why I was so depressed in the first place. Well, when I fell into The Arch World, Kibu found me, and he was real fascinated-like by the child. He promised to give me anything I wanted if I gave him my boy. The way I seen it, I didn't have no other choice… so I did."

Atlas stared at Freddy in disbelief.

"You gave Kibu your son?" Freddy nodded.

"I was desperate and the baby was real sickly," he said. "It's the only way I woulda done something like that. Anyways, Colin died not long after and Kibu felt cheated. Tol' me I owed him a favor. That turned out to be me helping him get to you."

From what Atlas had seen of Kibu, he realized that Freddy didn't have much choice. He now knew why Freddy had betrayed the Mirror People and tricked him into giving up his amulet. Atlas didn't know what he would have done if he were in Freddy's shoes. Instantly, he forgave Freddy for all his wrongdoing.

"Kibu gave me a life here," said Freddy, who was turning into translucent skin and bones. "Now, he's taking it back. I'm really sorry, Mr. Mapp. I really am."

Freddy's life was ebbing away, just like the E'lum warriors who had fallen in the battle in The Emaciated Forest. Atlas thought of how Image had provided comfort to them before they died and wondered if he could do the same for Freddy. Finally, he thought of the one thing he knew would make Freddy feel better.

"I'll make sure to tell Reflect and Vision why you did what you did, Freddy. I'm sure they'll understand that Kibu gave you no choice," he said.

A twinkle came to Freddy's eyes.

"Thank you. I'd like that very much," he said. "Reflect was like a daughter I never had. I loved the E'lum as much as I ever did my own family."

While Atlas consoled Freddy, Ormon, Pepper and the lone E'lum warrior stood by nervously, watching as an army of dark shadows loomed ever closer.

"We've got to go *now*, Atlas!" Ormon said in an urgent whisper.

But Atlas couldn't leave yet. Something about Freddy still puzzled him. For all that Freddy had explained, Atlas still had one more question.

"Freddy, why did you come back to help us?" he asked.

Freddy managed a smile. "You know that thing I said about people not being everything?"

Atlas nodded.

"Well, I was wrong," Freddy said, reaching up to hand Atlas a gold pocket watch dangling from a thin silver chain.

"If you ever get to Tennessee, I hope you'll look up the Bearer family. This here was kinda precious to 'em."

"I'll try, Freddy," said Atlas, who could now see the ground through Freddy's disappearing body.

"Goodbye, Mr. Mapp," Freddy said.

Freddy faded away. His clothes turned into a pile of gray ash, which an icy cold gust of wind then blew away.

The three boys were staring at the spot where Freddy had dissolved into nothingness, when gargoyles sprang from everywhere.

They were out of time.

"Watch out!" Ormon shouted, dodging several of the slimy creatures.

The E'lum warrior spun on his heels, blasting at the goyles with fireballs of light while Ormon and Pepper fired holy water. Atlas was shooting his soaker, too, but his acid rain spray had no effect.

Pepper tossed him Neffer's vial of holy water. "Put this in your gun!"

Atlas looked at the little bottle curiously – and nearly had his head lopped off by the sharp talons of a goyle – but Pepper killed the demon with a shot to the head.

"Don't read it!" Pepper cried, "Put it in your gun!"

"And aim for their heads!" added Ormon.

Atlas furiously emptied the vial into his soaker and joined the others in vaporizing the enemy. Goyles in the trees hurled rocks and shot at them with bows and arrows, keeping their distance from the deadly soakers.

To Atlas' dismay, the E'lum warrior collapsed with an arrow protruding from his chest. Like the other fallen mirror warriors, he glowed dimly for a moment, and then his light softly went out.

The boys were now alone, surrounded by gargoyles. They were also quickly running out of water.

"Toxic Circle," Atlas commanded.

Like true soldiers, the boys pressed their backs against each other to guard every angle from attack, and inched their way through The Emaciated Forest towards the portal to The Arch World.

Suddenly, Boroom and Sharibu appeared, blocking their path. "Take Atlas Mapp alive!" Boroom declared in a low voice. "The others… they're for dinner."

"Aaaaaaggggggghhhhh!" Pepper and Ormon cried in unison, sure that unless a miracle happened, they'd become gargoyle food.

At that moment, Atlas' amulet began to glow with an intensity he'd never seen before, its color a different shade than the crimson he had seen while fleeing Kibu's castle. A golden spotlight shone brightly from the charm around his neck and, to his surprise, a baby eagle fluttered forth with swords clutched in each taloned foot.

"Agle!" Atlas exclaimed.

"AWWEEE-AWWWEEEEEE!"

With each war cry, Agle grew in size, and, in the blink of an eye, she dwarfed the boys and their attackers.

Gargoyles ran for cover as Agle took to the bleak skies and attacked, lopping off heads with her gleaming pair of swords.

"Cool!" Pepper remarked, nearly so caught up watching the eagle that he forgot he was also in the middle of a fight. Ormon's yell brought Pepper back into the fray.

"Hey, Dude," he shouted, "The war's not over yet!"

Atlas mouthed a silent thanks to Neffer and Ahib, who had assured him that the amulet would someday protect him from danger. Still, he could hardly believe his eyes.

Neither could the goyles, who had never seen such a thing in The World Below.

In the face of Agle's relentless attack, some of the evil creatures fled, choosing to face Kibu's wrath rather than die by the sword of the boys' new protector. Other goyles hid in the darkness of the forest and fired arrows into the humongous bird, but they seemed to have little effect.

Agle was fearless in combat, swooping down at frightening speeds with a deafening screech, its swords dripping bright green blood, and leaving a trail of goyle heads and guts in its wake.

"We must destroy this thing," Boroom thundered, just as Agle bore down upon his unsuspecting brother.

"Sharibu, watch out!"

Sharibu tried to duck, but was too late. Agle's blade sliced clean and sure. Boroom watched in horror as Sharibu's severed head plopped onto the ground and rolled off into the weeds.

Enraged, Boroom unleashed an unholy howl and charged the boys, his black eyes glistening.

"I will kill you all! You will not leave The World Below alive!"

They faced the angry beast and took aim with their soakers. Pepper nodded to Atlas and Ormon with a smile.

"Let's have some fun with this one, guys," he said.

"We shall see how much you laugh while I rip you to shreds!" Boroom roared as he stalked toward the boys.

Atlas' knees were shaking and Ormon's teeth chattered as Boroom menacingly lumbered closer, right into Pepper's trap.

"That's right. Keep on coming, big guy," Pepper taunted coolly. Once Boroom was in range, Pepper gave the command. "Kneecap 'em, boys!"

With their aim true, Ormon fired at Boroom's right kneecap while Atlas blasted the left. Boroom tumbled face first onto the forest floor, his muscular legs incinerated by the acid rain spray.

But even with his legs missing, Boroom lifted himself up by his powerful arms and glared at Pepper.

"You shall pay for this!" Boroom said defiantly. "I work in the service of the great Kibu. I have never been defeated."

Pepper's smile faded as he took aim at Boroom.

"You've never fought against Toxic Soldiers," he retorted. Boroom growled, but without legs he could not attack.

"You're one gone goyle!" Pepper said, blasting the evil Boroom right between the eyes.

Boroom's head exploded, showering Pepper with green goo from head to toe.

"Ewwwww, Dude!" Ormon uttered, holding his stomach and cringing while Pepper wiped the sticky ooze from his face with a broad grin.

"Now, that's what I call teamwork!" Pepper crowed.

Atlas, exhausted, stood with his soaker dangling limply at his side, only then noticing the eerie quiet of The Emaciated Forest. Far off in the distance, he saw the fleeing silhouettes of limping and battered gargoyles in retreat. Still, he felt that they remained in danger.

Just then, Agle smoothly landed on the path before Atlas and lowered its head. He climbed onto the huge bird's back and beckoned to the others. "Come on. Let's go."

Pepper and Ormon clambered on, holding tightly to each other as the war eagle rose into the perpetually dark sky over The Emaciated Forest towards the portal back to The Arch World.

Atlas kept watch behind them, expecting the shapeless black figure to attack at any moment, but Kibu never appeared.

"He's not coming, Dude," Pepper said. "Kibu lets those gargoyles do all his dirty work."

"I hope you're right," Atlas replied, with his heart still in his throat.

Agle flew high above the heavy stone steps that the boys had navigated on their way down into Kibu's world, and soon, the eagle burst through the portal into the bleak city of Polema.

Their sighs of relief quickly turned to dread when they noticed the Arch World sky was much gloomier than before, darkened as if by the approach of a thunderstorm. Up above, the two suns were on a collision course.

Without a word between them, Atlas, Pepper and Ormon knew that the convergence of the Novi was nearly underway - and they had no protection from its cleansing light.

"Can it get any worse?" Pepper said in a resigned tone. Ormon and Atlas were wondering the same thing. For all the danger they had just survived, it seemed unfair that they would die so close to safety.

But Ormon remembered Reflect telling he and Pepper that life in The Arch World was not always fair. Ormon had heard his father say much the same thing of his own world. He

250

recalled Reflect's answer when he had asked why the convergence also destroyed the good with the bad.

"I do not know why things are the way they are," Reflect had said. Neither did Ormon.

Atlas was also lost in thought, but his musings were not of death here in a world so far from his comfortable home in Seattle. Instead, Atlas replayed in his mind all that had happened since he had begun his search for his father. He wondered how long he had been gone. Was it just a few days, or weeks?

Atlas glanced at his pals and knew that they were afraid. Right then and there, Atlas promised himself that they would all survive.

He leaned forward and whispered into the eagle's ear.

"Agle, you've got to get us out of here. We've got to get to The Black Pyramid. I know you can do it."

The eagle shrieked as if it understood and beat its enormous wings faster, picking up speed. Just as Agle knew the way out of The World Below, Atlas hoped the big bird would also know the way to E'lum Village.

Agle flew over Fossil Mountain and the Five Kings, and then sped over The Lazantine Forest. The boys held on tightly, watching the two suns about to converge in the sky, and searching for any sign of the Black Pyramid.

"Do you think we'll make it in time?" Ormon asked solemnly.

"We *have* to," Atlas replied. "We've got no other choice."

TWENTY-TWO
Atlas' Sacrifice

Ahib's head was buried in the book, *Mythological Curses from A-Z*. He hadn't been able to tear himself away since the words miraculously appeared on the pages of the book revealing the story of the curse on the Diamonds of Bushawri. Ahib had read it several times since and continued to stare at the book in hopes it would tell him even more.

Sarah, however, did not need to read the story again. The first time had been difficult enough. And after hearing the worry in her husband's voice on the satellite phone from Althanar – telling of Denai's knowledge of this same ancient curse – Sarah did the only thing she could do at a time like this: she went back to the large map in her living room and waited for a sign.

She did not have to wait long.

Three heartbeats suddenly appeared in the city of Polema. At first, Sarah thought her eyes were deceiving her, but when she heard Jenny gasp upon seeing the red blips, she knew it was true. Atlas, Ormon and Pepper had somehow escaped from The World Below and the evil spirit whom she now knew was also King Attanan Bushawri.

But how?

"They're out!" Sarah screamed with joy. "They're out!"

Sarah hugged Jenny so tightly that in her joy she almost squeezed the breath from her sister.

"I told you he would make it," Jenny said.

Ahib rushed over and stood with Jenny and Sarah in disbelief - and relief - tracking the heartbeats moving across the map over The Lazantine Forest.

"I do not understand," Ahib sputtered. "According to the book, Atlas had to sacrifice his soul. So how could he-"

"I don't know and I don't care, Ahib," Sarah interrupted. "The most important thing is that he's away from that terrible place and he's with his friends. They're free."

But Ahib was not so sure. In his mind, until the boys were back in their own world, preferably where Ahib could see them with his own eyes, they were not safe. Ahib did not think it was yet time for a celebration.

"I do not mean to be pessimistic, Mrs. Mapp," he said, "But one is not home free until one is home."

Jenny and Sarah shared a glance. Ahib was right. While they had gained new hope, in reality, the boys still were a world away.

Speeding on a plane toward Seattle, Field was staring at the little map in his hands when he also saw the red blips appear.

Field realized these were indeed the heartbeats Neffer had spoken of, but as a man of science, he simply could not grasp that the lights on this animated map represented the life forces of Atlas, Ormon and Pepper.

"Neffer, something's happening here," Field said.

Neffer leaned forward, gazed at the map and smiled. It didn't take him long to gather that somehow the boys had escaped from The World Below without a sacrifice to Kibu. He also knew that they were still in danger, and would be so until they were out of The Arch World.

"It appears," Neffer said with a pause, "that Atlas and

his friends are fighting to make their way home."

Field didn't reply. He simply stared at the blinking red lights, wondering which one might be the heartbeat of his only child.

Now, with Denai's tale of the curse on the Diamonds of Bushawri fresh in his mind, Field was beyond questioning Neffer. He was growing more convinced by the hour that everything his old friend said was true.

During his life, Field had traveled to many strange and mysterious places. He respected the customs and belief systems of the many different peoples he had come across, but to believe in what he was seeing on the map challenged nearly everything he had learned about the world.

Field, however, had to accept that The Arch World was not *his* world.

Neffer watched Field in silence, knowing there was nothing more he could say in such moments of desperation.

As Field continued to focus on the map, his eyes were drawn to the gentle, pulsing rhythm of one particular heartbeat – the one in front of the others. Something about it felt vaguely familiar, and as Field's anxiety waned, he became aware of the feeling of his own heart beating deep inside his chest. A warm sensation filled him as his heartbeat became one with the bright little blip on the map.

It was then that Field knew for sure. The blip *was* Atlas. "I love you, son," he said, softly, gently touching the map.

Neffer watched Field and nodded a knowing smile.

Meanwhile, the pace of Atlas' heartbeat quickened in the heat generated by the two suns as the boys flew over The Lazantine Forest. Atlas, Pepper and Ormon alternated between looking ahead for signs of The Black Pyramid and up at the dual suns, knowing the convergence could happen at any moment, and fry them like scrambled eggs.

"I don't think we're going to make it," Pepper said, seeing nothing but a glacier of green forest below. "Maybe we should land and find a place to hide until the convergence is over."

"That won't work," Ormon said. "According to Reflect, the only two places we'll be safe are The Black Pyramid or in The World Below. I don't think you want to go back to Kibu's house, do you?

Pepper didn't answer.

"The Black Pyramid is our only chance," Atlas said seriously. "I'm sure they'll wait for us as long as they can…"

His voice trailed off. All he could do was hold on to the feathers of the great war eagle and hope that Agle would get them there in time.

At the entrance to the pyramid, Vision's face was grim as he, too, stared up at the sky.

Vision had witnessed the convergence many times and he knew that he could not wait. At his side, Reflect watched her father slowly place his hands atop two glowing crystal orbs. She knew it had to be done, but she also couldn't help but protest.

"Please, father, just a little while longer," she cried, in a voice almost too soft to hear.

Vision scanned the anxious faces of the Arch World races packed inside the once-spacious Black Pyramid. All of their lives were in his hands.

Their fearful expressions told Vision that the decision was not his alone to make. He had a responsibility to all of those who had come to E'lum Village seeking protection.

"We can wait no more," he said. "The pyramid must be

sealed."

As Vision simultaneously pressed down on both orbs, they emitted small flashes of light. Silently, a hidden door began to slide down over the entrance, blocking light from the suns outside. All over the pyramid, lightproof panels locked into place and the interior grew dark except for the light emanating from small spheres in holders on the walls.

Vision saw that Reflect was crying, and this hurt him deeply. He knew there was nothing that he could say to console her, so he offered the only words he could muster.

"Reflect, I am sorry."

Atlas, Pepper and Ormon desperately searched the treetops of The Lazantine Forest for sight of The Black Pyramid. Suddenly, Pepper's eyes opened wide. "There it is!" he said, pointing excitedly.

In the distance, the tip of The Black Pyramid came into view, but the boys noticed something else unusual about the sight: as they approached, large square panels rose and fell into place flat against the large structure, almost like a shield. Atlas instantly knew what was happening.

"Vision's sealing the pyramid," he said, hope fading from his face.

"We're too late," Ormon wailed, afraid to consider what this meant.

As if the pyramid being sealed wasn't bad enough, a small cry came from Agle. The eagle whimpered and struggled to keep its altitude.

"What's wrong, Agle?" Atlas asked, only then noticing the arrows protruding from the bird's side. A golden fluid seeped from the wounds.

"Guys, Agle's hurt. She's bleeding," Atlas said grimly.

"Dudes, what are we gonna do?" Pepper asked, "The Black Pyramid's sealed. We've got no place else to go."

As Agle descended, the two suns were now nearly one. It was much hotter and the air grew thick, making it nearly impossible to breathe. The sweaty trio was fearful and fast running out of options.

Ormon grasped Atlas and Pepper's hands.

"If this is the end," he declared, "I'm glad I'm here with you guys."

Pepper and Atlas choked up and they all hugged.

They were now close enough to The Black Pyramid to see that the crystal pyramids were empty. As far as they could see, there was no sign of a living thing. All the creatures of The Arch World had taken cover either inside The Black Pyramid or in The World Below.

"I guess that's why Kibu didn't come after us," Ormon said. "After he realized he had the wrong kid, he probably knew we'd get fried in the convergence."

"Or *he'd* get fried," Pepper added.

But Atlas wasn't thinking of Kibu anymore. He was worried only about his friends. Their lives would not be in danger if they hadn't come to rescue him. For this reason, Atlas felt terribly guilty.

Dying together provided little consolation.

He stroked Agle's neck tenderly and whispered into the eagle's ear, "Can you get us to the Monkey Bar Bridge?"

Agle weakly shrieked and continued fighting a losing battle to stay aloft. It was then that Atlas saw the wide path cut through The Lazantine Forest. He didn't remember it being there when he first came to E'lum Village with Image, Reflect and the others.

"Where did that path come from?" he wondered aloud.

"Your mom made a shortcut for us," Ormon said. "I guess she figured out that since she painted the picture, she could change it."

Atlas had no idea how Ormon came to this conclusion, but the new path gave him an idea. Maybe there was a way out of this.

Unable to continue, Agle landed with a jerk and skidded to a bumpy stop in front of The Black Pyramid, nearly toppling the boys over. Then, she collapsed in a heap beneath their weight.

The trio climbed down and examined the eagle's injuries, only noticing then that many arrows had hit their mark during their battle with Kibu's gargoyles in The World Below.

"I don't know how Agle made it out of there," Ormon said. "I think she's dying. She's a very brave bird."

"Yeah," Pepper managed, a lump growing in his throat. Atlas gently rubbed Agle's crown.

"Thanks for helping us," he said. "I know you did the best you could." Agle weakly shrieked, and the mysterious glow enveloped its body.

Before their eyes, Agle transformed into a small ball of light that shot back into Atlas' amulet so quickly that it startled him.

"Whoa!" Pepper said. "That was wild."

"I'll say," Ormon added as Atlas caressed his magical medallion.

A bolt of lightning in the sky drew their attention back to the dual suns. The suns were nearly touching, creating a very intense white light. The boys had been so entranced by Agle's transformation that they'd nearly forgotten about the danger they faced.

Atlas stole a glance at The Black Pyramid, where, if not

for the large glowing Sphere of Norova in front, he would have never known that an opening ever existed. It was sealed as tight as a drum. He figured that it would be useless to pound on the structure in hopes that Vision might open it for them before the convergence.

There was only one thing they could do.

"Guys, we've got to get to the door of desire!" he declared. "Run!"

The threesome galloped off down the path Sarah Mapp had created through The Lazantine Forest, moving as fast as their legs would allow.

Every so many steps, Pepper turned to wait for Ormon. Atlas was a very fast runner, but he labored because of the heavy glass shards in his backpack.

Finally, Atlas stopped and stood in the middle of the path.

"Dude, what are you waiting for?" Pepper shouted in a panic. "We're gonna get fried any minute!"

"You guys go ahead," Atlas said, turning back toward The Black Pyramid. "You can make it. I'll catch up."

"Atlas, c'mon. You'll never get there in time," Ormon panted. "We're not leaving you. Not now."

But Atlas was already sprinting away. "I've got to do somebody a favor," he said. "You guys just get to the door of desire. Go!"

Ormon and Pepper didn't know what could possibly be important enough for Atlas to risk his life at a time like this. At any moment, the two suns would come together and that would be the end of them. Pepper considered running after Atlas before Ormon grabbed his arm.

"I don't know what Atlas is doing, but if it means that much to him, I think we've got to trust him, Pepper," Ormon said. "If he says he'll catch up to us, he will. We've just got to have faith in him."

Pepper watched Atlas disappear into the distance and nodded as Ormon's words sunk in. After several moments of contemplation, he picked up Ormon's pack and said, "Okay, Bookworm, let's go."

Back at The Black Pyramid, Atlas knelt before the Sphere of Norova and took out the mirrored shards of glass that had been Image's body. He carefully placed them inside.

"I hope this works, Image," he said, standing and taking a long final look. "Goodbye, my friend."

Atlas then made a mad dash to catch up with Pepper and Ormon, who were already far ahead. This time, however, he didn't dare look up at the two suns to see how close they were. Atlas knew that with so little time left, he would either make it or he wouldn't. Whether he lived or died was in the hands of fate.

Sarah, Jenny and Ahib were on pins and needles watching the scene unfold on the large map that was back on the easel in the living room. Sarah had nearly fainted when she saw one of the red blips turn back while the other two ran through The Lazantine Forest toward the edge of the map.

"This doesn't make sense," she said in a frightened voice, looking to the others for answers. "Why would the boys split up when they're so close to making it back home?"

"I do not know, Mrs. Mapp," Ahib said, shaking his head slowly. "Only they know the answer to your question. I recommend that we go to The Door of Desire and wait for them."

Sarah was afraid because she instinctively knew that Atlas was the one who had turned back. But Ahib's suggestion gave her hope that they would discover all soon.

Sarah grabbed the painting and headed out the door. They were all in such a rush that none of them noticed that the third little heartbeat was racing against time to catch up to the other two.

High in the sky not far from Seattle, Field and Neffer were also intensely watching their miniature map. Field focused on the lone red blip in The Lazantine Forest, and, like Sarah, felt certain that it was his son. The unease was apparent in his face as he tried to imagine what was actually happening to Atlas and his friends.

Neffer watched Field, and his thoughts were transported to a long, long time ago, when he once saw Compass Mapp wearing this exact expression. It had been ages since Neffer recalled the reason for Compass' angst, but now seemed as good a time as any to recount it.

"Field, I was hoping that you might indulge me a story," Neffer said.

"Sure, Neffer… sure," Field replied, pulling his eyes away from the map.

Neffer moved closer and locked eyes with Field to make sure that he had his full attention.

"For days now, we have all been worried sick about you and Atlas," Neffer began. "It was quite a terrible feeling at first, wondering if I had lost two members of my family at the same time, but hope always has a way of replacing despair. And, as I hoped, you both were indeed alive."

Field nodded, although he was not sure what Neffer was getting at. "Now, as I look at you and find your face creased with concern, I am reminded of a time similar to this, and of the adage that there is a time when a father teaches a son, and another time when a son teaches a father."

Field smiled at the thought as the old man spoke.

"Many years ago, I accompanied your father on an expedition into the dangerous jungles of Katrina in search of the lost tribes of Monteneyo," Neffer said. "You were a small boy, maybe three or four years old, but the occasion was special, for it was the first expedition that your mother allowed Compass to bring you."

Field's face softened. "I think I remember that," he said. "It's hazy, but I can recall bits and pieces."

"Yes," Neffer said. "Your father hired a nanny to accompany us because you were such a curious child that it was difficult for him to both work and keep an eye on you. In a flash, you would amble away on your own, which was a constant source of worry for us all.

"Well, on the fourth day of the expedition, the worst actually did occur. You wandered off into the jungle when no one was looking."

Field sat up, suddenly very interested in Neffer's tale. "I don't remember that. My father never-"

"Compass never told you about it because it was the most painful thing he had ever experienced," Neffer explained. "A search party was hastily organized to look for you, a mere child lost in a dense jungle populated with poisonous spiders, venomous snakes and all manner of danger lurking… I shudder to think about it even now."

"What happened, Neffer?"

"Well, since you are here, it is obvious that the story turned out well, but I can tell you, I was not so sure then that this day would ever come to pass," Neffer said. "You see, darkness fell and the search was suspended until morning. Your father could not risk the lives of so many others, so he made the agonizing decision to wait until daybreak. And we did."

Field raised his brows, incredulous. "You mean, that I was- "

"Yes, alone in the darkness of a hostile jungle for the entire night. We did not sleep a single wink. For hours on end, your father wrung his hands in great despair – and I admit, so did I – worrying that we might not find you alive. But we also realized there simply was nothing we could do."

A gleam came to Neffer's eyes.

"But at the first sign of light, as the somber men gathered to search once more, there you were, sleeping peacefully among the guard hounds," he said, his eyes glistening as if to hold back fresh tears of joy. "It was the most beautiful and magnificent sight in the world. Somehow, the dogs chose not to bark to alert us of your return."

From the look on Neffer's face, Field could see himself back in the jungle as a little boy across many, many years.

"Oh, you regaled us with great nonsensical accounts of all that you had seen and experienced, great adventures that only a child can know - but you were much too young to realize the great pain your father had endured in your absence," Neffer related.

"As overjoyed as Compass was to have found you, he vowed to never bring you on another expedition. He knew he would never be able to forgive himself if bad fortune were to befall you."

Field sat back and turned silent. Neffer allowed him a moment with his own thoughts.

In that quiet moment, Field recalled the many adventures he and his father shared during his youth. He could not remember a time outside of when school was in session that he had not been by his father's side in some remote and interesting corner of the world.

As a boy, Field had been all over the globe. Now, he couldn't imagine growing up any other way.

"What made my father change his mind?" he asked.

Neffer's face turned serious.

"Well, a wise old man who had seen many things informed us that it was not the first time a child had survived a night in the unforgiving jungle," Neffer said. "He told us that there is a time when fathers teach sons and another time when sons teach fathers. That old man, you see, had also been a little boy who was once lost. And he survived. That was when we knew for sure."

"Knew what, Neffer?" Field asked.

"That you were a Mapp. A born adventurer and explorer," Neffer said, as if he were a proud father. "Being lost and finding the way home is your birthright. And I suppose that you will learn the same is true of your son."

Slowly, a smile crossed Field's face. Neffer's incredible stories always left him speechless. The old man had told him many over the years and always at the most appropriate time.

Field carefully folded the little map and placed it in his pocket. Neffer patted Field's hand, then nestled his head into a pillow and fell fast asleep.

Although rest did not come to Field quickly, after a little while, full of renewed hope and faith, he eventually joined Neffer in the land of dreams.

Ormon and Pepper staggered up to the sandy cliff where they first landed in The Arch World. Above them was the long hand ladder spanning the chasm over the river below.

Ormon glanced up and saw small explosions of fire

radiating from the two suns. The convergence was beginning. Knowing there was precious little time left, he turned to look down the path for Atlas, but there was no sign of his friend.

"What are we supposed to do now?" Pepper asked. "How do we get out of here?"

Ormon grew frantic, only now remembering that they had fallen into The Arch World from the sky and had no idea how to find the way back to their own world.

"Check the map, Pepper. There's got to be another way out," he said.

Pepper dug his hands into his pockets, only finding lint, a few coins and scraps of paper. Suddenly, he realized they had an even bigger problem.

"Bookworm, we gave our map to that funny-looking little guy back in Kibu's cave," he said. "I... I think we're stuck here."

Ormon deflated. At any moment, they could be turned to cinder by the converging suns. Worse, Ormon felt that it was his fault. After all, he reasoned, it was *his* idea to give Ekim their map instead of Atlas' in hopes that the little Byab would not make it into their world. That decision had now doomed he and Pepper's chance to escape the convergence.

With all that had happened since fleeing Kibu's castle, Freddy's death and the battle with the gargoyles, Ormon forgot that they had given away their only key to get out of The Arch World.

Ormon glanced across the divide and saw the mouth of a cave slowly appearing in the mountainside. Pepper saw it, too. "That *must* be the way out!" he exclaimed. "Atlas climbed across The Monkey Bar Bridge to get over here."

"We'll never make it in time," Ormon said. "Besides, we can't leave Atlas."

But Pepper was desperate. Though he didn't want to abandon Atlas, he also didn't like the alternative of becoming a human French Fry. "Well, what are we gonna do, Ormon?"

Ormon calculated. Without a word, he rummaged through his backpack, finally pulling out a plastic bottle with a few drops of water remaining inside.

"I've got an idea," he said, quickly removing the cap and sprinkling water onto the sandy ground.

"Hey, friend!" he shouted. "Are you here? We need your help!"

Pepper didn't know what Ormon was doing, or *who* he was talking to. But when the ground began to shake and shiver. Pepper got the idea. "Bookworm, tell me you aren't-"

Before Pepper finished his protest, the form of Waheel the Salt Monster rose from the sand.

"He's our only chance, Pepper," Ormon said.

"Yeah," Pepper sputtered, "but he tried to kill us – unless you've forgotten."

"Trust me, he'll help," Ormon replied.

Soon, Waheel towered over them, but he wasn't as menacing as when the boys first encountered him. Instead, the lonely monster almost seemed, well, *happy,* to see them.

"Boys come back!" he bellowed, with a jagged smile.

Ormon nodded uneasily, noticing that Waheel's left hand – the one he and Pepper had blasted with their holy water-fortified Super Soakers – had not returned. He felt guilty about asking a favor of the same monster that they'd nearly killed, but he couldn't see another way.

"W-w-we're real sorry to bother you, Mister, but we need you," Ormon said, taking a chocolate bar out of his backpack. "See, we're going to die if we don't get out of here before those two suns up there come together. We really want to get back home."

Waheel looked at the sky curiously. Being made of salt, he was not affected by the light of the Novi and, therefore, wasn't afraid.

"Ormon," Pepper whispered, "How can that thing help us?"

"Shhh!" Ormon whispered back with urgency, edging closer to Waheel and extending the chocolate bar. "This is all I can pay you," he said. "It's the last one I've got."

Waheel smiled at the sight of the sweetest thing he'd ever tasted and gingerly took it from Ormon with his good hand. He gulped it down and flashed a satisfied smile.

"Do you think you could get us over there?" Ormon asked, pointing across to the cave in the mountainside.

Waheel nodded.

Pepper regarded Ormon and the Salt Monster with amazement, unable to believe that another one of his pal's crazy plans was actually working.

"You're a genius, Bookworm," he said quietly.

"Thank me when we get home," Ormon replied, searching the path for Atlas, "When we *all* get home."

He turned to Waheel and pointed to The Monkey Bar Bridge. "See that?" Ormon asked, "I figure you can carry us over one at a time faster than we can climb across. Can you do it?"

When Waheel smiled, little flecks of salt fell from his sharp, gritty teeth. "Waheel have better idea," he said.

With that, the Salt Monster scooped up an unsuspecting Pepper and nestled him under his powerful arm.

"Whoa, Dude!" Pepper yelled, helpless in Waheel's mighty grip as the creature lumbered toward the edge of the cliff. "He's not going to do what I think-"

Pepper's screaming voice trailed off as Waheel took flight with a leap over the canyon. Pepper squeezed his eyes shut, too afraid to look. Waheel glided gracefully through the air and landed hard against the side of the mountain with the talons on his feet and his good hand dug firmly into the rock.

Effortlessly, he lifted the dazed Pepper onto the small ledge in front of the cave.

His heart pounding, Pepper squeaked, "Thanks."

With a loud grunt, Waheel then heaved himself off the mountain back to the other side, where Ormon waited.

"Uh, that wasn't really what I had in mind," Ormon began before Waheel snatched him off the ground and turned toward the cliff's edge.

The words stuck in Ormon's throat once Waheel gathered speed and raced ahead. Ormon tried to scream, but simply couldn't.

Pepper, who had recovered enough to sit up on the ledge, watched in awe as Waheel soared through the air with Ormon's round body dangling from his deformed arm like a rag doll.

It was then that Pepper noticed a look of despair cross the creature's face. To his horror, Ormon and Waheel began descending rapidly. They wouldn't make it. Too terrified to imagine Ormon and the monster plummeting hundreds of feet into the river below, Pepper covered his eyes.

Waheel had not accounted for the fact that Ormon was much heavier than Pepper. Only now, with the added weight bringing them down much faster than anticipated, did Waheel realize his fatal mistake.

Through sheer force of will, or maybe a miracle, Waheel reached for the mountainside and shielded Ormon from the unforgiving rock.

The crash sounded like a large fly colliding with an equally large windshield. Pepper heard Ormon gasp as if the wind had been knocked out of him. For several seconds, there was only silence and the slight gurgling of the river below. Pepper gathered the courage to peek through his fingers, at first not seeing anything.

"Ormon?" he called out hopefully. There was no reply.

And then, Pepper saw Waheel's talons scraping the tiny ledge in front of him. He inched to the ledge and saw Waheel struggling to lift Ormon to safety.

Ormon wasn't helping. He was stiff as a board, dazed and hyperventilating. Pepper shouted his name, but Ormon did not respond. His eyes were glazed over, locked on the multi-colored Arch World sky. Pepper realized Ormon was in shock.

Pepper lay flat on his belly and cautiously reached over the ledge. "Grab my hand, Bookworm," he said softly, trying to reassure Ormon.

Ormon blinked several times, slowly becoming aware of his surroundings. Just as Pepper uttered, "Don't look down!" Ormon gazed at the river and imagined his impending doom.

"Aaaaaaaaahhhhhhhhh!!!!"

Ormon's eardrum-shattering scream echoed off the canyon walls. "Ormon, take my hand!" Pepper commanded, like a military drill sergeant. "C'mon soldier!"

Pepper's Toxic order snapped Ormon to his senses, and, despite his intense fear, Ormon reached for Pepper's hand, barely touching his fingertips. Helped by a final mighty push from Waheel, Pepper pulled Ormon onto the ledge where they both collapsed in a heap.

Pepper, out of breath from the ordeal, smiled and wearily patted Ormon's chest. "You okay, Bookworm?"

Before Ormon could answer, the boys heard what

sounded like fingernails on a chalkboard. Waheel was losing his grip. The boys tried to form a human chain with Ormon grabbing Waheel's arm and Pepper holding onto Ormon for dear life, but Waheel was too heavy.

"C'mon, you can make it," Pepper said through clenched teeth as they strained to keep the monster that saved their lives from falling.

"Yeah, you can do it," Ormon implored, even as he felt Waheel slipping from his grasp. They tried as hard as they could, but there was nothing they could do. To their astonishment, Waheel looked up at them with a peaceful smile.

"Boys safe now," he said. "Boys go home." Tears welled up in Ormon and Pepper's eyes.

Waheel fell. They heard a sickening thud as he bounced off the mountain and tumbled towards the water. The boys peered over the ledge, just in time to see Waheel splash into the water and dissolve into a million individual grains of salt.

They looked at each other, wordless.

Then came a yell, as startling as it was familiar. "Hey, guys! Over here!"

Pepper and Ormon saw Atlas across the divide, frantically calling their names as he made a beeline for the Monkey Bar Bridge. Their elation quickly faded when they saw that he was not alone.

Not far behind Atlas, waddling like angry leprechauns, were hundreds of little Byab creatures. Ekim was out front, clutching Pepper's map in his tiny hand.

Ormon and Pepper jumped to their feet, helpless. "Run, Atlas!" they cried. "Get to the bridge!"

At that moment, a huge flash of light exploded in the sky, as if an atomic bomb had been detonated. Pepper and Ormon's eyes burned when they looked up to see the two suns becoming one.

"It's the convergence of the Novi!" Ormon exclaimed.
Ormon and Pepper saw Atlas running for the cliff's edge.

"No, Atlas! No!" Ormon shouted, afraid that Atlas had
decided to do something unthinkable.

Without warning, a strong wind from behind pulled
Ormon and Pepper toward the cave and whisked them inside.
They were headed home.

On the other side, Atlas heard Pepper scream his name
and saw the cave disappear into the mountainside.

He looked up to see a sheet of white erasing the once-
purplish-pink Arch World sky, and then whirled in time to see
the angry Ekim and his army approaching. There was nowhere
to go. He was trapped.

"You fooled us, Atlas Mapp!" Ekim wailed, his beady
eyes burning. "There must be another-"

Ekim never finished. There was a loud boom and the
sky exploded.

Atlas covered his eyes, trying to shield himself from the
most intense light he'd ever seen. A huge laser of light beamed
from above, blasting Ekim and the other Byab into
nothingness. Their wicked little bodies were no match for the
radiant light of the Supernovi.

Atlas felt his skin burning and collapsed to the ground
in pain. He curled into a ball to protect himself. By now, the
light had wiped away all color from the horizon and he could
no longer see even The Lazantine Forest.

As he closed his eyes, he saw only an incredible,
indescribable whiteness. And then, he saw nothing.

TWENTY-THREE
A Blank Canvas

Sarah went ashen. Ahib stood perplexed. Jenny turned away.

Ahib attempted to say some words of solace, but Sarah's attention was so focused that she did not hear him. Instead, she stared in shock at the large map of the Arch World that had been her only connection to Atlas and his friends since they had gone missing.

The canvas was now *blank*.

There was nothing there. No little red heartbeats. No E'lum Village. The Lazantine Forest, with its exotic trees and deep green foliage, and the rich, black rock of Fossil Mountain was gone. The city of Polema, once marked by angry, dark clouds hovering over its center, had also disappeared beneath a sea of pure white. Even the hideous World Below was nowhere to be found. Everything had completely vanished.

The canvas was fresh and bright as if the mythical Arch World painting that Sarah spent weeks working on had never been there at all.

Sarah sobbed inconsolably. Ahib and Jenny were pained, because neither knew what to do.

"Maybe Atlas *did* sacrifice his soul to Kibu," Sarah said, between a flood of tears and violent sniffles. "What else could it be?"

Ahib and Jenny hugged Sarah, who ignored the inquisitive stares of passersby. Customers inside the

McDonald's restaurant stopped munching on their burgers to watch the curious spectacle in the parking lot. Indeed, it was a strange sight to see: a bereaved young woman crying over a canvas with absolutely nothing on it.

Not long before, Sarah's desperate hopes had been lifted when they'd piled into Ahib's cramped pickup truck and headed for The Door of Desire. But that hope turned into despair once Ahib retrieved the covered canvas from the truck bed to find the picture erased.

Baffled by the strange happening, Ahib's sole wish was for Neffer to be there to help. Neffer was wise and understood many things. Ahib, however, was a simple man prone to confusion when faced with circumstances out of the ordinary. *Times like this.*

But Ahib could not have known that, miles away, Neffer and Field were also perplexed by their own map. It, too, had gone blank.

Field noticed the transformation only after being awakened by the screech of the jet's tiny wheels touching down on the runway at a small airport near Seattle. As he rose from his seat, Field unfurled the map and was stunned to see that the image was no longer there.

Neffer was equally dumbfounded when Field showed him the empty piece of paper. Several times, the old man nodded thoughtfully, and a serious expression crossed his withered face.

"I am sure there is some explanation for this, Field," he said finally. "We must keep our heads about us until more information reveals itself. We must remember, as your father once said, 'Nothing is ever lost. We simply have to keep looking until it is found again."

But Field's mood remained grim.

He couldn't help but feel a surge of guilt over how he had escaped certain death many times over the past week, and now, Atlas might not.

"I just don't understand, Neffer," Field said. "Why did I get a second chance when I'm the one who's responsible for all of this? Atlas is just a child. He doesn't deserve what's happened."

Neffer gently took Field by the arm and led him to a waiting sedan where their bags were being packed away.

"Field, I know that you would gladly trade places with your son, but it is not a question of what one deserves," Neffer began. "Although it may be of little consolation to you, for all the years that I have known your family, the Mapps have never been handed a burden too heavy to bear. This was true for your father and for you. Trust me, Atlas will survive."

Neffer suddenly felt faint and staggered. Luckily, Field caught him before he could fall to the ground.

"Neffer, are you all right?" Field asked with alarm in his voice. Neffer struggled to regain his bearings and the dizziness passed. "I am fine, just a little light-headed," he said.

In truth, Neffer was extremely weary from all of the activity of the past several days. Nearly a week had elapsed since he answered Agle's call that Atlas was in danger and he had barely taken a rest since that time. The stress and strain had finally caught up to the old man.

Neffer averted his face as Field helped him into the car. He didn't want Field to see that he was very worried about Atlas. More importantly, Neffer could not relax until the Mapp family was once again whole.

"Neffer, let me take you home so you can get some rest," Field offered.

But Neffer stubbornly refused, saying, "I have the rest

of my life to rest, Field. Now, we must get to The Door of Desire. I am sure the answer to all of our questions lies there."

Reluctantly, Field agreed. Soon, they were headed towards the city. Twenty-five miles away, Neffer's words were proving prophetic.

As Ahib and Jenny attended to the grieving Sarah in the parking lot, the answers they all sought were being revealed. It began with a rush of activity on the lawn near the recently-repaired McDonald's sign.

The ground wheezed and blew puffs of dirt into the air, shaking violently. Slowly, the earth split unevenly apart and a large black door rose to the surface, opening with a lazy yawn before slamming backwards onto the lush green grass.

As the astonished people inside the restaurant watched, Pepper and Ormon floated up through the strange door as if on a geyser of air.

In seconds, before the incredulous onlookers could squeeze out a collective gasp, the door slammed shut and disappeared, and the boys fell sprawling to the ground.

For several moments, Pepper and Ormon were disoriented, lying on their backs staring up at the pale blue sky. As they slowly regained their senses, a semi-circle of people formed around them, staring down wearing bewildered, curious and even frightened expressions.

Pepper, whose hair stood on end as if he'd stuck a finger into an electrical socket, gazed warily at the collection of strangers.

"You okay, Bookworm?" he asked, while slowly sitting up.

"Yeah," Ormon replied, adjusting his spectacles. Only then did he notice that they were surrounded by a small army of people who gawked at them as if they'd come from another world.

"They can't be *aliens* because aliens come from up there," a woman pointed out to a little girl.

"They look just like regular boys – *almost human*," added a thin man in a baseball cap.

Pepper did a quick check to make sure that he was still…well, himself, and then snapped, "Whaddya mean *almost*? We *are* human."

But those in the crowd didn't listen; this was quite understandable considering that they had just witnessed the pair flutter out of a now-missing hole in the ground.

"Where are we?" Ormon asked, more to himself than anything.

"It's called, SEEE-AT-TOLL," replied a grandmotherly woman with shimmering gray hair. She spoke slowly and deliberately to make sure that they understood her.

Ormon and Pepper exchanged glances.

"D-d-d…did you say 'Seattle?'" Ormon asked.

"Why yes, young man," the old woman replied. "It's in A-MER-I- CA," she added.

"AAaaaaaaaaaa-hhhaaaaaaaaaa!!!" they boys screamed with delight.

The leapt to their feet, yelling and dancing in euphoric disbelief. "We're home! We're home!!"

In mid-jig, Pepper declared, "I knew we'd make it back, Bookworm!"

Ormon rolled his eyes. With no more danger facing them, Pepper had already resumed the role of conquering hero.

"Don't worry," Ormon said, "What happened in The Arch World – stays in The Arch World."

Just as Ormon's secret pact left his lips, three familiar faces pushed their way to the front of the crowd. Ahib, Jenny and Sarah.

"Mrs. Mapp!" they boys cried.

Sarah rushed over, fell to her knees and wrapped both in a bear hug. Overcome, she kissed their grubby foreheads and cheeks.

"Thank goodness, you're safe," she said, her voice trembling as tears of relief welled in her eyes. "We didn't know if you'd make it."

"We're sorry if we worried you, Mrs. Mapp, but we had to go," said Ormon apologetically. "We thought if we told our parents...well, they wouldn't have let us-"

Sarah shushed Ormon and hugged him again. "All that matters is that you're home now."

Pepper, his face red with embarrassment from the public display of affection, allowed Sarah to cuddle him, nonetheless. Locking eyes with Ahib, Pepper felt remorse for having been less-than-truthful several days before.

"Hey, Mister Ahib," he offered, as politely as he could, "Tell Mister Neffer that I'm sorry for taking his holy water. It really came in handy down there, but I figure he might be missing it. I'm really sorry."

"I will tell him gladly, Mister Pepper," said Ahib, who had no idea what Pepper was talking about. Pepper's transgressions did not matter to Ahib. Instead, as he and Jenny scanned the crowd, Ahib was much more concerned about *something else* that was missing.

It was then that Sarah pulled away from Pepper and Ormon and asked a question that Ahib could not bring himself to ask.

"Boys," she said in a quivering tone, "Where's Atlas?"

TWENTY-FOUR
Haven

A world away, Atlas' eyes softly fluttered open.

He blinked several times, no longer feeling the burning sensation that had filled his entire body when the convergence of the Novi began. In fact, he felt pleasant and peaceful.

Looking around, Atlas didn't recognize anything. There was no cliff or mountain. There were no dual suns up in the sky. The canyon with the gurgling river below had disappeared and there were no arches in the distance to give him a sense of where he was.

Stranger still, there were no sounds and the air smelled of freshly-cut flowers. As he sat up, Atlas noticed that there was nothing to see except bright, fluffy white clouds all around.

He blinked several more times to make sure he wasn't dreaming, and then noticed for the first time that even his clothes were white.

It was if he had died and gone to-

"Wait a minute," he said to himself. "This must be-"

"Haven," said a voice from somewhere within the clouds.

"Who's there?" Atlas called, slowly rising to his feet, then noticing the tall figure of a man walking towards him.

The approaching stranger, dressed in white with thinning hair and a reassuring smile, said nothing as he came closer.

"Who are you?" Atlas asked again, before a warm and familiar feeling grew inside of his chest. In that moment, he knew.

"Grandpa?" he said, in a tentative voice. "Is that you, Grandpa?"

Compass Mapp nodded and knelt before Atlas, taking in the boy's features for the first time.

Atlas had never met his grandfather in life, but he recognized the steely eyes that were much like his father's, and his own. For a moment, he was leery, fearing that this might be yet another attempt by Kibu to gain his trust. But the feeling quickly dissipated when he realized that Kibu was far too evil to be capable of exuding such kindness.

"It *is* you, Grandpa," said Atlas, who was filled with emotion as he wrapped his arms around the man who had died long before he was born.

"And you, Atlas, are just as I imagined. Strong, handsome and brave, just like your father," Compass Mapp said, with a chuckle.

Atlas stared into his grandfather's eyes, unable to comprehend all that was happening. Atlas had spent hours looking at photographs and hearing stories of the man now before him. He often imagined what expeditions would have been like had Compass Mapp been there with he and his father.

As happy as Atlas was to see his grandfather, his feelings were mixed.

Now, he had a very strong sense of what death was, and he knew that his grandfather had died years earlier. His own father, Field, had explained it as the natural course of life, that all things – and people – live for a while, and then, inevitably, they die. Never to return.

Sarah, however, explained death in a way that was

much more comforting to Atlas.

A scary thought came to him. "Am I dead, Grandpa?" he asked.

Compass Mapp smiled. "No, no, no. I believe that you have a long life ahead of you."

"But, I don't understand," Atlas stammered, "How did I get here with you? Am I dreaming?"

"Well, that depends upon what you believe," said Compass Mapp. "Belief is important to possess, as is faith. Both qualities have been important to our family throughout history, for it takes both to search the world for things that others believe do not exist. Would you not agree?"

"Well, I *think* so," Atlas replied, although he didn't grasp everything his grandfather was saying, or why.

"It is true," Compass continued, "for what little boy would go on such an arduous and terrifying journey as you have without belief in himself?"

At this, Atlas felt ashamed.

"Grandpa," he said, lowering his head, "I don't think I'm really like you and dad. I mean, when I left home, I didn't know what was going to happen. I can't honestly say that I believed that I would find anything. I only knew that I had to try. So, that's what I did."

Compass lifted Atlas' chin and looked into his eyes.

"And I am proud of you for that," he said. "My father once told me something that I carried with me for all of my life. He said, 'Youth and wisdom don't come in the same box.' Now, at the time, I didn't understand what he was talking about. But as I grew older, I figured it out. Youth is lost as we unwrap the box of wisdom.

"One does not start off brave, Atlas, but one's actions determine his bravery, and you have shown this in abundance,"

Compass continued. "You have also shown great compassion in your willingness to sacrifice your personal desires to help others. And, whether you know it or not, you learned to believe in yourself along the way, which saved Field's life."

Atlas looked around expectantly, his eyes searching. "Dad's here? Where is he?"

"He is safe at home, where you will soon be."

Atlas shook his head. "But Mom said Dad was in Haven," he protested. "He's got to be here. That's why I followed the map to find him."

Compass stood and took Atlas by the hand.

"There are many havens in the universe, places where one feels safe and secure," he said. "This is but one. Home is another. Now, it is time for you to return home. Your mother and father are waiting for you."

Tears welled in Atlas' eyes. He felt torn. Although he desperately wanted to get back home, he also wanted to remain with his grandfather. He had so many questions.

"Can't I stay here with you, Grandpa?" he pleaded. "Can't we talk just a little while longer?"

Compass hugged Atlas once more.

"We have talked ever since you learned how, Atlas. I just happen to be a very good listener," he said. "Whenever you feel the desire to talk to me, I will be there, as always."

"But, Grandpa!" Atlas sputtered.

"You must go, Atlas," Compass said. "It is not yet your time. You have many worlds to explore. There is much wonder and adventure waiting for you. I will be with you."

Atlas nodded and hugged Compass Mapp one last time. "I love you, Grandpa," he said.

"And, I love you, Atlas," Compass replied, before walking away.

Atlas waved until Compass Mapp disappeared back into the white clouds. And though Atlas now stood alone, he didn't feel alone. He closed his eyes and marveled at the warm feeling, knowing that it was the spirit of his grandfather within him.

"Atlas Mapp? Atlas, can you hear me?"

The voice was near, but seemed to come from far away at the same time. Each time it called out, Atlas felt himself being drawn toward it, moving closer and closer.

When he opened his eyes, he saw bright yellow light all around him – and then, he saw the bright shiny smile on Reflect's face.

"Image, Atlas Mapp is alive. He's alive!" she shouted with glee.

Atlas quickly recognized the golden light that enveloped him. He was inside the Sphere of Norova. Atlas sat up and looked out to see hundreds of Mirror People and citizens of The Arch World looking back at him with grateful smiles.

He rose and stepped out of the glowing sphere. That's when he saw someone he wasn't sure he would ever see again.

"Image, you're okay!" he exclaimed.

"The Sphere of Norova returns life to us both," Image said.

Atlas quickly noticed that The Arch World seemed different, cleaner and brighter. The sky was a smooth pink and the two suns appeared much smaller in the sky than when he arrived.

The crystal pyramids shone like diamonds in the sun, and the trees in The Lazantine Forest exuded a youthful shade of green, like in springtime.

"It's really beautiful," Atlas said, "Like a whole new world."

Vision, looking much stronger than when he was held captive in the dungeon at Kibu's castle, stepped forward and shook Atlas' hand.

"I am Vision, Atlas Mapp, and I am honored to make your acquaintance."

"Thank you, sir."

"My daughter has spoken much of you and informed me that because of you, many lives were spared," Vision said. "Our world has been cleansed of evil and for that I thank you. All of The Arch World thanks you."

Deafening applause erupted from the thousands of creatures who had waited to thank the boy from The World Above. Vision then handed Atlas a golden bracelet with a sun symbol emblazoned upon it.

"It is time for you to return to your world," he said. "With this, you may call us whenever you wish to return. Your friends are also welcome."

Reflect stepped forward and lightly kissed Atlas on the cheek. "I will miss you, Atlas Mapp," she said, "and your heartbeats."

"I'll miss you, too, Reflect," Atlas replied, as Image produced a Skyrider and lowered it so that Atlas could climb aboard.

"Let us go," Image said. "I am sure there are many who await your return home."

"Home," Atlas said softly to himself, repeating the word for a place he hadn't been so sure he would ever see again.

Already, he could see his mother and father, Pepper and Ormon, and Neffer and Ahib. Only now, as he prepared to leave this wonderful world, did he realize just how much he missed his own.

Atlas climbed onto Image's fantastic flying board of light and waved goodbye to the denizens of The Arch World, who quickly became ant-like specks as they flew over The Lazantine Forest. In the blink of an eye, the two hovered at the cave where Atlas would begin his journey home.

"Thank you for everything, Image," Atlas said, nearly choking on the lump in his throat as a wave of sadness overcame him.

"Do not be mournful, Atlas Mapp," Image said. "Here in The Arch World, we do not say 'goodbye.' We say, 'See you soon.'"

"Okay, then," Atlas said, "Well, Image… see you soon."

Image zoomed from sight, leaving Atlas alone on the small cliff. For the final time, Atlas gazed at a world that was no longer strange.

He thought of the unusual beings that he had encountered – from Waheel the Salt Monster, to the E'lum, Freddy Bearer, the Byab and the evil gargoyles, Boroom and Sharibu – and he wondered if he really would ever see this place again. He even wondered what had become of the evil Kibu.

Atlas did not resist the tug of the wind behind him. He went limp and allowed himself to be pulled inside the cave. A happy thought echoed through his mind, so much so that he simply had to say it aloud:

"See you soon, Arch World. See you soon."

TWENTY-FIVE
Home

It was near dusk in Seattle. The sky was a hazy mixture of pale pink and light blue, the kind of color that could confuse one as to whether dawn was approaching or night was falling.

Hours had passed, and the curious crowd that earlier hovered around the mysterious boys had filtered away, once they determined that Ormon and Pepper were, indeed, earthlings. After discussing the unusual happening among themselves at length, the gathering of strangers realized there was simply nothing more to see or say, so everyone went home.

Neffer and Field, who arrived in the midst of the hubbub, stood in an anxious huddle with the others, hopefully awaiting Atlas' return.

Sarah and Field's reunion was joyous, though tinged with melancholy.

Now, they held each other tenderly as if to never let go, but looked incomplete, like a puzzle with a very important piece missing.

Ahib and Jenny sat side by side on the grass not far from the McDonald's sign, keeping an eye on the large blank canvas, and ruminating over the wild stories Pepper and Ormon told about their experiences in The Arch World.

Their heads swirled as they tried to imagine this parallel universe where demons, gargoyles, mirror people and adult babies roamed.

The tale of Freddy Bearer particularly saddened Ahib, for as a man with a young child of his own, he could not fathom being in such a situation, widowed and helpless to care for a sick infant.

"I do not believe I could give my child away to anyone, much less an evil spirit like Kibu," he said, after much deliberation. "I would rather die."

Jenny pondered Ahib's words. Although she did not have a child, for her, such an exchange was unthinkable.

"Your family is lucky to have you, Ahib," Jenny said. "I'm sure they miss you very much."

"Thank you, Jenny," Ahib said, his voice trailing off. Only now, for the first time since Neffer arrived, did he consider how long he had been away from his wife and child. It had only been a week, but felt like months.

"I will return to them once Atlas is home," he said. "They will understand."

Jenny began to reply, but hesitated.

"What is it, Jenny?" Ahib asked.

"Well," she said, "You seem so sure that Atlas will come home. How can you know that?"

Ahib patted Jenny's hand.

"How do I know? Well, first of all, because he is a Mapp. And, secondly, because the gods do not punish the young and brave," he said. "He will come home. You will see."

Ahib's encouraging words brought a smile to Jenny's face. Her spirits lightened. "Thank you, Ahib," she said. "Thank you."

Off to themselves, Pepper and Ormon sat quietly. For more than an hour, they hadn't spoken, each fluctuating between hope and despair, but keeping their feelings inside.

Finally, Pepper ended the silence.

"I've been thinking, Bookworm," he said in a low voice so as to not be overheard by the others, "Maybe we should break up the Toxic Soldiers. You know... without Atlas, it won't be the same."

Ormon gazed sadly at Pepper, but did not reply.

Pepper continued, "I mean, we broke a fundamental rule. Toxic Soldiers don't ever leave anybody behind. That's, like, our basic motto. But that's exactly what we did with Atlas."

Pepper looked off into the distance, fighting off tears.

"Every time I close my eyes, I can still see him over there calling out our names," he said, choking up. "And we left him down there, Bookworm. We just... left him."

Ormon shook his head.

"We didn't leave Atlas, Pepper," he said, "We did what he wanted us to do. We had no choice. He was more worried for us than he was for himself. That's what Toxic Soldiers is about, caring for your fellow man, taking care of your brothers. And that's what Atlas showed us.

"The way I see it, Toxic Soldiers is just a game that teaches us about life, and what happened in The Arch World was a real-life experience. But what really happened down there is that Atlas *saved* us.

"And in case you've forgotten," Ormon continued, "there's another rule in our manual that's the most important rule of all."

Ormon stopped. This time, he wasn't going to give Pepper the answer. It took only several seconds for Pepper to realize what his pal was saying. Blinded by grief, he had forgotten the final line in the Toxic Soldiers handbook that they'd spent months writing and revising.

"Never give up," he said.

A slight smile crossed Pepper's face as he repeated the words aloud. "That's right," Ormon said.

"I almost forgot about that one," Pepper said, extending his hand. "Well, don't ever forget it – soldier," Ormon said, as the two performed their secret handshake. "This one's for Atlas."

"Yeah," Pepper replied, heartily. "For Atlas."

Nearby, Field and Sarah were engaged in a serious discussion of their own. Exhausted from his ordeal in Althanar and growing despondent over Atlas' peril, Field spoke of selling Mapp Excavations and retirement.

Sarah, too, was under great strain, but realized that her husband was in a state of helplessness. It was a feeling he seldom experienced, even during the most dangerous explorations, where disaster was a constant companion.

She didn't know what to say to make him feel better, but she did know that she had to say something. *Anything.*

Then, it came to her, a story from long ago. "Field, remember the celebration we had on the night that Atlas was born?" she asked.

Field nodded, pondering the memory, which was shrouded in the haze of a decade past.

"You were feeling so good that night. You had found the Diamonds of Bushawri and Atlas was born and christened by Neffer. Our future was bright and everything was perfect."

"I remember that," Field replied softly.

"Well," Sarah continued, "The moment I remember most is when Ahib came up to us and was afraid that you would retire because you had found that treasure. Do you remember what I told him?"

Field struggled to recall, but could not.

"What I told Ahib that night was 'Mapps don't retire,' Field," Sarah said, firmly looking into her husband's eyes. "Even when I was saying it, I was frightened to think of the days ahead when I might be alone with Atlas while you were off working in some strange, scary place. But I also knew that what you do is the reason I fell in love with you in the first place."

She tenderly caressed Field's face, wiping his unkempt hair away from his eyes, and seeing her young son's face in that of his father.

"I looked around the camp that night and saw the faces of all those happy people and I realized that they were all there because of you," she said. "You care about the world and unlocking its secrets to share with others. I knew then how selfish it would be for me to want you all to myself.

"So, no, you can't retire – because Mapps don't quit and Mapps never give up. I really hope that Atlas grows up to be just like you."

Tears trickled down Field's face, but they were not tears of sadness. He cried because as he looked at Sarah's beautiful face, it dawned on him how much she meant to him. She had been there for every important event in his life, a beacon of encouragement, patience, strength and compassion.

When he was at his lowest point – on the day Ada stole the Diamonds of Bushawri and took away his hopes for a comfortable future – Sarah was the one who convinced Field that everything would work out.

Field embraced her, and felt their hearts beating together as one. "I love you, Sarah," he said. "More than you know."

"I love you, too, Field," Sarah replied. "And our love is strong enough to bring our little boy home. You must believe that."

"I do," he replied. "I really do."

From a distance, Neffer watched the couple. He loved Field and Sarah as he did his own family. Witnessing them in pain had been difficult, but Neffer knew that they would find strength in each other.

Over the past several hours, Neffer had prayed to every god and goddess he could think of for help in this matter. He did not know if they were listening – for the gods were usually busy with more pressing concerns than that of a lost boy – but when his medallion began to glow and dance upon his chest, Neffer felt that his prayers might soon be answered.

At that moment, Ahib unleashed an urgent squeal. "Professor Mapp, come quickly! The painting!"

Ahib was so overcome with excitement that he could not finish his sentence. Field and the others crowded around the large canvas. Slowly, the painting began to reappear, coming into focus like an instant photo from a Polaroid camera.

Two small moons appeared, as did four different-colored arches marking North, South, East and West. Pepper and Ormon gasped as the Monkey Bar Bridge faded into view, along with E'lum Village deep inside The Lazantine Forest.

Towards the eastern side of the map, Fossil Mountain re-emerged. The City of Polema now sparkled against the horizon as night fell. Gone were the gloomy clouds that had covered the city with a sense of foreboding.

"Wow, Bookworm," Pepper declared, "It's like the whole Arch World has been cleaned up."

"More like *cleansed*," Ormon corrected him, "by the convergence of the Novi."

In minutes, the entire map had returned, with two

notable exceptions. "Where is The World Below?" Jenny asked, although she did not really wish to see the hideous place.

"Where's Atlas' heartbeat?" Pepper asked. "It's …gone." A hush fell over the group.

Then, the ground shook beneath their feet.

"The Door of Desire!" Neffer announced, as the earth split apart to reveal the large black door. It eerily swung open to show a swirling mass of purple and black that looked like a scene from Outer Space.

They were all transfixed by the sight when, suddenly, an unconscious Atlas floated out from within, right into Field's waiting arms.

"My baby!" Sarah shrieked, as Field laid Atlas' limp body down on the soft grass and checked for a pulse.

"Is he… alive?" Ahib asked, edging closer.

"He's breathing," Field replied.

"That is a good sign," said Neffer, who had his eyes glued to the open Door of Desire. "Very often, those who have traveled between worlds sleep throughout much of the journey and arrive home without injury."

Ormon and Pepper looked on, speechless. They were both worried about their pal, but remembered their own feelings of drowsiness both when descending into The Arch World and upon returning.

Actually, Ormon had considered the trip quite relaxing and pleasant, once he adjusted to the feeling of weightlessness.

At that moment, Atlas' opened his eyes, slowly focusing on the face of his father.

"Dad?"

An intense wave of emotion overcame Field as he gazed into Atlas' eyes.

"Are you really here?" Atlas asked, wondering if he were in a dream.

"I'm here, Atlas," Field said softly. "We're all here."

"Mom!" Atlas cried at the sight of Sarah, "I just had the most awesome dream." Then he saw the happy and relieved faces of Ormon and Pepper, "You guys were there, too. It was this really crazy world full of strange people and monsters!"

"I've got news for you, buddy," Pepper said, cutting him off, "That wasn't a dream. We were in The Arch World with you."

Atlas sat up with a look of disbelief. Pepper was the king of practical jokers, but when Atlas looked at Ormon, he knew Pepper was serious.

"The convergence of the Novi had just started when we got out," Ormon added.

Field and Sarah helped Atlas to his feet. It was then that he saw The Door of Desire.

"That was all real? Image, Freddy Bear and Kibu were really there?"

Ormon and Pepper nodded.

"Don't forget about Reflect. She was pretty cute for a mirror girl," Pepper quipped. "I think she liked me."

"So that means that I really did meet grandpa," Atlas said. Field, Sarah, Neffer and Ahib all exchanged glances.

"He lives in Haven and he told me all about you, Dad. Even the story about the wisdom box," Atlas said.

Atlas' words sent a shock through Field's body. He knew the story that his son was speaking of. It was one that Compass Mapp had told him when he was ten years old. In fact, Field had planned to share this story with Atlas on *his* tenth birthday, but was stopped by the mine collapse.

Sarah immediately believed Atlas, for she had heard the

story from Compass many times before, but never shared it with Atlas.

The others, including Pepper and Ormon, did not know what to think, for *this part* of the adventure had been Atlas' alone.

"This is worrisome," Ahib whispered to Neffer. "Maybe Atlas has experienced some trauma to his brain. Compass, is, after all... well, you know!"

Neffer, too, was startled. Although Atlas had jumbled the details of the old tale of youth and wisdom, Neffer knew the story well – for Compass had also related it to him many, many years before.

"The boy is fine," Neffer said. "However, what concerns me is that the door remains open. In my experience, a Door of Desire always closes immediately – unless there is unfinished business."

Instead, the strange portal emitted a low and steady hum.

"It is like looking into the insides of the earth," Ahib mused, although he did not know what the insides of the earth looked like, of course.

"Daddy! Come quickly. These are the boys who broke our sign!"

Pepper and Ormon were startled by the shrill cry of the Indian boy who had accused them of smashing the McDonald's sign days earlier. "Hey, chill kid," Pepper said. "We've been through a lot. 'Sides, we already told you we didn't break anything."

But the Indian boy did not stop with his loud accusations. He jumped up and down animatedly, as if pointing out criminals to the police.

Atlas stepped forward.

"They didn't do it," he said. "I didn't mean to, but I broke your sign trying to get into The Arch World."

Atlas' admission quieted the boy, who was confused by his explanation.

"Does your father own this restaurant?" Field asked. The boy nodded.

"Well, I'm Atlas' father. Go get your father and tell him that we'll gladly pay for any damage my son has caused."

But, just as the boy turned to run inside, a statuesque woman in traditional Indian clothing walked out. Her appearance startled Ahib.

He stared long and hard, and then blurted out, "Sanji?"

The woman was equally stunned at the sight of Ahib, whom she had not seen in more than ten years.

"Ahib??" she stammered.

A suave, well-dressed Indian man then walked out of the restaurant, and stopped short at the sight at the sight of Atlas' family and friends.

"This can not be-" he stammered.

Field, Neffer and Ahib were equally shocked.

"Ada?" they said together as they laid eyes on the man who had absconded with the Diamonds of Bushawri a decade earlier.

It suddenly dawned on Ahib that Ada had fled to Seattle after stealing the diamonds because it was the only place in America that he had ever heard about while working for Mapp Excavations.

"You thief!" he scowled as his blood began to boil. "All of these years you have been here in Seattle right under our noses?"

Sanji was confused. Obviously, Ada had not informed her of the source of their newfound wealth.

"Ada, what is Ahib talking about?"

Before Ada could answer, a sound much like a cold wind blowing through a tunnel was heard. It turned into a howl as it came closer to the surface, from deep within the bowels of The Door of Desire.

Atlas, Pepper and Ormon recognized the shapeless black figure instantly.

"Kibu!" they shouted, terrified as the evil demon appeared and snatched the Indian child right out of his shoes. For a moment, he glared angrily at the petrified Ada.

"*Now* the curse is fulfilled," Kibu growled, before darting back inside The Door of Desire with his captive.

Sanji fainted on the spot and fell into her husband's arms. The cries of the boy rang out as Kibu carried him deep into the recesses of the earth.

"Daaaaaaaaaaaaaaddddddddddyyyyyyyyyy!!!!!!!"

"Ada Junior!" Ada shouted helplessly into the night.

The Door of Desire slammed shut with a frightening finality, disappearing into the ground with no evidence it had ever been there.

No one spoke. The only sounds were Ada's tortured wails of grief.

"Please, Professor Mapp, I beg your forgiveness," Ada desperately cried. "Ada junior is my only son. I will gladly return to you the remaining diamonds if only you will help me rescue him. I will give you anything."

Despite all the anger he had felt over the past ten years whenever he thought of how the once-trusted Ada had betrayed him, Field harbored no malice now. Having suffered through the experience of not knowing the fate of his own son just hours before, he felt compassion for Ada.

"I don't want the diamonds, Ada," he said, wrapping

his arms around Sarah and Atlas and pulling them closer. "I've found the only treasure worth searching for. I'm sorry. I can't help you."

"But, Professor," Ada sputtered, "What can I do?"

"You should have thought of that before," said Ahib. "You knew of this curse and deliberately put the professor and his family in harm's way."

Like Field, Ahib also did not feel the rage for Ada that had filled his nightmares over the years.

"All this time I have dreamed of wringing Ada's neck, Neffer, but now I can find in my heart only pity," he said, softly.

Neffer had lived long enough to understand that retribution often left one empty. He, too, was sad to know that Ada would now have to pay for his crime for a lifetime.

"In this, and every world, Ahib," he said, "There is justice – always."

"As always, dear Neffer," said Ahib, "You are right."

Ahib's words hung in the air as nightfall suddenly took another unexpected turn.

"Look at the painting!" Atlas said, suddenly. "It's a heartbeat."

Sure enough, moving quickly over The Lazantine Forest was a rapidly pulsating red blip. There was no doubt who the heartbeat belonged to.

Field removed the small map from his pocket and saw that it also contained a little red heartbeat. He walked over to Ada and handed him the piece of paper.

"Ada, this map can show you how to find your son," he said. "I'm sorry, but there is nothing else that I can do."

Sarah then picked up the large canvas and placed it beside the grieving Ada, who comforted Sanji as she regained consciousness.

"Maybe this can help," she said. Turning to Field, she added, "I've destroyed the others. I don't want anyone else to find out about this place."

Field nodded. "Let's go home," he said.

"I never thought I'd be so glad to hear somebody say that," said Pepper, bolting to retrieve his bicycle.

"I'll say," added Ormon, running to catch up.

Atlas, however, was still riveted to the spot, unable to take his eyes off the pained Ada and his wife Sanji.

"Mom, Dad," he asked, "Can I ride with Ormon and Pepper? I promise we'll come right home."

Sarah turned to Field and said, "Let him go with his friends, Honey. He's proven he's a big boy."

Field smiled and ran his hands through Atlas' hair. "I'll see you at home, son."

"Thanks, Dad," Atlas replied happily, running to catch up to his pals, who had already strapped on their packs for the long trek back.

"Let's go, Adventure Boy," Pepper chortled, waiting for Atlas to hop onto his handlebars.

"What do you mean, 'let's go?'" Atlas replied in a secretive tone. "We can't just let Kibu keep that kid. We've got to help him."

Ormon looked at Atlas warily.

"You heard your father, Atlas," Ormon protested. "He told the guy there's nothing we can do. Besides, your mother destroyed all the maps."

A gleam came to Atlas' eyes. Then, he reached into his pocket and pulled out a small piece of paper.

"Not *this* one," he replied. "And you know, Toxic Soldiers don't ever leave *anyone* behind."

Pepper's eyes widened. "Dude, you can't be serious."

But Ormon could tell by Atlas' determined look that he was, indeed, serious.

"Okay, Atlas," he said, "What's the plan?"

Nearby, Neffer and Ahib watched as the boys performed their secret handshake and came together in a huddle.

"I believe that young Atlas has been bitten by the family bug," Ahib whispered to Neffer with a laugh. "Now, even you cannot retire. Something tells me he will keep us busy for a long time."

Neffer exhaled and looked up to the heavens.

"Something tells me, dear Ahib," he replied, "that Atlas and his friends will keep us all busy for a very, *very* long time."

THE END

37133129R00179

Made in the USA
Middletown, DE
23 February 2019